# THE HARD WAY HOME

## THE STAR AND THE SHAMROCK - BOOK 3

### JEAN GRAINGER

*To my children,*
*Conor, Sórcha, Éadaoin and Siobhán*

\* \* \*

*'There are only two lasting bequests we can hope to give our children. One of these is roots, the other, wings.'*
*Johann Wolfgang von Goethe*

# CHAPTER 1

*D*ublin, Ireland, 1950

Liesl sat behind the podium, focusing her attention entirely on the speaker from the other team, mentally noting his points, formulating her rebuttal. The crowd was respectfully listening to her opponent, so despite the ornate hall being packed to capacity, his voice was the only sound. Ancient books rested behind grilles the length of both walls, and the entire place smelled of a rich cultural and academic heritage dating back centuries. Liesl loved it. Trinity College Dublin were proposing the motion today. Not her chosen position at the best of times – she preferred arguing against – but it was the luck of the draw.

It required all of her analytical and oratory skills to argue in support of this motion – 'that this house supports Irish neutrality in the period 1939–1945' – something she personally vehemently disagreed with, but the Irish Varsity debating finals held no place for sentiment.

She allowed herself a quick glance down at the audience in Goldsmith Hall, where Elizabeth, Daniel, Ariella, Willi and Erich were sitting, proud as punch. She'd warned them in advance that she would be saying things she fundamentally disagreed with, but they said they

1

understood and insisted on coming to support her. She made them promise not to look at her, as it was going to be difficult enough without seeing them there: her *mutti*, who hid in a Berlin attic for years; her mother's husband Willi, who'd lost a leg in Russia but didn't let it stop him; her adopted mother, Elizabeth, who lost everything when the Germans bombed her house in Liverpool; tall, dark, handsome Daniel Lieber, her adopted father, who as a Jew had escaped Vienna only by the intervention of a friend in England; then her brother, Erich, tall as Daniel almost and filled out too, who looked so much like she remembered her father it took her breath away sometimes. Arguing that anyone should have been neutral in the face of the evil that killed their father and forced her and her little brother on a train and into the arms of strangers was going to be hardest of all.

She risked a glance at her brother. She was ten and Erich seven when they left Berlin, and they were very close. His sleek dark hair was a little longer on top now as was the fashion, and his dark-brown eyes gave him a soulful look. How she loved them all. She was delighted they'd finally made the trip down to Dublin together, though it was time enough for them since she was in her final year of her degree programme, majoring in international relations with a minor in French and German. Elizabeth and her mother visited sometimes, taking a day trip on the train, and Erich visited often because he loved socialising with her college girlfriends, but the men were always busy with something. Normally, she caught the train to Belfast every few months and Daniel picked her up from the station and brought her home to Ballycreggan for a visit.

She missed them all, and though returning to the bosom of both of her mothers, her brother and her father was wonderful, she loved her life in Dublin.

She looked around the room. She liked Trinity. It felt nice to be part of something, but like always, she wondered when, if ever, she would feel like she truly belonged. Her teammates were Irish, born and raised, as were most of her fellow students. Those who weren't had left home, wherever that was, to study at the famous Dublin university. As a German Jew, raised first by her parents in Berlin, a

Jewish mother and a Gentile father, and then cared for by a lapsed Catholic, Elizabeth, and moved initially to Liverpool and then on to Northern Ireland, she struggled to feel that sense of belonging. Ireland was divided; the North where her family lived was part of the United Kingdom, and here she was in the Irish Republic. It seemed like nowhere ever felt like home.

She focused on her opponent. If she caught the eye of anyone in the family, she'd lose focus. Her team had come so far; it would be a shame to lose now. The final speaker from University College Dublin was mesmerising. He spoke with such passion against neutrality, his argument being that it was not the time for politicking and that it was a moral question. The defeat of Hitler and the Nazis was imperative, and Ireland should have left her own issues with Britain aside and done the right thing.

The tall young man with a lilting accent that suggested he was from the south of the country held everyone enthralled as he painted graphic pictures of concentration camps, death marches and the relentlessly cruel and ruthless suffocation of human rights perpetrated by the Nazis across Europe. His eyes blazed with venom for an Irish administration that refused to allow Jewish refugees into Ireland, and he railed against those who put religious dogma and bigotry ahead of humanitarianism. Liesl found herself falling under his spell. He pushed his reddish-brown curls out of his eyes. She didn't dare make eye contact, choosing instead, as she'd been taught, to look nonchalantly into the middle distance while taking in every word.

He finally sat down, and she could feel the backing for him, even from the Trinity supporters, those from the Protestant college as it was seen in Ireland. The reality of the war, and in particular what was done to the Jews and other marginalised groups, was becoming more and more apparent every year as survivors gave testimony, wrote books and allowed the world to hide no more behind a curtain of ignorance.

But Liesl didn't need books or diaries of Jews who'd been victims of National Socialism to know what it was like. She knew on a deeper, more personal level. But that would not be apparent from her speech. She was determined to remain true to her argument, even if she didn't believe a word of it.

This was it, her chance to win the coveted trophy. Her teammates had done a solid job – they had been clear and committed to defending the motion – but she knew she was the one who would make or break it.

Though she'd warned her mother before the debate about the topic, to say what she was about to with her mother in the room felt so wrong. She mentally shook herself. This was not about her or her family, or what they'd experienced. This was just a college debate, and while it wasn't life or death, she would like to win. She could do this.

'Mr Chairman, distinguished guests, fellow students, the motion for debate this evening is the question of Irish neutrality during the last war.' Liesl looked around the room, making eye contact here and there, establishing a connection with her audience. 'And the proposition have done a thorough job outlining where the Irish government went wrong. They have brought us close to tears at the fate of the Jews of Europe, and indeed, one would need to have a heart of granite not to be moved. But I put it to you that hindsight is perfect vision.'

She wondered if the audience could hear the trace of a German accent in her voice, a slight lingering even after ten years in Ireland. She looked Jewish, she knew that. Her first name was German but her surname was Irish, so while her friends and family knew who and what she was, this audience and the judges did not.

'This country was at war with Britain since the arrival of the Anglo-Normans in 1169. Think about that, ladies and gentlemen. Eight hundred years of armed resistance to subjugation, mistreatment, abuse and even genocide that was perpetrated on the Irish people by our next-door neighbour. The Irish were forbidden to speak our language, to educate our children, to own land, to enjoy our culture. Every single human right, every aspect of human dignity, was denied the Irish people by their oppressors.' She paused and looked around, her voice low and determined. 'They didn't force the Irish into concentration camps, it's true, and they didn't exterminate them with poisonous gas, but they killed, they beat and tortured, they exiled, and they spread fear and hatred throughout the entire country. And when we finally achieved freedom, through centuries of Irish blood being spilled for the cause, the demand was made from London, the birthplace of every decree of misery for this nation, that we forget our old silly grievances, put aside our petty harking back to the past and join up with them to fight a people with whom we had no quarrel.'

She could sense the room shifting. The next few moments were crucial.

'Why should a young man from Carlow or Kerry don a British uniform, the uniform that had struck fear and loathing into every seed, breed and generation of his family for centuries, and go to Europe to shoot Germans, who had never harmed a hair on their heads?'

She could see a few slight nods at the rhetorical questions – she was winning. The opposition had brought up that de Valera, the Irish Taoiseach, or prime minister, visited the German ambassador in Dublin in May of 1945 and expressed his condolences on Hitler's death, but to that she had no answer. Nor could she bring herself to try to vindicate such an action, so she chose to ignore it.

'When Winston Churchill accused us of "frolicking with the Germans and the Japanese", it was with the knowledge that the Irish people had, in so many ways, assisted the Allied effort. This country fed Britain during those years, we gave radar and weather information, we returned Allied airmen and tried to repair and return their crashed aircraft – all facts, ladies and gentlemen, of which Mr Churchill was well aware.'

She took a sip of water.

'We did what we could, and what we should have done in support of the cause of what was right. But allying ourselves to an enemy as tenacious and duplicitous as Great Britain proved herself to be was unconscionable. Historians are doomed, ladies and gentlemen, for they are trying to analyse the actions of those in the past, with the benefit of knowing what comes next. We know now what Hitler and his followers did. Of course we do. But we didn't know then. Mr de Valera was dignified in his response to Churchill, who described so eloquently how Britain stood alone against an occupied European continent, when our Taoiseach asked, and I quote, "Could he not find in his heart the generosity to acknowledge that there is a small nation that stood alone not for one year or two, but for several hundred years against aggression; that endured spoliations, famines, massacres in endless succession; that was clubbed many times into insensibility, but that each time on returning consciousness took up the fight anew; a small nation that could never be got to accept defeat and has never surrendered her soul?"'

The words that had so rallied the Irish people in the face of Churchill's criticism sank in around the room. Liesl stayed silent, allowing their impact to resonate fully before going in for the kill.

'Should we have taken more refugees? Yes. But should we have thrown away the sacrifice of so many dead generations who fought to free our island from British oppression? Never. We were neutral. And we were right to remain so. Thank you.'

As she sat back down, she caught her brother's eye. Erich was a strapping eighteen-year-old now, but to her he would always be her little brother, entrusted into her ten-year-old care by her mother on the platform of Tempelhof station in Berlin in 1939.

Unlike her, Erich wasn't studious and couldn't wait till he left school. They'd been educated together in Ballycreggan Primary School, with Elizabeth as the teacher. It was an incredible stroke of luck that Elizabeth's home town was the location of the only Jewish refugee camp in Northern Ireland, so they'd grown up with Jewish friends, boys and girls from all over Europe who'd been brought to the farm on the Ards Peninsula in County Down to escape the Nazis.

Erich and Daniel had a business going. Daniel was an engineer, and Erich was serving his time as a carpenter. They were father and son, in every way but blood.

He made a face at her, trying to make her laugh. She gave a hint of a smile but looked away. The judges had yet to decide, and she didn't want to throw it all away.

The judges withdrew to deliberate, and the volume in the hall rose with the hum of conversation.

Beside her, Val and Jerome, her teammates, were equally inscrutable. They'd done their best, but it was a hard motion to support. However, as Professor Kingston was constantly reminding them, the judges were not making a moral judgement; they were judging the standard of oratory and rhetoric and the debaters' ability to adapt and reply.

Liesl glanced across at the UCD team and flushed when she was caught staring at the lad with the brownish-red curls. He looked back at her, his green eyes dancing with merriment, the earnestness of his performance moments earlier seeming dissipated. He was tall and muscular, and now that the debate was over, he loosened his tie and collar rakishly. He joked with his teammates, and they seemed to hang on his every word. She risked another glance, and again he caught her, this time giving her an almost imperceptible wink while simultaneously listening intently to the studious-looking teammate beside him.

The chairman of the judges led his fellow presiders back into the room, and both teams stood. He made all the usual remarks, praising both the Trinity and UCD teams for an excellent debate. He singled out Val and the last speaker from the UCD team, the young man with the curly hair, for particular praise. It was impossible to tell how he was going to vote. She was sure he was finished and was about to make his judgement when he paused and looked at her.

'I must make exceptional mention of the captain of the Trinity team. Not only is it wonderful to see our female students represented, but to see a debate so ably argued and with such passion is something unprecedented, even in these hallowed halls. Therefore, I and my panel of judges find for the proposition and Trinity College Dublin.'

The crowd burst into thunderous applause, and Liesl caught Professor Kingston's eye. He was over the moon, accepting hand-shakes and congratulations coming from every direction.

The chairman invited the dean of students onto the podium to present the trophy, and Liesl went forward to accept it. Val and

Jerome were beaming, and Liesl looked down to see her family standing and applauding vigorously.

Eventually, the photographs were finished, and as she walked backstage, she felt someone grab her hand. In the darkness and the crush of people trying to get out of the small exit, it was impossible to see who had done it, but a note was pressed into her palm.

She felt a surge of excitement – was it from the UCD captain? He was only a few feet away, but when she risked a glance, he was deeply engaged in conversation with someone. She wouldn't read the note until later, not wanting to be caught looking too eager if it was from him.

She put it in her pocket and went downstairs, where she was immediately enveloped in hugs from her friends. Daniel and Elizabeth stood to one side, looking so proud, and Erich was trying to make room for Willi and Ariella to get in to greet her.

Once all the hugs and congratulations were complete, Daniel announced, 'Everyone, to the Shelbourne! The drinks are on me.'

# CHAPTER 2

*L*iesl's friend Abigail linked her arm through hers as they sat in the corner of the Shelbourne bar. They were both Jewish, so had gravitated to each other on the first day of university and had been inseparable since.

'Did you see the UCD dreamboat making eyes at you?' Abigail whispered. She giggled, sipped her lemonade and nudged Liesl to look towards the bar, where the UCD team had also congregated. She was right; he was looking over.

'I…I don't know who you mean,' Liesl objected.

Something about his gaze was disconcerting. Was the note from him? She was dying to find out but needed to be alone to read it.

Erich sidled up beside them. Every time he met Abigail, he flirted most amateurishly, but she was always nice to him.

'Erich Bannon, so good to see you again,' Abigail said. 'Join us!' She patted the seat beside them.

'Hello, Abigail, you look lovely tonight,' Erich said, trying to sound suave and sophisticated.

Liesl fought the urge to laugh.

'Thank you, Erich, so do you. I like your tie.'

Erich blushed to the roots of his dark hair. He had grown up to be handsome, Liesl supposed. It was hard to tell when it was your little brother, but according to Elizabeth, all the girls in Ballycreggan had an eye for him. But he was after someone a little more exotic than the girls of a small rural village.

'I was just asking your sister if she noticed her admirer from the UCD team. He couldn't keep his eyes off her.' Abigail nudged Liesl again.

The two girls were as opposite as chalk and cheese. Abigail was short with a rounded figure and had what she called mousy hair, though in reality it was light brown. She constantly bemoaned the fact that Liesl was so pretty compared to her, but Liesl thought her friend was lovely and told her so frequently. However, Abigail had yet to have a boy ask her to a dance or the pictures, and they were in their final year.

'The lad with the curly hair? Aye, he seemed keen, right enough.' Erich grinned.

Erich was pure Ballycreggan these days and, unlike her, showed no trace whatsoever of his German identity. He looked, spoke and dressed like an Irishman, and that's how he saw himself. He was proud of her, Liesl knew that, and they were very close. But he couldn't understand her studying German of all things, the language of the people who killed his father and tried to kill his mother and who snatched him and his sister from the happy life they had in Berlin before the war.

Things had worked out well for them. Elizabeth was their father's first cousin and had agreed to take them from the Kindertransport, but for so many others, the future had been much less certain at the time.

'He wanted to get inside my head. That's what debating is all about, rattling your opponent. He was so fiery in his delivery, he would have wanted to put me off. That, my dear Abigail who sees the romance in every single thing,' Liesl teased, 'is what you witnessed.'

Later though, when she went to the ladies, she took the note out of her pocket. Her heart pounded. Something told her it was from him.

The writing was rushed and scrawled, and Elizabeth would have had a fit if she'd seen it. As a schoolteacher, she insisted on neat hand-writing.

*Liesl, you are the most incredible woman I've ever seen or heard. I have to get to know you. You intrigue me. Will you meet me in Bewley's tomorrow at eleven for coffee or tea or any beverage of your choosing? I'll throw in a cream cake to sweeten the deal. I'll be there, waiting impatiently.*

*Jamie Gallagher*

She smiled. He was as confident in his note as he was in his speech.

She put the note back in her pocket and left the cubicle. As she washed her hands, she took a moment to think. Winning the debating final had been all she'd thought about for the last few weeks, and she'd spent her time researching and writing her speech and collaborating with her teammates every evening. But now that it was over and they'd won, she had some free time. Her final exams were not until May and it was only October now, so she could probably allow herself a little diversion. And there was something fascinating about him.

'Jamie Gallagher,' she whispered, then caught herself in the mirror. 'Ah, would you catch yourself on,' she muttered as she gazed at her reflection.

Abigail was like a broken record telling her how pretty she was, but she didn't think it was true. Her dark hair and brown eyes combined with creamy skin that took the sun just made her look unusual in Ireland, but she was nothing special. Anyway, she didn't go on dates; she wanted to focus on her studies, and that was what she had come to do. She'd had one boyfriend, David, back in Ballycreggan, but he'd been hurt when she said she wanted to come to Trinity and so the relationship kind of fizzled out. She missed him. He was a nice boy, but they wanted different things from life. He'd accused her of being restless, of never allowing herself to be happy, and maybe he was right. She was searching for something – she just didn't know what it was. Since then, she couldn't be bothered with boys.

Even her mother had suggested that she socialise a bit more. Because Ariella had survived the war by hiding in Frau Braun's attic – Frau Braun was Willi's mother and also now lived in Ballycreggan – she wanted everyone to really appreciate life, to take joy out of being alive. Liesl remembered how her *mutti* used to walk up to the Bally-creggan National School every morning to hear the children singing the *Modeh Ani*, a prayer of thanks, in Hebrew. Rabbi Frank taught it to everyone, and all of the children, Jewish and Christian, sang it together each day, first in Hebrew and then in English. It reminded them all of how wonderful life was and how lucky they were to be alive.

She pushed her way back into the crowd and saw Daniel buying more drinks for her friends at the bar. Her stepfather, Willi, was good-naturedly passing them back. Daniel was such a generous man. She loved him, and he was the patriarch of their family. She sat down with Ariella and Elizabeth, who were both sipping whiskey and soda.

'Oh, darling, I'm so proud of you! You were incredible up there. I could hardly believe this poised young woman was my little Liesl.' Ariella squeezed her hand, her face suddenly wistful. 'When I met your papa, he was at university and he too was a debater. He was excellent, and I went to some of them just to see him in action. He would never argue for or against things he didn't believe, though, which was ridiculous of course. I mean, you had to fight that Ireland was right to remain neutral, when I know you don't believe that. But he was young and pig-headed and stubborn.' She laughed at the memory, a lovely sound that always reminded Liesl of a little bell ringing. 'He got thrown off the team in the end, but oh, how proud he'd be of you, Liesl. Erich looks so much like him– sometimes when he steps into the room, for a moment I have to do a double take – but you are the one who really takes after Peter.'

'Do you think I shouldn't have argued –' Liesl began, feeling like she'd betrayed her father's memory. He'd always done what was right; he'd died doing so.

'Oh, of course not, darling! That would have been ridiculous, and it's why you will succeed.' Ariella smiled. 'You're passionate but also pragmatic. I often wonder if Peter had been less rash, maybe if he'd not been as forceful that day he intervened with that Jewish lady in the street, maybe he could have stopped those Nazis abusing her a bit more diplomatically, then perhaps things would have been different. But that's how he was, all or nothing.'

'But I'm afraid I sounded like I was forgiving them…' Liesl wasn't convinced.

'Liesl, my love, it's peacetime now. That's what all those millions of people who fought back died for. Of course we must move on, try to put it behind us. Otherwise it was for nothing if we are going to relive it every single day and hold onto grudges and hurts.'

Liesl nodded but knew her mother wasn't practising what she preached. She would never return to Germany and could never forgive them, and Liesl didn't blame her.

'Your papa would be bursting with pride if he could see you.' Ariella took her hand and kissed it.

Liesl loved to hear about her birth father, but her mother rarely spoke of their lives before. Liesl knew that any happy memories had been obliterated by the way their country turned on them, what Ariella had endured during the war years and the horrors she saw in those final months.

'You were so impressive, Liesl, honestly. We knew you'd be good, but the judge was right – you were exceptional. Especially since we knew you didn't believe a word of it.' Elizabeth chuckled. 'You are a worryingly convincing liar, Miss Bannon.'

Liesl grinned. 'Ah, yes, what else am I lying about?' she said dramatically, and her mother and stepmother laughed.

'We were just saying on the way down how we wished you did a little more of the things girls lie to their mothers about,' Ariella said wryly.

'*Mutti*, believe me, you don't. If you heard some of the shenanigans the girls in my halls get up to, you'd never sleep a wink with worrying about me. I've told you before, I want to get first class honours, and they don't hand them out like sweeties, so I need to work hard.'

'We know you do, sweetheart, and I'm sure you'll pass with flying colours, but a little fun isn't going to do you any harm, you know. You're young, free and single in a big city – you should be enjoying it, not stuck in books from dawn to dusk.' Elizabeth patted her hand.

It was as if she'd always had two mothers, and in every way that mattered, she had. She and Erich had not seen Ariella for six years when their mother arrived in Ballycreggan, undernourished and overwhelmed. But she'd stayed alive as a Jew in Berlin for the entire war, determined to be reunited with her children. Elizabeth and Daniel had cared for them, had even adopted them because they had all assumed that Ariella was dead, and what could have been an awkward or fractious reunion turned out to be the complete opposite.

Ariella married Willi Braun, Frau Braun's son, and since there was nothing for any of them back in Germany, staying in Ireland seemed the sensible thing to do.

'I am enjoying it here,' Liesl insisted. 'I love Dublin, and I really appreciate that I'm studying at Trinity. The fees are huge, and I just want to make the most of the opportunity – it's not one many people get.'

'Your papa would have wanted it for you,' Ariella said with a sad smile. Luckily, Peter Bannon had made some investments in America when he saw how things were going in Germany, which Ariella was able to recoup after the war. The money from those investments allowed her to rebuild her life with plenty to spare.

'So tell me, how is everything at home?' Liesl asked, changing the subject. 'How are Frau Braun and the rabbi and everyone? I haven't heard from Viola for a while – how is she?'

Elizabeth and Ariella shared a glance that Liesl caught.

'What? What's happened?' she asked.

'Did Viola not write?' Elizabeth asked.

'No. I've written to her three times but got no reply. I was getting worried.' Liesl raked their faces for a clue. 'Do you know something?'

'Liesl, Viola and David are together.'

'Oh.' Liesl struggled to find words. 'Together?' She swallowed. 'As a couple?'

'I think so,' Elizabeth said.

So that was why her friend hadn't written. Viola and her sister, Anika, had been Liesl's best friends growing up, and David was her old boyfriend. She'd tried to keep the relationship with David going when she came to Trinity – he was from Dublin but was working in Belfast now, having moved up to Ballycreggan to be with her as a boy of seventeen – but it was impossible. Finally, after many fraught letters and a few disastrous weekend visits, Liesl broke off the relationship. David was hurt and angry. He said he loved her and had moved up to Ballycreggan to be with her, and now that she had a much more exciting life, there was no room for him. She hated to admit it, but he was right.

At university, she met all sorts of people, with exciting ideas and plans for the future. David had been her first boyfriend – well, her only one – but he didn't fit in her new world. She'd told Viola all about it last time she was home, and now that she knew about Viola and David, her friend's reaction made sense. She'd said that Liesl was too sophisticated for them all now, and the conversation had ended awkwardly, something she'd only once before experienced with Viola.

'When did this happen, that Viola and David started going out together?'

'A while ago,' Elizabeth said gently. 'Look, I told both of them they should tell you themselves, but...'

'They didn't,' Liesl said dully.

It felt like betrayal, but she knew she had no right to complain. She'd broken it off with David, and she was the one who'd left Ballycreggan and Viola. The one weekend her friend had come down to Dublin was a disaster. A friendship that worked in Ballycreggan just didn't seem to translate to Dublin. She found her friend prickly and hard to talk to. Perhaps something had been going on with David at that stage; she didn't know.

'Will it last, do you think?' Liesl asked Elizabeth. She had no right to feel hurt, but she did. Viola and David were both free to go out with whomever they chose, but she wished they felt like they could tell her.

'I don't know,' Elizabeth replied. 'Though they seem quite serious.'

'I'm happy for them.'

Liesl's heart was heavy. She inhaled. Ballycreggan as she knew it was changing – she and Viola, Erich and his friends, school, the synagogue on the farm. It had felt almost like where she belonged, but each time she went back, things were different, and it was hard not to feel sad.

'So how about everyone else? Anything else exciting happening?' she asked, trying to insert some brightness into her voice. She could see by their faces that Ariella and Elizabeth were worried about her.

'Oh, nothing,' Ariella said. 'Rabbi Frank is fine – he sends you his blessing and good wishes. And Levi and Ruth have decided to go to Israel. Some of the children – well, they are all growing up now, but some of the older ones are going with them.'

'To live, you mean?' She was surprised.

'Yes, they want to live in their homeland, and they see Israel as that. It's both sad and exciting. The rabbi and I have exhausted almost every avenue in trying to find the families of the children of the farm, and in most cases, there is nobody left. But we've been lucky a few times. Remember Benjamin?'

Liesl nodded. Benjamin Krantz was only a toddler when he arrived and so had been in the kindergarten group, but she knew him; they all knew each other.

'Well, incredibly, his grandfather and one aunt survived Bergen-Belsen, so he's going back to Prague to be with them. Though he cried, the poor child. He's thirteen now and Ballycreggan is the only life he knows, but we hope it works out. I tried to teach him whatever Czech I knew, but it is going to be hard. They might be family, but they are strangers.'

'Poor Benjamin. I hope he'll be all right. He's just a little older than I was when I left Berlin, but at least I had Erich. I suppose he could always come back if he hated it?'

Ariella nodded. 'We will give him some money for the fare and keep in touch by letter until we're sure he's happy, although I'm not sure legally we have the right to take him back. Rabbi Frank has corresponded with the grandfather and he seems very anxious to reunite with him, so we can just hope.'

Liesl nodded. 'What about the Schultz boys? Last you told me, Dieter and Abraham were waiting on a letter?'

'Yes.' Elizabeth nodded. 'Their older brother is married in Vienna and has asked them to go to him. They're thinking about it, but they are sixteen and eighteen now so they can choose for themselves. They and Erich and Simon spend a lot of time together playing football. Dieter is going to the technical college in Strabane to study motor mechanics and Abraham finishes school this year, so they are going to see how they feel.'

'Maybe they should go for a visit first, see how it works out,' Liesl suggested. 'I keep trying to imagine what it would be like to go back to Berlin. Would I feel at home or like a stranger? It's hard to know until you actually do it, I would think.'

'The Berlin I left in 1946 was nothing like the one you remember, darling,' Ariella said sadly. 'It's up to you of course, but for me, if I never see that city again, that is fine. It was just rubble and suffering, and so many people just wandering, lost. Willi and Frau Braun feel the same. They speak English all the time now, never a word of German.'

'I can understand that, but you know, studying German and reading Max Weber, Thomas Mann and Chekov is good – it reminds me that Germany was once a place of culture and learning and art and that it can be again. The Nazis might as well have won the war if we allow them to rewrite our future as well as our past.'

'I'm glad you see it that way, darling. It's right that young people should be optimistic and forward looking,' Ariella said with a sad smile.

'You always try to see both sides. It's one of your many talents, Liesl.' Elizabeth smiled.

'And so who is going to Israel with Ruth and Levi?' Liesl asked, and she saw that look pass between Elizabeth and Ariella again.

'Well, originally it was just Max, Rosa, Gretchen, Paul and Anika...' Elizabeth paused. 'But I think Viola and David are considering it now as well. There's been a huge take-up of people going now, from all over the world, I'd imagine, since the Law of Return was passed. Levi has always been a Zionist at heart, so he is happy to go. Ruth is nervous though. And the children who have nobody left are drawn there too. They want to be with people who understand. So now Michael is going, Malek and Katarina, Josef... Who else, Ariella?'

'Anika is gone already – she went straight from Poland. She wanted to go back. She knew there was nothing left in Warsaw, but she wanted to see for herself. Viola said she'd rather remember it as it was. So the sisters will be reunited.'

Liesl was lost in thought as her mothers talked. After years of upheaval and chaos, everyone seemed to be finding where they were meant to be. Everyone but her. Erich was going to stay in Ballycreggan, that was for sure. Her parents were all secure and happy there too, and now her oldest friends were leaving for Israel.

Something told her that Israel was not her calling. She might go someday, for a visit, but she had no desire to live there. Was it because she was German? Or because her father was a Gentile? She didn't think that was it. She just didn't feel that connection to the homeland so often talked about in her faith. The trouble was, she didn't feel that connection anywhere else either.

# CHAPTER 3

*L*iesl didn't even tell Abigail that she was going to meet Jamie. It was so uncharacteristic of her to do such a thing, but once she'd had breakfast with the family at their hotel on Baggot Street and sent them on their way back to Ballycreggan amid promises to visit soon, she rushed back to her room in the university hall and got ready.

She was still hurt by the revelation that David and Viola were together and leaving for Israel. All night she'd lain awake thinking about it. She didn't love David anymore, not in that way anyway, so it wasn't jealousy. She wanted him to meet someone else, and Viola was a lovely, gentle soul. She would be good to him and he deserved it. But it felt so disappointing that neither of them had told her. If they'd have just said it, she'd have been happy for them.

The idea that she was so irrelevant to both of them hurt her deeply, more than she would ever admit. Elizabeth knew how much it cut her. Elizabeth was the one she'd turned to when she and David first fell for each other. She was only sixteen, and David had begged to be allowed to take her to a dance in the village. Daniel had behaved like David wanted to take her hot air ballooning around the world. She smiled at the memory.

This move to Israel was a huge thing, and yet Viola had never expressed a desire to go there to Liesl. Maybe the full realisation that Warsaw was in ruins, her family was all gone and there was nothing and nobody left had been so hard for her and Anika that it had made her seek a new home. Liesl had tried to understand when they were younger and the news of the annihilation of the Polish Jews filtered through, but Viola rightly pointed out that she didn't know what it was like. Liesl and Erich had lost their father and their home, but Elizabeth and Daniel had given them another one, just as warm, just as welcoming, and then their mother appeared almost back from the dead, so there was no comparison.

Viola and Anika were truly alone, not one person to call their own, so she shouldn't begrudge her friend a boyfriend. She didn't; she just wished they'd have told her.

*Well*, she thought as she brushed her dark hair, leaving it loose, and put on a little lipstick, *if they can move on so easily from me, so can I from them.*

She was wearing a blood-red flared skirt and a little cream fitted jacket with a red collar and cuffs that she'd bought on sale. It had been too big, but Elizabeth was a genius with a needle and thread and remade it to fit Liesl's tall, willowy frame. She inserted the pearl earrings Willi and Ariella had bought her for her birthday and sighed. She was as ready as she would ever be. She almost stopped at the door, thinking she might be totally overdressed. Normally students just wore skirts and jumpers and macs with college scarves thrown around their necks, but Elizabeth's words rang in her ears. 'Everyone is a work in progress. Dress as the person you aspire to be in any situation.'

Elizabeth dressed formally for school every day, hair always done, light makeup, even though the children of Ballycreggan hardly noticed, Liesl was sure. Mrs Lieber could come dressed in a flour sack and nobody would care, as she was loved. But Elizabeth explained why she did it.

'Clothes are our armour sometimes. Dress up, you feel confident and ready. Dress down, you feel calm and relaxed. But if you need to go into battle, be sure to have the right uniform.'

Liesl knew she looked nice in the suit, so she would keep it on.

Bewley's Café on Westmoreland Street was a Dublin institution. The interior was beautiful: vaulted high ceilings, ornate woodwork and a beautifully tiled floor. Diners weaved between wrought iron tables and chairs. Exotic artwork was everywhere, decorating the space.

As she stepped into the café and out of the blustery autumn wind, she was conscious of the steam and heat making her flush. It had rained on the way but then it got too warm to wear her coat and walk, so she was carrying her wet rain mac and an umbrella. As she caught her reflection in the beautiful double doors, she realised she was very far from the poised, confident young woman she'd hoped she could be.

She was nervous – what if he wasn't there? Maybe that would be better, save her the embarrassment of meeting a total stranger.

She saw him the instant she stepped into the dining room, as he stood and waved to get her attention. He was even taller than she remembered and very broad and muscular. He looked more like a footballer than an academic. He'd managed to get one of the much-coveted booths at the back, and she smiled and gave him a wave. She took a deep breath – she could do this.

'Liesl, I'm so glad you came. I really wasn't sure if you would. Here, have a seat. Let me put your brolly down here.' He took her umbrella and placed it on the floor, folded her coat on the seat beside him and moved along to make space for her. 'Did you walk?'

'I did. It's not far though. I'm living in halls.' She settled herself into the booth beside him. He felt very close and must have sensed her discomfort because he moved along the banquette to give her more space.

'Lucky you. I'm in digs in Belfield with the world's worst cook and most miserly woman ever created. She recycles the eggs. My friend Donal has started putting pencil marks on all of the uneaten boiled eggs to see how often she serves them up. So far, the same one has been offered nine days in a row.'

Liesl giggled. Nightmare landladies were the stock-in-trade of Dublin students.

'She loves me though,' Jamie went on. 'Well, love is a strong word. I'm not sure Henrietta Hanratty – I swear that's her real name – ever loved anyone, but I stood up for her when one of the Kerry lads asked for honey for his toast and the tiny bit she brought him made him remark, "I see you keep a bee." She nearly threw the poor gombeen out for that, but I soothed her ruffled feathers by cutting the grass, so she thinks I'm wonderful.' He chuckled. '"Not as bad as the rest of them" I think were her exact words.'

Liesl laughed. It felt nice to be with someone funny. He was dressed much more casually today, in dark trousers and an open-necked shirt that had seen better days. She could see that the collar had been turned and the new side was very well worn. His hair was damp from the rain and formed corkscrew curls, which he had to push back from his face. His green eyes were ringed by long lashes, and a sprinkling of freckles covered a nose that had definitely been broken at least once.

As he pushed back his hair yet again, he noticed her watching the gesture. 'My hair is a disgrace, I know. I'm playing Macbeth though in the dramatic society's production, and I need to look all wild and highlander. The director says he'll have my guts if I cut it, so apologies. The minute the play is over, I'll get a short back and sides, I promise.'

'I could lend you a hairband,' she said with a smile.

'Oh, that'd be lovely. I can just imagine the lads' faces – would nearly be worth it. Ah, here we are.'

A waitress in a black uniform with a white apron and a frilly hat appeared with a notebook. 'What can I get you?' she asked.

Liesl was still full from breakfast, and anyway she suspected Jamie hadn't much money, so she just ordered a cup of coffee. Most Irish people drank tea only, but Daniel had introduced her to the world of coffee. All through the war, when rationing made getting such luxuries close to impossible, he'd had a small but steady supply from an importer in Belfast. Daniel kept the man's old car going despite lack of parts, and in return, the importer furnished the Austrian with an occasional small bag of beans, which Daniel used to make one good cup each week.

'Better one proper cup than lots of weak ones, that's my philosophy,' he would say as the Sunday-morning coffee ritual took place. Even after the war, he would grind the beans and smell them, savouring the aroma, before brewing the coffee. Then when it was ready, he would sit in the garden all on his own, on the seat he'd made for her and Erich, and drink his coffee and smoke a cigarette. Elizabeth, who loved him and understood him better than anyone else, knew he needed that time. He, like so many others, had lost everything. He'd been raised Catholic by Jewish parents trying to get ahead in an anti-Semitic society, long before the rise of Adolf Hitler and the Anschluss of 1938, and only learned he was a Jew when the Brownshirts came knocking on his Viennese door. He'd been lucky to get out.

Liesl wondered what her adoptive father would make of Jamie. Daniel was like Liesl in so many ways – a hybrid, struggling to figure out who he was. She found herself hoping Daniel would like Jamie.

'Surely you'll have cake? The almond slices here are only gorgeous. Or a cream puff maybe?' Jamie offered.

'No thanks, I'm not long after breakfast. Just the coffee would be lovely.'

'If you're sure.' He turned his attention to the waitress, who blushed as he spoke. 'Then two of your finest cups of coffee, please. This is our first date, so I'm trying to impress this lady.' He winked, and the waitress giggled. 'How do you think I'm doing?'

'I...I'm sure the lady is very happy,' she stammered, then blushed and rushed off to fill the order.

Liesl could have seen him as very forward, but he wasn't at all cocky. He was just funny and cheerful, and she found herself warming to him.

'Now then, first things first, congratulations on beating us. Don't feel one bit bad about it, even though we were working our backsides off for weeks.' He winked.

'Thank you. We did nothing, just breezed in there and made it up as we went along,' she said sweetly, and he guffawed.

'You're so good I'd nearly believe it. Anyway, fair play to you. The toffs won the day fair and square.'

She was used to the friendly banter between both universities in the city. Trinity was seen as the posh college, full of Protestants and all sorts, and UCD the Catholic one, full of culchies – a word for people from the country – and obsessed with the Gaelic games of hurling and football.

'We did. Probably it was the caviar and champagne we have every day for lunch. It makes us smarter.' She winked.

He chuckled again. 'You're well able for me, I can see, Miss Liesl. There's no fear of you.'

His accent was not Dublin, and it certainly wasn't Northern Ireland where she was from. It was soft and lilting.

'So, Jamie, where are you from?' she asked as the waitress delivered their creamy coffees. She sipped hers gratefully. Café coffee wasn't something she indulged in very often. She had an allowance, but she didn't like to use it for such things. Books and supplies were expensive, and while Ariella was comfortably well off, Liesl wanted to be as self-sufficient as she could be.

'I am from the kingdom of Kerry, God's own country,' he said with a flourish. 'And yourself, what part of this fair land produces such beauty?'

'Och, can ye not tell?' she said, hamming up her best Ballycreggan accent. She didn't usually tell people her story. Not that she was ashamed of it, quite the opposite, but it made people behave differently when they discovered she was a German Jew. It instantly made her the outsider.

'Somewhere up north?' he asked, then sipped his coffee. He winced.

'Is it not nice?' she asked.

'No, no, it's lovely altogether, just a bit hot.'

'Oh, right. Well, yes, I'm from the Ards Peninsula, a little place called Ballycreggan, County Down.'

'I was never up there. I'd like to go sometime.' He took another sip.

'Well, there's a bus and a train, so you could go any time you liked.' Liesl smiled innocently.

'But a poor little Catholic boy like myself up there might be out of his depth with all those Protestants. I'd need a guide, you see.'

'Are you afraid of Protestants, a big strong lad like you?'

Though the tone of the banter was jovial, she needed to see what kind of person he was. It had surprised and hurt her to experience as much anti-Semitism as she did on a daily basis. Though nobody was rude to her face or had said anything mean to her directly, she had overheard cruel jokes about Jews, and once in the college bar, a fellow student accused another of being Jew-like because he didn't buy his round. There was a casualness to the anti-Semitism that she found hard to reconcile with a nation that was generally warm and welcoming.

At Trinity, it wasn't so bad, as there were lots of non-mainstream people there, but the wider community was not like that. She'd understood before she came to Dublin that Ireland was predominantly Catholic and was inherently mistrustful – at least, if not downright hostile – of Jews. Oliver J Flanagan, a member of the Irish parliament, went so far as to say Hitler was right in the way he dealt with the Jews, and the Irish record on refugees was terrible. But Trinity was where she'd set her heart.

Because Ballycreggan was in Northern Ireland, and therefore technically part of the United Kingdom, her family had been worried about her moving to the Republic – they'd all heard the stories. But she was determined. Many of the volunteers at the farm during the war years were from the South, and they were kind and welcoming. She didn't believe an entire country would be anti-Semitic, especially now, when everyone knew what Hitler and the Nazis did.

And she was right. Most people she met were kind and mad for the craic, always joking and laughing, but she would be lying if she said there was nothing, that people didn't do a double take when she said she was Jewish, and a German. She never knew which made them more uncomfortable, but she had yet to experience open resentment.

Jamie looked at her, and she found herself returning his smile.

'You've such a lovely smile, Liesl,' he said quietly and with such sincerity that it changed the tone of the conversation from jokey to serious.

She blushed, unused to such compliments, but she realised she liked this boy with the wild hair and the square jaw.

Jamie's speech at the debate would indicate he wasn't a racist, but then he may not have been expressing his true feelings – she certainly wasn't – and she needed to know before this went any further. Was he like her father? Only capable of arguing what he believed in? Why did she think that about him? Maybe he was just as capable of arguing against his personal beliefs as she was.

'Tell me about yourself.' His eyes never left hers, and though the merriment still danced in his green and amber-flecked eyes, he was gentle and honest.

'Well, my name is Liesl Bannon, and I was born in Berlin, Germany, where I lived until I was ten. I moved first to Liverpool and then to Ballycreggan in 1940, and I grew up there.' She searched his face for a reaction, but the usual awkwardness when she mentioned that she was German was absent.

'What brought you from Germany to Northern Ireland?' he probed.

Liesl held his gaze, deciding to tell him. 'A train. It was called the Kindertransport, and it was a scheme to get –'

'Jewish children out of Germany,' he finished for her.

'Yes.' She noted his stricken expression and wondered what caused it. Was he sad that she'd had to leave her home? Was he shocked to discover she was a Jew? A German?

'And you are Jewish?' he asked.

She nodded. 'Yes, a German Jew. My mother put my brother, Erich, and I on the train – I was ten and he was seven – and sent us to my father's cousin, a woman called Elizabeth Lieber. She lived in Liverpool, so we went there first, but then when Liverpool was bombed and we lost everything, we came here to Ireland. Elizabeth – she's my other mother really – is originally from Ballycreggan, so we moved back and lived in her late parents' house.'

He swallowed, and she could see he was struggling to say the right thing. She should probably tell him that there was nothing to say. Millions of Jews gassed or worked to death defied explanation. Often people tried to find words of condolence or sympathy, and her response was always that eleven million people died. Six million were Jews, but there were others: Jehovah's Witnesses, gypsies, homosexuals, anyone who resisted, communists, the physically or mentally disabled. The list went on and on.

'And your parents...' She could see he was almost afraid to ask.

'My father was a Gentile, and one evening in 1939, he and a colleague were walking home. They saw a patrol of Nazis abusing an elderly woman in the street. She was Jewish, of course, and my father and his friend intervened. He was arrested and taken away for his trouble. We found out later that he died in a camp.'

'Oh, Liesl, I'm so sorry. That's terrible. He must have been a very brave man.'

Liesl shrugged. 'I don't know, I always thought he was just an ordinary person. Anyone would have done the same, or at least that's what you'd think, but, well, clearly he was different. Because if more people had stood up to them...well, who knows?' She smiled. 'My mother told me last night that when she met my papa, he was a debater – I never knew that – but that he could only argue the side he believed in. I wondered what he would make of me arguing that Ireland should have stayed neutral.'

'He'd be proud. Being able to see both sides is a skill that goes far beyond debating,' Jamie said quietly.

'That's what Elizabeth said too.'

'That's your adopted mother, right?'

Liesl nodded as she sipped her coffee.

'So what about your birth mother?'

'My *mutti* – that's the German for mum – went into hiding. She spent the entire war in the tiny attic of her now mother-in-law, Frau

Braun, who was a neighbour of ours. But *Mutti* only married Willi, her son, after the war. Hers is an incredible story of bravery and determination, but for some other time. Tell me about you?'

'Woah.' He grinned. 'Don't mind my boring life. This is an incredible story – it sounds like a film. Tell me more.'

Liesl shrugged. 'I suppose it is, but it's my reality, so I never see it as strange as it is, I suppose. We were well off, so we had a lovely apartment in Berlin. My papa worked for a bank, and my *mutti* was a linguist. She speaks – oh, I don't know – twenty languages? It comes easily to her. So she spoke to my brother and me in French, English, Greek, different languages, and it was really helpful when we had to leave because Elizabeth had no German but Erich and I had fluent English. So after my papa was taken away, his best friend, a man called Nathaniel Richter, arranged for us to get on the train. Tickets were very hard to get, so we owe him our lives. He and his wife, Gretel, and their children were like family. So we left, not knowing what the future held.'

'Go on.' Jamie was captivated.

'Well, we'd never met Elizabeth – her mother didn't like my grandpa for some reason – so we arrived in London terrified, but she was lovely. Her first husband, Rudi, had been killed in the Great War, and she had no children, and so we kind of became hers. And then her house was flattened in the bombing of Liverpool in the summer of 1940. By then, Elizabeth's mother was dead and the house was empty in Ballycreggan, so we went there. Elizabeth got the job as the local schoolteacher, and to our amazement, there was a farm where other Kindertransport kids were being housed, and they attended the school too. So I grew up with lots of children in the same position as my brother and me.'

'And your mother?' he prompted.

'Well, my *mutti* was in hiding, and then she had to survive on the streets of Berlin as a submerged Jew – that's what they called Jews living on false papers. And she did it, terrifying as it was, and finally managed to cross Europe to get to us. Frau Braun and her son, Willi, helped my mother, and she and Willi fell in love and now they're

married. They all came to Ballycreggan, and now my whole complicated, convoluted family lives there. The end.' She chuckled.

He smiled ruefully, a lovely crooked smile where one side of his
mouth was raised higher than the other. 'What an incredible story. I...
I'm speechless, honestly.' He seemed genuinely bowled over.

'Well, it's all true. But enough about me. Tell me about you.'

'I'm very uninteresting anyway, and compared to that, I'm as dull
as ditchwater. I'm one of four boys, from outside Killarney in County
Kerry. My mam and dad are farmers, and I'm the second youngest.
My eldest brother, Brendan, is a priest – he was ordained last
summer. The next one, Sean, is a Kerry footballer on the county team,
so he lives and breathes football. Then there's me, and then the
youngest is Derry, and he's still at school.'

'And you're a UCD student. What are you studying?' She liked him
more with every passing minute.

'Second year medicine.' He sighed. 'But I'll tell you what, Liesl, it's
fierce hard altogether and I'm forever getting my ventricles mixed up
and what have you.' He grinned.

'That would be problematic, all right.' She nodded. 'But are you
happy? Is medicine your calling?'

He sat back and observed her for a long moment. 'Do you know
what?' he asked. 'You're the very first person to ever ask me that. It
was always like Brendan has the collar, and sure Mam is dining out on
that since he came in and said he was going to be a priest aged thirteen. And Sean will get the farm, though he's only interested in
kicking footballs. And Derry will probably be made into a national
schoolteacher or an engineer. And they decided a doctor would be a
fine fit for me. My uncle is the local GP and on his last legs. Not one
person ever asked me if I was happy.' He stirred the coffee that was
hardly touched and cold by now, and he seemed as surprised at this
realisation as she was.

'And are you?' she asked.

'No then, Liesl, I am not indeed. I hate it, truth be told.' His attention never left the spoon, stirring and stirring in the cup.

'Then why do it?'

He exhaled and finally looked back at her. 'I don't know. I was bright at school, I suppose, and the master told my mother I was clever enough for medicine, and that was kind of it. I could have objected, I guess. I mean, they didn't have a gun to my head or anything. But I just kind of went along with it in the absence of any better idea, y'know?'

'And now you don't want to do it?'

'I don't. And I'm rubbish at it. It's too scientific for me. I should have done something else. I love college life, the sport especially, and I love debating actually, but it's too late now.' He shrugged.

Liesl knew her perspective on life wasn't usual. Her life experience to date, the losses and gains she and Erich had had over the years, the manner in which they were forced to confront the best and the worst of humanity long before they should, meant she didn't see things the way other people did. Abigail was like Jamie, imagining things were set in stone, feeling the social pressure to conform, failing to imagine any present but the one they inhabited. But Liesl knew everything was fluid. Certainties could dissipate in the blink of an eye; nothing was permanent.

'It isn't, actually,' she said with certainty, and he looked at her, puzzled.

'What do you mean?' he asked.

'Too late. It isn't. Nothing is set in stone. We only get one life, and we have no idea how long it will last or where it will take us. But one thing is for sure – it's too short to spend it pleasing others at the expense of our own happiness.'

He looked intently at her, and she could tell he thought she wasn't like other girls.

'But doesn't everyone have to conform in the end? We all have dreams, but for almost everyone, they end up doing what everyone expects. Join the priesthood, or get a good job and marry and have children, work, live the life you were born to live.'

Liesl shrugged. 'Maybe, if you allow it. But I'm living my life on my terms. The law of averages would suggest I shouldn't be here, that I should have died in a Nazi camp like so many others. But I didn't, because some people were brave and kind and didn't conform. It wouldn't be much of a repayment to them if I just plodded along and didn't make the most of my life, would it?'

Jamie's sea-green eyes held hers, and she didn't break his gaze. When he spoke, there was a huskiness to his voice that betrayed the emotion he felt. 'You're incredible. Honestly, I've never met anyone like you.'

Liesl smiled. 'Not really. I just played the hand I was dealt, I suppose, and I was lucky. At the end of it all, we only have our own lives to live, our own choices to make. Your parents, mine, anyone really, they have their own lives and they made their choices, or they didn't. But either way, they don't get to live your life too.'

Jamie chuckled. 'I'm sure you must have been a right handful with such headstrong views. So what would you do if you were me?'

'Well, I just think you should write to them, tell them medicine isn't for you. If they love you, and I'm sure they do, they may not like it at first but they'll understand. They won't expect you to give up your own happiness in favour of their plans. But don't keep going and then just drop out and spring it on them. Give them notice by letter and then go home and discuss it once the initial shock has worn off. If my mad life has taught me anything, Jamie, it's that we have to take our chances to be happy, it's too short to spend it pleasing others at our own expense, and nothing is guaranteed. If people love us, they'll support us.'

'So your folks would be all right if you decided to drop out, would they?' he asked.

'I think so. They know it's my life and they encouraged me to live it, so they'd trust me to know what was right for me.'

'That's where we're different, Fräulein.' He grinned. 'None of your German liberalism down in Kerry, I can assure you. People believe in tradition, duty. Our farm has been in the Gallagher family for six generations. People do what is expected of them, and that's just how it goes. I wish I could be more like you, but it's not how I was raised. You're braver than I am, I think.'

'Not really.' She smiled. 'I was just lucky. Both my birth parents and my adoptive ones are all interesting and brave people. They always supported me, and they're actually the ones who gave me the power to believe I hold my destiny in my hands.'

He turned his large frame so he faced her, and spoke sincerely, all messing around gone. 'Liesl Bannon, you are undoubtedly the most fascinating person I've ever met. Not to mention the most beautiful.'

Liesl laughed. 'Would you go on out of that with your sweet talk. I'm not falling for your old patter. I've seen your powers of persuasion in action, remember?'

He pretended to be hurt, clutching his heart theatrically. They both laughed, but then he placed his large hand over hers. 'I mean it though. You're amazing. Can I take you out again?'

# CHAPTER 4

*L*iesl should have been studying but all she could think about was Jamie.

He hadn't been joking when he said he had little interest in medicine. He was very clever and so managed to pass each exam, but only just, and with no enthusiasm whatsoever. She'd encouraged him to write home, telling them the truth, and though he'd been reluctant at first, he did it and said he felt happier, though his family had not replied yet. He was anxious, but she assured him they probably just needed time to get used to the idea.

They'd been going out for a few weeks now, and Erich had come down for a visit. He and Jamie really got along, both obsessed with sport of course, and they were in touch now independently of her. They wrote, discussing the British football leagues, a subject in which Liesl had not a shred of interest.

Jamie had spoken to the dean of the school of medicine and explained he wasn't cut out for being a doctor and asked him what his options were. The dean was nice and assured Jamie he was doing the right thing if medicine wasn't for him. He just needed his parents to agree, and he was free. Jamie had no idea what he wanted to do. He was a talented footballer and an excellent actor and debater, but nothing on offer at the university seemed to interest him. He was worrying that not only was he dropping out, but he had no better idea.

She was sure he was fretting over nothing, and assured him it would all be fine. He told her she had no idea what it was like coming from his background. It could have turned into a fight, but as usual he made her laugh. Then he kissed her and told her how beautiful she was, but that if she looked like an old boot he'd still adore her because she had an incredible intellect.

She'd grown used to his flowery compliments – it was part of his flamboyant personality – but there was a sincerity to Jamie, a genuine streak that ran through him, and when he told her on their fourth date that he loved her, she believed him.

They'd gone for coffee again, but she realised that he hated it and had only ordered it the first time they met to look sophisticated. Instead, he preferred to drink gallons of milk, and he ran the roads of Dublin for two hours every day to burn energy.

She'd gone to see him as Macbeth. He was wonderful, and that was the moment. As he stood on stage, commanding everyone's attention, looking so gorgeous and wild that every girl in the audience lusted after him, she realised that she loved Jamie Gallagher.

She couldn't wait for everyone to meet him. She'd written and told them all, tried to describe him, but the full force of nature that was Jamie Gallagher had to be experienced to be understood. He could be like a force ten gale, wild and rough on the football pitch or on stage, but when he was with her, he was gentle and kind and so funny, with a streak of mischief that she lacked. She adored him.

LIESL LOOKED up with a start as Professor Kingston touched her arm in the library. Aware that the librarians would murder anyone who made noise, he beckoned her outside into the corridor. All around her, students were cramming for the end-of-term exams before dispersing for Christmas.

'Can you come to my office, please, Liesl?' the professor whispered, despite being outside. Everyone lived in fear of the college librarians, who were strict to the point of ridiculousness. Abigail was banned for two days for sneezing two weeks earlier.

'Is everything all right?' Liesl swallowed. Her life experience to date had made her wary of people wanting to discuss things in this manner; far too often it had been bad news.

'Everything is fine.' He smiled and walked ahead of her, his black academic robes billowing out behind him. She followed and soon they were at his office.

'Please come in. Have a seat.' He gestured that she should sit opposite him as he took his position in a beautiful brown leather Chesterfield chair behind his very untidy desk. He was a popular lecturer, and passionate about his subject. Not everyone took up his modules, usually medieval German, perceiving them as too difficult, but Liesl loved them.

She turned her attention to her professor, who was rummaging about on the desk looking for something.

'Ah, here we are,' he announced triumphantly, extracting a letter from under a tea cup and a box of chalk.

He handed the letter to her, and Liesl read it, struggling to absorb its contents.

'Read it aloud.' He smiled.

Liesl had already scanned it, so she went back to the beginning.

*Dear Professor Kingston,*

*Congratulations on your university's victory in the Irish Intervarsity Debating Competition. I am assured that the entire team performed admirably and were worthy winners. I am sure their success was a result of your expert tutelage, so I commend you.*

Liesl looked up, and her professor was beaming. 'Go on,' he urged.

*It is with great pleasure I invite your nominated candidate, Liesl Bannon, to represent your university at the European Intervarsity Union Debates.*

It was a standard letter, and her name had been inserted.

*The vision of the organisers is to promote understanding and friendship between students and academic staff in the wake of the hostilities we have all endured. In a gesture of this friendship, the debates are to be held in Berlin, Germany, in February, 1951.*

*Please notify us as soon as possible if your candidate is willing to attend. The Debating Symposium will take place over two weeks, and all transport and accommodation is included in this invitation.*

*I look forward to hearing from you.*

*Helmut Koffer*

*Humboldt-Universität zu Berlin*

Liesl finished reading and put the letter down, speechless.

'Well?' Professor Kingston asked. 'What do you think? The theme is reconstruction and moving forward, healing the wounds of the past.'

'I...I'm overwhelmed...' Something occurred to her, and she had to ask. 'Do the authorities know my personal story? Is that why they invited me?' She wondered if her invitation was based on how good it might look for the organisers to have a fully functioning, academically attaining German Jewish refugee on the podium. Was she being used as a symbol of how the world would go on?

She'd written a piece for an assignment in her first year that was an autobiographical account of the impact of the breakup of her family. Professor Kingston had called her in and asked if it was a work of fiction. When Liesl told him that every word was true, he asked about her life, her family in Germany and all that had happened.

She saw now that her question hurt him, but she'd needed to know; she didn't want anyone's pity.

Sadly, he shook his head. 'Oh, Liesl dear, I would never reveal your story to anyone. That's yours to tell to whomever you see fit. So no. You've been invited because of merit, nothing more. I nominated you. I nominate students every year, but this is the first time anyone has been accepted. They only take the very best, and you are exactly that. But please, do not feel you have to attend. If going back to Berlin is something you have no wish to do, that is completely understandable. I debated about nominating you for that reason, but then I thought about it. I would certainly have suggested you if I didn't know your story, so to be invited is a great honour, of which you are richly deserving.'

'And what would I have to do, if I go?' she asked.

'Well – and again, no pressure – it's a two-week-long competition, with twelve individual debaters. In the early rounds, the candidates are given the motion in advance, but for the semi-final and the final, the competitors are only given fifteen minutes to formulate their arguments and then they are placed head-to-head. It is open to all manner of people, not just university students, and so the competition will be very stiff, though I have no doubt in my mind that you would be more than a match for them should you decide to go.'

'And they arrange everything?' She was still trying to process it.

'Yes, they transport you to the city. This year, it's Berlin. They choose a different European city each year – it was in Dublin in 1930, as I recall, a marvellous event. They put you up and take care of everything.'

'I…I'll have to think about it,' Liesl said. 'It's a huge honour, as you say, but I haven't been back to Berlin since I was a little girl. I need to think, to discuss it with my family. Can I let you know after the Christmas holidays?'

'Of course, Liesl.' He nodded kindly, smoothing his pointed grey beard. The students called him Lenin behind his back, and the resemblance, she had to admit, was uncanny. 'Take your time, and please know this – I will be happy with whatever you decide.'

She stood and nodded. 'Thank you, Professor Kingston, for your support and for nominating me. I appreciate it so much. I'll have a think and let you know.'

Returning to the library was pointless. She couldn't concentrate on Voltaire now that she had to consider whether or not she should – or even could – return to Berlin.

She wished Elizabeth and Daniel weren't so far away. She loved her mother and was very close with her and Willi, but on this matter, she needed her adoptive parents' counsel. Ariella went through hell in Berlin to get back to her and Erich, and she'd vowed never to return there. Willi and his mother too had emotionally cut all ties with

Germany; there was nothing there for them as far as they were concerned. Would they see her going as a betrayal? Would they want her to go? What would Erich think about it?

She and her brother were so close, as close as siblings can be, but they were very different. She was a contemplative and serious person, she knew, despite Jamie telling her she was funny, and she thought deeply about things. Erich, on the other hand, was much more happy-go-lucky. He was Irish as far as he was concerned, and though the dark days of National Socialism had hurt him as much as anyone, he just chose to leave them behind him. He loved his life, working with Daniel, being doted on by both Elizabeth and Ariella and having all the girls in Ballycreggan making eyes at him. She knew he wouldn't understand why on earth she would want to go to Germany.

But she found herself getting excited at the prospect of returning. Berlin was her first – and in lots of ways, her only – real home. She and Erich, living with *Mutti* and Papa, being friends with the Richters, going to school and dance lessons and the synagogue…that was the last time she truly felt she belonged. If she went back, could she recapture that feeling? Should she try? Would it hurt her mother? That was what was stopping her, she realised. The fear that Ariella would see it as a betrayal.

She walked up Grafton Street until she arrived to Stephen's Green. Jamie had a lecture in the Royal College of Surgeons until five. They'd arranged to go to the pictures that night, but she didn't want to sit in a cinema now; she needed to talk this through with him.

She thought she'd surprise him by meeting him after the lecture and they could go to Beshoff's for their tea and to talk about the opportunity. He worked part time in the Shelbourne hotel as a night porter but was off tonight. She missed him, but he was working hard to save some money for when he was out of college digs and on his own.

They'd had a discussion the previous night about which film to see – she wanted to see *All About Eve*, but Jamie tried to convince her that Gregory Peck in *The Gunfighter* would be much better. Of course, he gave in finally.

But the conversation with her professor had put her off the idea of sitting in the dark for two hours. She wanted to talk it out with someone, and Jamie was a great listener.

They normally talked for hours as they walked on Dollymount Strand or around Phoenix Park despite the wintry weather. They'd pop into a café for a cup of cocoa to warm their hands before walking home hand in hand. Abigail and all Liesl's gang of friends really liked Jamie, and he was always happy to join in with whatever was going on. It felt like he fit so easily into her life. Erich thought he was great, and she knew once the Ballycreggan lot met him, they would love him too.

His digs were in Belfield while she was in halls on campus, so they usually met at her accommodation rather than his. The tales of his horrible landlady, Henrietta Hanratty, were legendary, and though Liesl suspected Jamie was hamming it up for storytelling purposes, she was in no doubt that young ladies would not be welcome.

It was ten to five, and the smoke from the fires of the households of Dublin filled the air. It would soon be Christmas, a season she always loved despite her faith celebrating Chanukah at this time of year. In Berlin, they'd celebrated both holidays, and Elizabeth kept up the tradition. Each year, Elizabeth put up a tree as well as lit a menorah, and Santa Claus always came to her and Erich. Even in the worst of the rationing, Elizabeth and Daniel managed to make both holidays special.

Jamie was going home for Christmas as was she. Their last lectures were this week, and once she was finished, she'd be on the train to Belfast. He was nervous, dreading the confrontation with his parents. They'd still not responded to his letter, which was worrying him.

Normally, her Christmas trip home filled her with anticipation of home-cooked meals, latkes and kugel, turkey and Christmas cake, warmth and love, but this Christmas she would miss Jamie, who would be all the way down in Kerry, as far from her as it was possible to be.

Adding to her lack of enthusiasm was the thought of seeing Viola and David. It was impossible to avoid anyone in Ballycreggan, and so she'd have to face them. It annoyed her that she was the one dreading it, as she'd done nothing wrong, but she hated the awkwardness it was sure to bring.

She stamped her feet on the ground outside the College of Surgeons. It was bitingly cold and she thought about the fish and chips and big mugs of tea at Beshoff's. The twinkling lights of the Shelbourne were visible through the corner of the park and they were very inviting, but the fancy hotel was outside their budget; besides, Jamie wasn't allowed to socialise there because he was staff.

She could see her breath as she waited, and she wrapped the bright-yellow scarf Elizabeth had knit for her tighter round her neck. She wore her royal-blue warm winter coat, an old one of Elizabeth's left in the house from her childhood, but it fit Liesl like a glove. It was a colourful outfit and it turned heads. Jamie had told her she looked like a beautiful parakeet when he saw her with the coat and scarf, topped off with a yellow beret to match her scarf.

She could hear the movement inside. Like Trinity, the lectures began and ended on the hour, so it was time for the old university to spill its students out into the night air, their heads full of scientific facts and figures.

She saw Jamie before he saw her. He towered over his fellow students, and his dark-red hair that he'd kept long at her request even after the play made him stand out in any crowd. She thought he was gorgeous, and she knew other girls did too.

As she was about to call to him, she saw him shake hands with a man waiting on the other side of the door from where she was. He'd never mentioned he was meeting anyone.

Soon they were deep in conversation, and it looked serious. As the man spoke, Jamie bowed his head. They started to walk in the opposite direction, and she wondered if she should let them at it. Clearly the conversation was important. But something about Jamie's body language worried her. Was the man bringing bad news? She decided to just check he was all right and then be on her way.

She ran after them and tapped Jamie on the shoulder from behind.

He turned and saw her, and there was a slight hesitation, a reticence about the split-second delay, before he acknowledged her.

It was only then that she realised the other man was dressed in a black suit, black shirt and a white Roman collar. In his black overcoat and trilby, the priest had a forbidding effect.

'Liesl, I didn't know you were going to be here.' Jamie smiled but didn't give her his usual warm hug – and kiss if he could get away with it. 'I thought I was to pick you up?'

'I finished early. I thought I'd surprise you.' She stood by his side, waiting for an introduction.

'Ah, right. Great.' But his tone didn't suggest he was delighted. 'So, Liesl, this is my brother, Father Brendan Gallagher. Father Brendan, this is Liesl Bannon.' Jamie's smile as he made the introductions lacked its usual warmth and merriment.

Liesl stuck out her hand, trying not to betray her hurt that she wasn't introduced as his girlfriend. 'A pleasure to meet you,' she said with a smile. 'It must be a lovely surprise to see your brother?'

The priest cast a look at Jamie she couldn't read. 'This visit was arranged, so not a surprise.'

# CHAPTER 5

*J*amie's brother shook her hand, and his skin felt cold and dry. Liesl wished the ground would open and swallow her. Why hadn't Jamie told her his brother was visiting? And why hadn't he said she was his girlfriend? Was he ashamed of her?

The priest nodded but didn't smile. He looked like Jamie in some ways – the same square jaw and tall frame – but he was thinner and his eyes were grey.

'What manner of name is Liesl?' he asked directly.

'Ah...' She glanced at Jamie, who looked helpless. 'It's German.'

'I see,' the priest replied, his tone leaving no doubt how distasteful he found that information.

'So, ah, will we go for a cup of tea?' Jamie seemed less confident than usual; he was clearly very uncomfortable with the situation.

Liesl felt very much in the way. 'No, I'll go back to my halls. I'm freezing anyway and need to get warm and drop off my books. I'll see you, Jamie.' She gave him a brief smile to take the edge off her abrupt departure and then turned to his brother. 'Nice to meet you, Brendan.'

'Are you not a UCD student?' Brendan asked, and Liesl couldn't ignore the imperious tone in his voice, which was ridiculous in someone only a few years older.

'No. I go to Trinity,' Liesl said, her hackles rising. She could sense the animosity from him.

Father O'Toole back in Ballycreggan was a lovely man. He was great friends with Reverend Parkes, the Protestant vicar, and Rabbi Frank from the farm made up the trio. The three men were often seen chatting or enjoying a cup of tea at Maisie McGovern's tea rooms, recently opened in Ballycreggan. Father O'Toole was the only priest she'd met, but she'd read enough about the Catholic position on Jews to know that he was not the norm.

'So are you a Protestant then?' Brendan asked directly. He might as well have asked if she was a murderer. Who did he think he was?

'No, I'm not. I'm Jewish,' Liesl answered, casting a glance at Jamie, who was examining the pavement. 'Look, I have to go.' She started to walk away, but Jamie called after her.

'I'll see you, Liesl.'

She didn't answer. All the way home, she fought the tears. How could Jamie have behaved like that? Pretended to that horrible priest that she and he weren't close, and allowed him to speak to her like that? She felt so let down. She'd thought Jamie would always defend her, that he was on her side, but she was wrong.

She was recounting the extraordinary encounter to Abigail when she heard the doorbell ring. It was Jamie. Each of the girls in halls had their own ring that they gave to their visitors, saving people constantly opening the door for others' visitors. Hers was three short rings and one long one.

'Will I go down?' Abigail asked.

Liesl sighed. 'No. Thanks though.' She gave her friend a small smile.

As the hours had worn on since the unpleasant encounter, she became more and more disappointed in Jamie. If he hadn't the guts to stand up for her, was he even worth bothering with?

She took her coat and scarf from the hallstand and went downstairs. They needed to talk, and the women's residence was like a

43

cornfield, full of ears, so they would have to find somewhere to speak in private.

She opened the door. He stood there, his face flushed from the icy wind, his hands buried deep in his coat pockets.

'Hi, Liesl.' He gave her his crooked smile, and for the first time since they'd met, it didn't give her butterflies.

'What do you want?' she asked, standing in the doorway, her coat over her arm.

The smile was gone, and he looked miserable. 'Could we go for that cup of tea now? Or a drink if you like?'

She refused to melt at his boyish charm. He was a Pioneer of Total Abstinance, meaning that he didn't drink alcohol – it was to do with a pledge he'd taken when he made his Confirmation– but she did. Not to excess, but she liked a glass of wine now and again. He always teased her about it.

'Now that your precious brother is gone, I'm suddenly good enough again, is that it?'

'What? Of course not! I mean, you are good enough, always…' Jamie was flustered.

'He was so rude. Why didn't you tell him I am your girlfriend?'

'Look, Liesl, I'm sorry, all right? Father Brendan was sent by my parents after getting my letter. I didn't tell them about you, and I didn't want you to meet him because I knew how he'd be. My family would only want to blame someone for me leaving college, and I didn't want it to be you.'

'Jamie' – she had to ask him the question that had been plaguing her all evening – 'are you ashamed of me?'

'No, of course I'm not. You're amazing, funny and clever and beautiful, and you're so brave and confident. I just…' His voice was filled with pain.

'Just what?' she prompted.

'Look, you say I can't understand your background, Berlin and the Jews and all of that, and you're right, but you can't understand mine either.'

'That's nonsense. I grew up in an Irish village. I understand perfectly.' She was indignant.

'But you don't understand. You grew up in Northern Ireland, Britain essentially, and in a community of all sorts of people, so everyone knew people who were different and they got along and all the rest of it. I grew up in Kerry. There was one Protestant family that had a big house about six miles from us and we knew them to say hello to, but that was it. You were the first Jew I ever met. I know up here in Dublin it feels all cosmopolitan and there are people here from all over the world, but where I come from, it's not like that. They are wary of change or anything different. So of course I'm not ashamed of you – I'm the proudest man in Dublin walking around with you on my arm – but they just need a bit of time to get used to…' His voice trailed off.

'Used to what?' Liesl asked slowly and calmly.

'Used to the idea that I have a girlfriend at all for a start, and then that she's not Catholic or from Kerry.' He turned and tried to take her hand, but she pulled it away.

'Please don't be like that, Liesl. They don't matter. We're together up here, and what we do or who we do it with is not anyone's business but ours. Maybe I should have told Father Brendan you were my girl-friend, but he came up to discuss my studies – my mother sent him – so I thought I'd fight one battle at a time.'

She turned to go; she'd had enough. Being rejected by her country as an innocent child meant she had little patience for anyone who tried to make her feel less.

He reached out and grabbed her hand. 'Liesl, please don't go. I love you, and because of you, I got up the courage to tell them I don't like medicine. I would never have done it if you hadn't encouraged me.'

'Why do you call him Father Brendan? He's your brother, for goodness' sake.' She was so hurt and angry, it came out as a snap.

'Everyone does, even Mam and Dad. It's like a respect thing. Look, it doesn't matter what I call him, the point is I love you and they'll just have to accept it.' He swallowed. 'I should have introduced you properly, and I shouldn't have let him speak to you the way he did. I'm sorry. It won't happen again, I promise.'

She looked at him, his face illuminated by the flickering firelight, and her heart softened. Maybe she was being oversensitive. And anyway, it was Jamie she wanted, not his awful brother.

'You'd better be telling me the truth,' she said with a small smile.

'I am, I swear to you. Brendan's a pain in the arse, to be honest with you, but we aren't allowed to criticise him because he's a priest. He hasn't a clue about the real world – he's been locked up in the seminary for the last seven years and now he's got a parish. Though he's only a curate, you'd swear he could walk on water. Please, can you just forget you ever met him? I love you and I can't stand him, but if I'd have stood up to him, he'd have been straight onto Mam and Dad and blamed you for me dropping out.'

'So they're not happy, I take it?'

'Not one bit. They are appalled, and I'm in the horrors at the thought of going home. But I'll have to face the music. I just don't want you dragged into it. Do you understand?'

'I suppose so,' she said quietly.

'Liesl. You're so gorgeous and clever and just fantastic, I can't believe someone like you would go out with me. It's them I'm ashamed of, especially Brendan, the way he goes on. But my parents would never have met a Jew in their whole lives, or a German either, and they'd be – I don't know – mistrustful. You're so much more cosmopolitan than people are where I come from, more broad-minded. My parents, family and neighbours aren't bad people, but they haven't much experience of anyone other than people like themselves. It's hard to explain...'

Liesl thought for a moment, but his vulnerability and his damp curls got the better of her. 'All right. Let's have that drink,' she said, then wrapped herself up warmly before following him out into the night.

In the pub, she told him about the invitation to Germany. When she finished talking, he gave a low whistle.

'That's amazing, Liesl. Wow. Really, it's incredible to be invited!

46

I'm so proud of you. And it's well deserved. Congratulations.' He gave her a squeeze. 'When do you go?'

'Well, that's the thing. I don't know if I should. I remember Berlin well. I was ten, so my memories of our neighbourhood, my school, our apartment, the synagogue we went to are very clear. And then how scary it was as the Nazis got stronger, my father going to work and never coming home, my mother bringing Erich and me to the railway station to put us on the train. I remember it all like it was yesterday, and I...' She didn't usually get emotional when speaking about her past – it often amazed people how she could be so stoic about it – but now that there was the prospect of going back, she felt unsure and frightened.

'What's stopping you?' Jamie asked gently. 'You know you're safe now. Nobody there would hurt you. And it is an amazing opportunity.'

'I know.' Liesl took a sip of her wine. 'But two things. First, I don't know about being over there on my own, stirring up memories. It's hard to explain, but I feel like Germany rejected me, my family, because of who we are, and though Hitler and the Nazis are no more, it's hard to believe everyone is suddenly all right with the Jews again. The thing that shocked us, Jamie, more than the government decrees and the endless laws and rules, was the alacrity with which our neighbours and friends took up the Nazi cause. People we'd known all of our lives, local businesses, people like that, joined the Party. I'm sure now they'd say, "Oh, we were forced into it," or whatever, but I'm not sure that was true, nor am I sure they don't secretly still feel that way. And though I know nothing would happen, it frightens me to be there, surrounded by people like that.'

He nodded and rubbed his hand over her dark hair. 'I know I can never truly get it, but I can see why you'd feel that way. And what's the second thing?'

'Well, this is bigger really, because I do want to go despite all I told you, just to see how it feels, but I don't know if my mother would want me to.'

Jamie looked surprised. He often remarked at how much more

independent Liesl was compared with other girls. She loved her family deeply, but she was an independent young woman. He'd been shocked when she suggested they sleep together, and afterwards, as she lay in his arms, he'd explained that he was brought up to believe boys pushed the physical boundaries in relationships and girls pushed back, protecting their virtue. To meet someone like her, who wanted to have sex but wasn't a woman of loose morals as the priest might say, was rare, if not unheard of.

Liesl had explained that she was a virgin, but that she felt the time was right. She told him she was curious and very attracted to him, and that so long as they were careful, there was no problem. He'd chuckled at that, saying he could think of several people who would have all manner of problems with it, but if she was sure, then he was very happy to comply.

The first time was swift, messy and a bit painful – he was a virgin too – but once they got the hang of it, it was actually lovely. They lay together so many nights in her single bed, Abigail next door oblivious to what was going on, she hoped, and he'd slip out the back door in the early hours. His friend PJ left the window on the latch for him so he could slip in undetected by Horrible Hanratty. Perhaps it was because their relationship had moved on to that level that his calling her his friend to his brother stung so deeply.

'Why wouldn't she?' he asked, trying to understand.

'I don't know, maybe she wouldn't mind. But she fought so hard to survive and then to get out of Berlin with the advancing Russians... I don't know, it's a complicated thing.'

'Will you ask her when you go home?' Jamie sipped his lemonade. 'That might help you to decide? We could be going around in circles trying to second-guess how people might react to things. Best just ask straight out.'

'Like you do with your family, right?' she teased.

'I know... But you're braver than me, Fräulein.' He put his arm around her and kissed her. 'I love you.'

'I love you too, Jamie,' she whispered, snuggling up against him. It was going to be all right.

# CHAPTER 6

*L*iesl dragged her suitcase from the parcel rack of the train as it pulled into Belfast Central Station. It had become a tradition that the entire family come to Belfast the day she came home, and they all went for lunch at the Imperial Hotel, a lovely old building on the corner of Donegall Square and Castle Lane.

She'd telephoned home that morning, and Elizabeth assured her everyone would be there. Ariella, Willi and Frau Braun would meet them at the hotel, and Daniel, Elizabeth and Erich would collect her. Willi had bought a specially adapted car, having had his leg amputated from the knee. He always joked that he was grateful to the Russians because it got him invalided out of the army. She longed to see them all again.

Erich was on the platform, smiling, his hands in his pockets, too self-conscious to be waving madly, but she saw the love beam out of him, just as it always had. He deferred to her in all things, and her approval was vital to him. She loved him too. She wondered what he would think about the Berlin idea. Daniel and Elizabeth would be waiting in the car, as parking spaces around the station were at a premium. It was incredible how many people drove private cars now. She knew Erich was saving like mad to get a car of his own. He and his friend Simon, originally from Hanover but sounding now like he'd never spent a day outside of Ballycreggan in his life, were forever tinkering with any engine they came across.

She found herself wrapped in his hug as he picked up her bag. They walked out, chatting animatedly, as Elizabeth waved from their car that Daniel had double-parked.

Daniel got out and hugged her and kissed the top of her head, and she felt herself relax against the bulk of him. For the first time since the day Professor Kingston gave her the news, she felt like it was going to be all right. There and then she decided she would talk to Daniel alone first, seek his opinion. The two of them had always been close, and he listened to her and took her seriously, like the time he championed her cause to have a bat mitzvah when she was twelve. Rabbi Frank was an Orthodox Jew, and in that tradition, girls didn't have a bat mitzvah. But Daniel challenged his position, saying that all the Jews were being thrown together, Orthodox, Chassidic, Reform, everyone, as the Nazis didn't differentiate, and so they should at least respect each other and try to act as one. He won, Liesl and the other girls had the ceremony, and it was wonderful. So many times when she lived at home, she and Daniel would drink coffee and talk, and she knew she could tell him anything.

'How's my girl?' he asked, his Austrian accent as strong as ever. Life in Ballycreggan suited Daniel Lieber, because like her, he was a hybrid. Unlike her, though, he was very sure where he belonged, and that was with Elizabeth in Ballycreggan. He was Viennese, but that meant nothing to him anymore.

'Good. Glad to be home.' She reached up and kissed his cheek, and he smelled like he always did, the comforting scent of cologne, wood and leather.

'The mothers have been baking and cooking and preparing both houses, secretly competing, I think. It's Chanukah at Ariella's and Christmas at ours, and between them they are trying to make me fat.' He patted his belly, and she noted he wasn't as lean as he'd always been.

'Oh, Ariella is tying you down and shoving rugelach down your throat, is she?' Elizabeth teased.

'Well, not exactly, but they are so delicious…' He grinned.

'Not as delicious as my mince pies though?' Elizabeth asked threateningly.

'You see, Liesl? Battle of the cakes. I'm so glad you're here to save me from them.'

Liesl laughed as she got into the back and Erich slid in beside her.

'Push over, little man,' she said as she leaned over and hugged him, using the pet name Daniel had for him since his first day in Ballycreggan.

'I'm about a foot taller than you.' He rolled his eyes dramatically.

'True, but you are still my little brother, so don't forget it.' She slipped her arm in his and rested her head on his shoulder as Daniel backed out into the traffic.

'So what's new with you?' she asked Erich as Elizabeth and Daniel were distracted by a man doing a very silly manoeuvre with a van.

A police officer came to the window, instructing Daniel to back up and go out the other way.

'I've got news actually, really exciting news,' he whispered.

'Tell,' she whispered back.

Daniel was now in conversation with a policeman who'd been called because the van had backed into another parked car.

'We got a letter from Bud. He's invited us to his wedding in Biloxi in May.'

'Oh, really!' Liesl was thrilled. Bud was an American soldier who'd joined the RAF before America entered the war. He'd been stationed at the base at Ballyhalbert just a few miles from Ballycreggan, and had befriended Liesl and Erich as children. They had stayed in touch, and Bud let them know he met a girl in Italy – Gabriella was her name – and fallen in love. His dream was to bring her back to Biloxi, and it seemed he'd managed it. Liesl was thrilled for him.

'That's so exciting,' she said, 'but I'll be doing my finals in May so I'll be going from the library to my bed and back again for the next few months. But you should definitely go.'

'I was afraid you'd say that.' Erich looked disappointed.

'But you'll have a great time and you can take pictures and tell me all about it,' she reassured him.

'Well, if you're sure you can't go, I'll have to go alone. I'm going to save up. I know *Mutti* would pay for me, or Elizabeth and Daniel, but I want to pay my own way. Just imagine it, Liesl – me, in America.'

She chuckled. 'Just don't come back talking like a Yank now, y'hear?' She did her best imitation of Bud's drawl.

'I won't,' he promised. 'I've not said anything yet to…' He nodded at the front seat. 'Or to *Mutti* and Willi, so keep it under your hat for now. I want to buy my ticket first.'

'Mums the word,' she whispered.

'Loose lips sink ships,' they said simultaneously – they'd always found the posters from the Department of Defence during the war urging people to be cautious in their conversation funny – and they both collapsed into giggles.

'What are you two whispering about back there?' Elizabeth asked suspiciously.

'Nothing,' they chorused, and immediately started laughing again.

Lunch was a really jolly affair, and the hotel was decorated beautifully with twinkling fairy lights and a huge aromatic tree in the lobby. Frau Braun told the gathering about the winding down of the farm. She began working there as soon as she arrived, helping out with caring for the children, and despite her somewhat acerbic manner with adults, the children loved her.

Rabbi Frank and Ariella worked tirelessly to find family members for the children, but even now, five years after the end of the war, things were still fairly chaotic in Europe. Camps for those displaced were still full, and the documenting of survivors as well as the efforts to bring those responsible to justice was an ongoing project.

They'd had some luck finding relatives in some cases, but it was slow and difficult, and in many cases the children, especially the ones who had arrived when they were very young, had no knowledge or recollection of their family. For them, home was Ballycreggan.

Elizabeth and Daniel had promised each child that regardless of the outcome of the search for their loved ones, they would have a home in Ballycreggan for as long as they wanted it. The committee that ran the farm had decided that children were only to be automatically returned to parents, grandparents or siblings; otherwise, it would have to be the child's choice.

'The lease of the farm is due shortly, and we are at a bit of a crossroads,' Elizabeth explained as everyone tucked into lunch. 'Some of the children are gone back to family, some of the older ones have decided to go to Israel or are settled in Ireland, studying or working, and three have family in America, so they are going there, which leaves us with five children.'

'Who?' Liesl asked.

Ariella answered. 'Well, there's Clara and her brother, Leo. Rabbi Frank thought he might have found a Gentile uncle, but when the man responded to the rabbi's letter of enquiry, he said he wasn't any relation of theirs.'

Something about Ariella's tone made Liesl give her a questioning look. 'But you think he was?' she asked.

'Well, let's put it this way,' Erich said. 'Not everyone would be happy to see the rightful owners of businesses and property suddenly show up. Clara and Leo's father apparently was very wealthy – he owned several textile factories before the war and a beautiful house in Hanover. So a lot of people suddenly found themselves very wealthy overnight and they don't want to hand that over now.'

Liesl was surprised to hear the hard edge to her brother's voice. But she didn't blame him for being bitter. Relief and joy at having survived and having their mother return had given way to deep resentment at how the Jews had been left to their fate by everyone, and he wasn't alone in that. She was dreading even more telling them she was thinking of going to Berlin.

'So you think people are denying their Jewish family?' Liesl was horrified.

Daniel shrugged. 'It would seem so. Hard to imagine, but some people are greedy and don't want to give up what they acquired, however nefariously.'

'It's unbelievable and more common than you'd think, it seems,' Elizabeth said. 'Then there's Marek Seinfeld, who lost everyone in Dachau. And Beata and Gretta Hoffman – their father died early on and the mother was liberated but died in a displaced person's camp, it seems.'

'That's awful, to have made it so far,' Liesl said, her eyes bright with tears.

Ariella reached over and squeezed her hand. She'd only barely survived herself, and but for the kindness of strangers and friends, Liesl and Erich would have lost both their parents too, like the Hoffman sisters.

'It is,' Daniel agreed. 'But with Levi and Ruth going to Israel, that leaves the rabbi and Frau Braun running the farm. It's too big and somehow too sad anyway for them to be there alone.'

'Doesn't Rabbi Frank want to go to Israel too?' Liesl asked.

'He does,' Frau Braun confirmed. 'But he promised to care for these children, and until they are all settled, he won't leave them. The Red Cross have no more information for us, so it's like we've reached the end of the line. There is a possibility that people will still turn up, of course, and the rabbi has ensured that his name is given as a contact for all of the children from the farm. He's made each one of them promise to keep in touch with him and let him know when they move from the address we have so that if anyone ever does come, then he'll be able to find them.' She shrugged. 'But I think that's all we can do.'

'So what's going to happen to the five who remain?' Liesl asked.

'There are a few options, but staying in Ballycreggan seems to be the only real choice and the one they are happiest with.'

The rest of the lunch passed in cheerful catching up of all that had been happening with Daniel and Erich's business, with Frau Braun grumbling about how the rabbi was driving her crazy with his pedantic nature, and with Ariella and Willi talking about their involvement with a movement to identify resistance fighters so their sacrifice wasn't lost to history.

There was a plaque to be erected in the St Johanniskirche Catholic church in Berlin dedicated to Father Dominic Hoffer, a brave man who was the reason Ariella survived. He died defending one of his parishioners, a Nazi spy, from the marauding Russian troops that wreaked havoc on the women of Berlin as the city fell.

As they spoke, Liesl saw her chance. 'Are you going to go back to see the plaque?' she asked.

The look on her mother's face said it all. 'No.' Ariella was adamant, and Willi rested his hand reassuringly on her shoulder. 'I won't ever go back there. But I have Father Dominic's prayer book and his lighter, and now there is a plaque there so everyone who visits that church will know about his kindness and courage.'

'It was a great thing to do, *Mutti*,' Erich said, placing his hand on hers.

Ariella, despite her diminutive stature, had proved to have the courage of a lion. Ariella had loved their father dearly, Liesl knew that, but she was so happy her mother had found love again with Willi. He was seven years younger than Ariella, and in lots of ways, he was more like an older brother than a stepfather to Liesl and Erich, but he made Ariella happy.

'Did you hear about the *Blonde Poison*?' Willi asked after the waitress cleared their plates and offered the dessert trolley.

Liesl knew exactly who he meant. Stella Kübler, a Jew turned Jew catcher, had betrayed many submerged Jews to the Nazis. Ariella had been convinced the woman knew of her whereabouts when she was in Berlin and lived in terror of her.

'No, I didn't,' Liesl answered.

'The Russians got her. She got ten years, though I doubt she'll survive a Russian prison. Siberia isn't for everyone.' He smiled, then chose a trifle.

'Fingers crossed,' Erich said darkly.

Liesl sat quietly. These were her people, each in their own way damaged by the Germans, and she was thinking of going to socialise amongst them. She felt dishonest and ashamed. Would her papa be proud of her now? She doubted it.

# CHAPTER 7

*E*arly Christmas Eve morning, Liesl woke to the familiar sound of Daniel brewing his coffee. Elizabeth liked a lie-in on the school holidays, but Daniel had been an early bird all his life. Erich had stayed at their mother's house the previous night, as he and Willi were going out early.

Tonight was the final night of Chanukah, the Shamash. The last candle of the menorah would be lit in the synagogue, and Rabbi Frank had invited anyone from Ballycreggan who wanted to come for a little celebration, at which traditional Jewish food would be served.

Erich and Willi were going to help set everything up. Daniel had relinquished his role as general caretaker of the farm when he started his own business, and Willi slotted into the position. It gave him a purpose. He'd followed Ariella to Ireland, but once there, he would have been at a bit of a loss were it not for the farm.

Initially, people were mistrustful, as he was a German. Though everyone knew Ariella was Jewish, Willi and his mother were not, and in the eyes of many, they were perpetrators of the bloody carnage.

Liesl wondered, as she lay cosy and warm under the blankets, if Willi would ever tell everyone the truth: that he was in fact Jewish, that Frau Braun was not his birth mother and that his father, Hubert

Braun, was a deplorable man who'd had an affair with a Jewish woman and Willi was the result. Frau Braun, Hubert's long-suffering wife, took the child on as her own, being unable to conceive herself, and she and Willi shared a bond of love that equalled any mother and son related by blood. Willi and Ariella had confided in Liesl, Erich, Elizabeth and Daniel, but chose to keep the information in the family, which Liesl assumed was to protect the woman Willi saw as his mother. Instead, they vindicated their German nationality by both of them throwing themselves wholeheartedly into helping the children on the farm.

Reluctantly, Liesl threw back the blankets and got out of bed. The wool rug on the floor mitigated against the stone cold of the early morning. She pulled on her woollen dressing gown and put her feet in the warm fur-lined slippers Erich had bought her for her birthday.

As she crept into the kitchen, she saw her stepfather's broad back as he busied himself with his coffee.

'Can you spare one for me?' she asked quietly.

He spun round and beamed. 'Just like the old days, eh?' He took another cup from the dresser. 'Except now I can have coffee every day, and not one cup a week under cover of darkness.' He chuckled.

'It's hard to believe rationing is still necessary though, isn't it?' Liesl said. 'Even in Dublin, some things are still very hard to get. Abigail's cousin sent some sweets from America in the post, and I could hardly remember the taste. It feels like forever since we've had sweets.'

'I'd just love the petrol rationing to end. I'd live without the sugar, but it would be nice to take jobs further away – but I just can't get the fuel.'

'Well, if the Conservatives get in next time, then you'll have your wish. They're working hard to end rationing. But Labour seem to think we need to keep going.'

Daniel nodded and sat at the kitchen table. 'You could be right.'

They chatted for a while about the political situation and the reconstruction of Europe.

'It's hard to imagine what it must be like there now,' Daniel mused. 'I saw some pictures of Vienna recently, and I wouldn't recognise it.'

'Do you think you'll ever go back? For a visit, I mean?' Liesl asked. She then sipped her coffee gratefully, her hands wrapped around the warm mug.

Daniel reached into the pocket of his jacket, which was hanging on the back of her chair, and extracted two foil-wrapped chocolates. Bridie in the sweetshop got them for Daniel whenever she could, as he was always on hand to help with any jobs she needed doing. It was his only other indulgence.

He gave her one and put his finger to his lips with a smile. 'It's Christmas.'

She grinned and unwrapped it, smelling the rich chocolatey aroma before nibbling it.

'No,' he answered her question. 'I can't see the point. Vienna is so far in my past, sometimes I wonder if I ever really was Viennese at all. I miss the coffee and the chocolates and some aspects of the life I had, but that's all gone now – the Germans, the Allies, then the Russians saw to that. Maybe one day it will be the beautiful city it once was, but it's for others to build now.' He took a bite of his own chocolate, closing his eyes to savour the rare treat. 'No, home for me is Ballycreggan now, and this family. There's nothing back there for me or for anyone really. Even the children from the farm, this is their home now, and some of them going back to people they don't know, to a country where they don't belong anymore... I don't know. If it were up to me, I'd keep them all here.'

Even when she was little, she'd loved how Daniel never spoke to her as if she were a child.

'So are you going to tell me what's bothering you, or do I have to drag it out of you?' His kind gaze met hers.

'Is it that obvious?' She smiled sadly.

'Only to me. So what is it? Maybe I can help?'

'I've been invited to participate in a debating competition. It's very prestigious, and they've asked me to represent Trinity.'

Daniel took another sip of coffee, and she could see the pride in her achievement on his face.

'Well done! That's a wonderful honour, though I could have told them that it's close to impossible to argue with you. Seriously though, that's amazing. We're so proud of you, Liesl.' He grinned. 'When is it?'

'February. But I don't know if I'll go.'

'Why wouldn't you?'

'It's in Berlin.'

The words hung between them.

'I see.' Daniel sipped his coffee. 'And you don't want to go back there?'

She sighed. 'I do. I know you won't be hurt by this, Daniel. I love you and Elizabeth and my life here, but I feel like I don't ever completely belong anywhere. I'm German, I'm Jewish, I'm Northern Irish, which means I'm British now but I live in the Republic. And everyone else seems settled, you know, happy to be where they are, or making plans, going to Israel or whatever. And I just feel like I almost belong but not quite. The last place I felt truly secure was Berlin, and I just want to go and see if it still feels that way. But I'm worried about *Mutti*. She had to fight so hard to get out of there, to get back to us. Would she be hurt if I just go back and pretend like everything is fine? This is the city that killed her husband, my father. She can't forgive them, and maybe I shouldn't either?'

Daniel smiled and took her hand. 'Liesl, your mother moved mountains to get back to you and Erich. I don't think we'll ever fully understand what she went through. Only Willi and Frau Braun truly know, and that will bond them till the day they die. But she put you on that train to save you, so you could live your very best life. So she won't stop you doing the very thing she wanted for you – of course she won't.' He smiled. 'People get the wrong impression of your *mutti*, you know. Because she's so tiny and looks like a little bird, people think she's fragile, but she's the toughest person I know. And she loves you and Erich fiercely. If you tell her you want to go there, she'll be happy for you – I know she will.'

Daniel pointed to the window where a plump robin had landed on the windowsill. 'Look.'

'People here say robins are the souls of those gone before,' Liesl said, then stood and walked across the bright kitchen to the window where the robin sat, his tiny black eyes looking in. 'Hello, Papa,' she whispered.

Daniel stood behind her, his large hand on her shoulder.

'Do you think I should go?' she asked, turning to look up at him.

'I don't know that, but I just think you should decide, and don't let fear, bitterness or what anyone else thinks about it influence you. If you want to go, then go. If you don't, then stay home. But be true to yourself.'

'I think I do. It's for two weeks, and there are lots of lectures and symposia as well as the debates. The theme is reconstruction and reconciliation. I'd get to use my German again, and maybe meet some new people...' She weighed it up in her mind – speaking to Daniel always made things clearer.

'And what about this Jamie we keep hearing about? Is he a factor in the decision?' Daniel asked.

Liesl smiled. 'No, not really. He's happy for me.'

'Fair enough. Be sure he treats you properly or he'll have me to deal with, all right?' He patted her shoulder. 'Now, I'd better get ready. Elizabeth has a list of jobs for me that will take me until June.' He rolled his eyes in mock despair, but Liesl knew he adored Elizabeth and would do anything for her.

'Thanks, Daniel.' She gave him a kiss on the cheek.

'For what?' he asked.

'Just for always being there.' She smiled.

The days at home flew by in a haze of greetings and goodbyes. Christmas in Ballycreggan was such a lovely time, each house decorated with a sparkling tree and tinsel and paper chains strung everywhere. Daniel had arranged for a big tree to be placed in the village square, and all the local businesses had donated to light it up. There were menorahs too in several windows as a friendly gesture to their Jewish neighbours, and a new tradition was the Christmas-Chanukah tea party in the parish hall during which the bakers of the community did their best to ensure everyone gained five pounds. The smells of her childhood – cinnamon cookies and brown sugar latkes – intermingled deliciously with the traditional Irish fruit cakes and mince pies. The memory of the deprivation of the war years was fading, and there was a real sense of gratitude for the bounty they now enjoyed.

Levi and Ruth were due to sail to New York later in the year to visit with some of Levi's family who had settled there, and then they were going to join a group who were booked to fly to Tel Aviv from New York. It was the adventure of a lifetime, and Liesl was really happy for them, but it did feel like the end of a part of her life. Ruth was Irish and Levi had managed to get out of occupied Europe, and despite their taciturn manner – both were known to be grumpy – they had proved themselves to be loyal and loving to the children of the farm.

Liesl only ran into David and Viola once, in Bridie's sweetshop, their favourite place in Ballycreggan since they were little.

'Hello, Viola, David,' she managed as she entered, only discovering they were inside once she'd closed the door behind her. Bridie had gone out the back to find something, so they were alone.

'Oh, hello, Liesl.' David flushed. 'You're back for Christmas, I suppose?'

'Well, yes. The university is closed for two weeks, so...' She wished she sounded more cool and sophisticated.

Viola refused to meet her eye, and an awkward silence hung between them.

'I hear you two are going to Israel?' Liesl said to break the tension.

'Er...yes. We... We're going to give it a try,' David responded, and Liesl noticed him give Viola a nudge.

'Well, I hope it works out well for you both. Good luck.'

Again there was silence, and she wished she could just leave but she couldn't. After what seemed like an age, Bridie came through from the storeroom, her signature pink overalls matching the paint of her shop.

'Ah, Liesl.' She smiled. ''Tis yourself, and looking like a fine young lady too. You must be having a grand time down in Dublin to say you're looking so well.'

Liesl knew it was showing off but she couldn't help it; her heart ached at the way her two friends had shut her out. 'Oh, I am, Bridie, thanks! I'm really enjoying it, and next month I'm going to Germany representing Trinity in a debating competition, so I'm really looking forward to that.' She knew she shouldn't go on, but she couldn't help it. 'My boyfriend can't make it, unfortunately – he's studying for his College of Surgeons exams – but it should be wonderful.'

'Well, you mind yourself over there, do you hear me? There's all sorts of unexploded bombs and the devil knows what over there, so watch where you're walking.'

Bridie handed over whatever it was David had wanted from the storeroom and took his money. Viola and David left, and Bridie carried on, oblivious. 'Will you tell Daniel that I've no chocolate this week, but maybe there might be a bit on Tuesday?'

'I will.' Liesl smiled sadly.

'Don't you mind that pair,' Bridie whispered conspiratorially. 'I know they never said a blessed bit to you, and you and Viola were such good friends, but don't you give them one more thought, do you hear me?'

'I'm fine, Bridie, honestly. Thanks though.'

Liesl knew Bridie had a soft spot for her and felt bad that Liesl didn't know about David and Viola. But it didn't help that now as well as sadness at being excluded from her friends' lives, she had the sympathy of the parish too.

She bought some toffee. Abigail loved Bridie's home-made toffee, and Liesl had promised to bring some back. On a whim, she bought a little selection of sweets for Jamie as well.

'Cheerio now, Liesl, and I'll see you next time you're home.' Bridie waved as she left.

Liesl walked up the street to her mother's house, a beautiful Georgian two-storied place on an incline at the opposite end of the village from Elizabeth and Daniel's. Ariella had green fingers, and so the house was covered with a variegated ivy creeper, and in the summer that was supplemented by a ruby-red Virginia creeper. Pots of evergreen miniature conifers lined the little driveway, and Willi had strung some fairy lights in the copper beech tree in the garden. Ariella's house was very different from the apartment in Berlin, what with all its big windows and clean lines, but it was so beautiful. Decorated inside in pinks and aqua, with china ornaments and chintz fabrics, it reminded Liesl of a full-sized doll's house. Willi teased Ariella about all the cushions and tea sets she bought for the house, but the joking was gentle and good-natured, and after all her mother had endured, she deserved every ounce of comfort her home afforded her.

Liesl walked up to the house, rehearsing what she would say. It had been childish of her to mention Germany and Jamie in front of David and Viola, but she didn't want them to see her as pathetic. And now that the word was out, she'd *have* to have the conversation with her mother.

She was due to go back to Trinity the next day, and she'd still not found the right time. There were always people about. But she had to admit she was putting it off. Daniel was probably right, but what if he wasn't?

# CHAPTER 8

$\mathcal{A}$s Liesl had strolled along the footpath of the village she called home, waving to this person and that as she made her way, she'd thought about how convoluted her family situation must seem to someone from the outside. Yet to her, it was all perfectly normal.

When she'd told Jamie about her family, he'd been intrigued about how she and her mother and Elizabeth got along.

'Was neither of them jealous of the other? One gave birth to you and raised you until you were ten, but then the other took over. It must have been tricky. Do you feel torn sometimes?' he'd asked, and as she'd recalled the conversation as she walked, she was reminded of why she loved him so much. Jamie wasn't like other boys she'd met. He was thoughtful and intelligent and people fascinated him. He could be a joker, and he was popular for sure, but she knew that very few people really knew him. And she was one of them.

She'd considered his question properly before giving her answer. It could of course have been awkward, but it wasn't. She thought of both Ariella and Elizabeth as her mother, and she confided in both, neither one more than the other but maybe on different topics. Both women were practical and helpful. In lots of ways, she was closer to Elizabeth in that Elizabeth was more similar in personality. But then sometimes she just needed her *mutti*. It was hard to explain to anyone, but it just worked. She loved Daniel like her father, which he was in every way that mattered, and she loved Willi's company, though she didn't see him as a father figure really – he was too young and boyish for that. He was a bit like Jamie actually, a joker on the outside, but she suspected he ran deep.

She went around the back of her *mutti's* house, hoping Ariella hadn't left for the farm already.

Ariella dedicated so much of her time – and though she never said, Liesl suspected her money as well – to finding the families of the children on the farm. Together with Frau Braun and the rabbi, she was relentless.

Liesl smiled, remembering the descriptions of the high jinks between the stoic Rabbi Frank and the grumpy Frau Braun. Both were entirely convinced they were right, so though they might be sharing a goal, their methods would vary wildly, Liesl imagined. Rabbi Frank would be for keeping everything within the rules and going about everything correctly, but Frau Braun was more pragmatic. Daniel and Willi had had Liesl in stitches telling her about the fiery relationship the pair had.

The rabbi had been married years ago but his wife had died young, and since then, generally women held him in respect and never questioned him. But Frau Braun wasn't that kind of woman and she challenged him daily, resulting in the poor rabbi almost exploding on occasion.

Liesl peered through the back window for a sign of life. She had a key, but she and Erich had once, many years ago now, walked in on her mother and Willi in a romantic situation, and she never wanted to do that again. Whatever about her embarrassment – poor Erich had been traumatised. Now that she was in a relationship herself, she understood the role of physical intimacy, and after all her mother had endured, she was just glad Ariella was happy.

She heard her mother's heels on the tiled hallway. At only barely five feet tall, Ariella was rarely seen these days in flat shoes.

'Darling! I hoped it would be you. I was planning to come down before Daniel brought you to the train, but it is so nice to have you here instead.' Ariella embraced her daughter, and Liesl caught the delicate scent her mother always wore.

Before the war, Ariella always wore Chanel, but Coco Chanel's behaviour – she'd collaborated with Nazis and lived it up in the Ritz in Paris while her people were starved and brutalised by her boyfriend and his henchmen, and she sat idly by, sipping champagne, as French men and women were transported to camps under her nose – had ensured that no Jew would ever buy Chanel products again. She'd even gone so far as to use her position within the German elite to swindle her Jewish partners out of their share of her perfume business.

Ariella had switched to a Coty fragrance called Emerald, and despite the ration on such luxuries, she got a bottle from Willi every Christmas and used it very sparingly.

'Hello, *Mutti*.' Liesl smiled and allowed her mother to lead her into the sunny drawing room. The décor was bright and cheery, and as Ariella sat on the sofa, Liesl realised once again what an incredible woman her mother was. Ariella was a survivor in every sense of the word. She'd persisted through war, abuse, starvation, physical discomfort that was hard even to hear described let alone endure, all to find her way from Berlin to Ballycreggan. She'd stayed alive for Liesl and Erich, and Liesl was so glad she had. Her experiences had created a character of such resilience and strength that nothing fazed her. She got upset about the children, of course – you'd need to be made of granite to spend your days researching the Jews of Europe and not be heartbroken – but she didn't let her sorrow get in the way of the job that needed to be done.

'Something smells delicious.' Liesl sniffed the air.

'I'm baking a *Pfannkuchen* for you to take back to Dublin. Remember how I used to make them when you were little? We used to get those gorgeous black plums from Herr Gronz?'

'I remember.' Liesl nodded. It felt like a lifetime ago that she and her brother and their parents were carefree Berliners, worrying only if the plums were ripe enough for the cake.

'Would you like some tea, or coffee maybe?' Ariella asked.

'No thanks, *Mutti*, I'm fine.' Liesl swallowed. She was nervous, not that her mother would be cross or ask her not to go, but that she would see it as a betrayal.

'What is it, my love?' Ariella tucked a stray wisp of hair behind Liesl's ear. 'Something is wrong. Out with it.' She smiled.

'There's nothing wrong.' Liesl was quick to reassure her.

'Well, what is it then?' Ariella asked gently. 'Is it that boy you're seeing?'

'No, Jamie is fine, and we're fine, I think. But... Look... I've been invited to represent Trinity in a European debating competition. It's for two weeks in February, and...' – Liesl took a steadying breath – 'it's being held in Berlin.'

Ariella said nothing for a moment, and Liesl couldn't judge from her expression what was going on in her head.

Then she smiled gently. 'Congratulations, my darling girl, how clever you are. I'm not surprised in the least that they chose you. Such talent and quick wit, such eloquence is rare even in older people, but to you, it's natural.'

Liesl saw her mother's green eyes were bright with tears. 'But, *Mutti*, if you don't want me to go there after everything, I understand, and I'll tell them they need to send someone else.' She hated to see her mother upset.

'No... No, my love. You misinterpret the reason for my tears.' Ariella wiped her eyes with a lace handkerchief she had up her sleeve. 'I'm proud of you and happy that you are being recognised for the talented young woman you have become.'

'So do you think I should go?' Liesl asked, allowing a frisson of excitement to spark inside her. The final obstacle might not be such a hurdle after all.

'Do you want to go?' Ariella asked, her eyes searching Liesl's face.

'I think I do.' Liesl wanted to be honest. 'It is such a great opportunity, and a huge honour to be asked, but I was so worried you'd be hurt if I did, like I was forgiving them.'

Ariella took her hand and caressed it gently. '*Mein Liebchen.*' Ariella hardly ever spoke German to her, and hadn't even when she was a child. 'I don't know what came over everyone.' She was calm again. 'I honestly don't. The country Germany turned into was nowhere I recognised, but it is a funny thing. War brings out the worst in people. I've seen what it can do with my own eyes, and I pray you never do. But it also brings out the best. I saw and experienced indescribable brutality and hatred, but I also witnessed such extreme bravery and kindness that I hold in my head and in my heart that right always wins in the end. And what good was that victory if we can't face the future with optimism?'

'That's what Daniel says too,' Liesl said.

'He's a wise man, Daniel Lieber. Listen to him.' Ariella tipped Liesl's chin upwards to look into her daughter's eyes. 'Go, my love, and spread your wings, have adventures. Imagine you, competing against the best in the world, using your intellect and skill at debating. Peter's heart would be bursting with pride, I know it would. So if you want to go to Berlin, then that's exactly what you should do, my darling. It's what I want, and it's what your papa would have wanted.'

'Thank you, *Mutti*. I…I'm so relieved.' Liesl stood to go. 'I wish I had longer, but the train is at two and I need to go.'

'Of course. Let me wrap the *Pfannkuchen* for you.' Ariella went to the kitchen and called back, 'How is Jamie, by the way?'

'He's fine. He's really pleased for me. I'll bring him up next time so you can all meet him.'

Liesl accepted the pie and kissed her mother goodbye. Ariella embraced her and then said, 'Wait, I have something else for you.'

She disappeared upstairs, returning a moment later with a small brown paper bag. She handed it to Liesl, who opened it, looked inside and extracted a box. Liesl flushed and shoved the box back in the bag.

'*Mutti*, I…' She was mortified.

'Darling, you are a young woman in love, and I don't know if you and this Jamie are intimately involved – perhaps you are or maybe not, it's not my business – but Willi went to London to meet some former resisters recently and I asked him to buy those. I doubt Mrs

White in the chemist has ever heard of Durex, and she'd need to be stretchered out if you tried to explain.'

'*Mutti*! Willi knows these are for me?' Liesl was aghast. Jamie had explained that the sale of contraceptives was illegal in the Republic and so they'd been careful, but there was always a risk.

'No, of course not. I might look old, but I'm not that ancient yet that I couldn't get pregnant, and I have no desire to have any more children so...' She smiled. 'He won't miss that packet.'

'But, *Mutti*... Oh, no... I...' Liesl stopped. Her mother was one in a million. Most of her friends' mothers would be horrified at their unmarried daughters having sex, but Ariella was just concerned for her protection.

'You only get one life, my love – live it. You have one body – enjoy it. But be careful, with your body, your head and your heart.' She took the paper bag and tucked it in the bottom of Liesl's brown leather handbag.

# CHAPTER 9

'*I*t's an ill wind, Fräulein.' Jamie chuckled. 'God rest Mrs Hanratty Senior.'

Liesl lay on his chest, their hearts beating in unison, as a light film of sweat settled on her skin.

Henrietta Hanratty's mother had passed away in County Mayo, and once everyone in the boarding house got over the shock that someone as advanced in years as Horrible Hanratty's mother was still living, they settled into a joyous few days of freedom. She managed to bully the rest of the lads into finding alternative accommodation for the duration of her absence, but because Jamie was unfailingly charming, she allowed him to stay to take care of the place.

Without her sour surveillance, it was actually a lovely place, and Jamie and Liesl were enjoying playing house. It was so nice to wake up together and snuggle or make love again, and nobody was creeping about in their bare feet trying to get out before anyone saw them.

It was Saturday so no lectures, and Liesl had even agreed to take a day off from her preparations for the debating competition in Germany. She was as ready as she'd ever be; she had her research done, and her speeches were outlined perfectly. It didn't do to learn things off by heart, as the debater needed to go with the flow of the arguments in rebuttal, but she had all she needed at her fingertips. The motions were all on the subject of reconstruction, international relations and diplomacy, and she was nervous but very excited. The plans were all in place: She would take the ferry to England next weekend, then catch another to France and then take a train all the way to Berlin. She was to travel alone, but Professor Kingston assured her that there was a 'meet and greet' function arranged for the first night, during which she would meet her fellow delegates and the competition organisers. She was going to stay on campus in the women's accommodation, and she had been assured that everything was taken care of.

Since she'd come back after Christmas, things with Jamie were wonderful. He'd missed her over the holidays and showered her with affection and compliments. The girls in her halls loved him too. He was kind of famous around campus at UCD, and she had to admit walking around Dublin with the gorgeous Jamie Gallagher on her arm gave her a surge of pride and pleasure.

Apparently the conversation with his parents had been a disaster, with them extracting a promise that he would finish out the year and they would talk in the summer. Jamie seemed to think they would let him give up then, but something about the tone of the conversation, even relayed second-hand through him, told her they had no such intention.

Erich had come down for a night the previous week, and they'd all gone out with the gang from college, which was great fun. Jamie's group of boys had blended with the girls she was friendly with, so there was always a gang to socialise with. Erich and Jamie continued to really hit it off too, which was lovely to see. Liesl teased her brother that it was Jamie he was coming to visit, not her, as the pair blathered on for hours about football.

Upon arriving home, Erich wrote her a jokey letter telling her that Jamie was the best she was ever likely to get and she should cling on to him.

'And what am I to do here all on my own for two long weeks in the depths of winter, Fräulein?' Jamie nuzzled her neck. 'How will I survive?'

Liesl rolled away and giggled. 'Oh, here's a novel idea – how about a bit of study? If you really intend to do this year's exams as you promised your parents, you might as well do well. It will be something to bargain with if you change courses.'

Jamie rolled onto his back and groaned. 'I hate it, Liesl, you know I do. It's actual torture. Ventricles and arteries and lymphatic drainage… I'm only interested in one body, and that is my gorgeous girlfriend's.' He snuggled up to her and began kissing her neck, but as she gave herself over to the waves of pleasure, they were startled by a loud knocking on the front door.

'Who's that?' Liesl asked in alarm. 'Is it Miss Hanratty?'

'She has a key to her own house.' Jamie was for returning to the task in hand. 'Just ignore it. They'll go away…' He resumed kissing her, but the knocking was more insistent now. Then they heard foot-steps on the gravel at the back of the house.

Jamie crept over to the window and moved the curtain slightly. She saw him pale.

'It's Father Brendan and my parents,' he hissed. 'Quick, get dressed. I'll go down and distract them, and you slip out the back.' He was halfway into his trousers and was pulling apart his shirt and pullover, taken off together in their haste last night.

Liesl got up, that familiar feeling that he was ashamed of her threatening again. 'Why don't I just go down, dressed obviously – it's 11 a.m. so they needn't know I spent the night – and you can intro-duce me properly. This seems so silly and juvenile skulking around like this. We are grown adults, Jamie.' She dressed as she spoke, but her eyes never left his face.

'I… Look, now would not be the right time, Liesl, trust me. Just slip out. I'll call to you later.' Without another word, he left, and she heard him open the front door. With a heavy heart she gathered her belongings and tried to fix her hair before opening the bedroom door and going onto the landing of the large and sprawling house.

The voices were wafting up. A woman, she assumed his mother, was admonishing him.

'This is just ridiculous, Jamie, you lounging about in bed in the middle of the day when your examination is around the corner.' Her accent was very country so it was hard to catch every word, but she was speaking to Jamie like he was a little boy.

'Your father and I had to make sacrifices to pay for this fine education, and what are you doing? Frittering it away! My poor brother is putting off retiring, as you well know, keeping the practice for you. He is getting on and doesn't have time for you to be repeating exams. He needs you down there running the practice, fully qualified.' Her indignation was reaching a crescendo.

'Mam, if you'd just –' Jamie started, but now two men's voices cut across him.

'Do not interrupt Mammy,' they said in unison.

'James Gallagher!' She was off again. 'Father Brendan came up to see you, though he is very busy with the Lord's work, but he did it for me after us getting that ridiculous letter, and you give him the same old nonsense about not liking the course and then tried to introduce him to this woman. I'm sure she's behind this! Is she trying to lead you away from your studies, from your faith? Is that it? Because for the life of me, I can't fathom how a lovely well-brought-up boy, from a fine God-fearing family, could have gone so wild. You're a scourge to me, Jamie Gallagher, and I'm ashamed of you, and that's the truth.' This ended with a dramatic sob, and Liesl rolled her eyes.

This was pathetic. Jamie was supposed to be a man, but he was allowing himself to be bullied by that harridan. She was so hurt and disappointed. She crept along the corridor as quietly as she could, holding her shoes in one hand, her bag and coat in the other, and began the descent. The polished mahogany stairs to the second floor split halfway down on a landing, one side going to where the Gallagher family were, the other leading out the back via the kitchen.

'You need to do the First Fridays and go to confession for flouting the commandments in not honouring your father and mother, James

73

Gallagher. In fact, Father Brendan will hear your confession now, this minute.'

Liesl stumbled and dropped her bag, which she'd left open in her haste to depart. A bottle of perfume, a lipstick, her toothbrush and some spare underwear spilled out onto the polished bare wooden treads, and suddenly she realised the party had come to the bottom of the stairs, alerted by the noise of her falling belongings. She stood on the landing, rooted to the spot, blushing furiously.

'It's her, Mammy. That's the Jew he was with the night I met him.' The young priest, now dressed in a long soutane down to his ankles, pointed accusingly at Liesl.

'Are you telling me…' Jamie's mother was dumbstruck, and the group stood in a tableau.

Liesl fought the urge to giggle. She was terrified, but there was something so incongruous about the whole situation – it was like a scene from a French farce.

Jamie's mother rounded on him. 'You promised us, you *swore* blind that Jewess had nothing to do with you. You said you barely knew her! How could you lie straight to our faces like that?'

Mrs Gallagher was red-haired like her son but short and stout. She wore a headscarf rather than a hat and a sensible brown overcoat. Her eyes were Jamie's though – Liesl recognised the sea-green eyes that she'd fallen for. Beside Mrs Gallagher stood a tall, broad, balding man, clenching his fists into balls by his sides, his face puce.

Liesl decided she'd better take control of the situation and forced herself to walk down to where the tableau stood fuming.

'Good morning, Mrs Gallagher, Mr Gallagher, Father Brendan.' She tried to look as dignified as she could, ignoring her belongings on the stairs as she walked down. 'My name is Liesl Bannon, and I'm Jamie's girlfriend. It's nice to finally meet you – he talks about his family often.' She held her hand out to shake theirs, but the trio stood and simply stared.

'Did you sleep here?' Brendan demanded, then pointed at Jamie. 'With him?'

Liesl tried not to blush, and her eyes frantically sought Jamie's, but he was staring at the floor.

'I did,' she said, her head high, praying they couldn't hear the frantic beating of her heart. 'But we are –'

Jamie's mother stepped forward then, her face only inches from Liesl's neck, as the woman was easily six inches shorter, even with Liesl in her stocking feet. 'You dirty Jewish jezebel.' She was seething and spat each word. 'I know you're behind the fall of my child, but you may get your filthy heathen claws out of him, do you hear me? You're the reason he's not studying, you're behind the whole "I want to give up my course", and now you have him fornicating and damning his soul with a mortal sin for your own pleasure.' She grabbed the front of Liesl's blouse as the three Gallagher men stood behind.

'Mammy, please. It's not Liesl's fault. It's all me. I… Don't speak to her like that, it's not right,' Jamie pleaded.

But his mother spun round, not relinquishing the hold on Liesl, and shouted, 'You've done enough!' She turned to her husband. 'Get him out of here.'

Before Liesl knew what was happening, Jamie's mother dragged her by her blouse to the front door and shoved her out. Liesl stumbled with the weight and ferocity of the shove and only barely steadied herself when she heard Mrs Gallagher's final sentence.

'Never contact my son again, do you hear me, you dirty slut? Or I'll get the guards.'

The front door slammed and she was outside, alone.

# CHAPTER 10

*L*iesl knew the girls in her halls were finding it hard to keep repelling Jamie, but she would not speak to him. She knew she would have to get him to stop calling on her. With a sigh, she pulled a notebook towards her. She was leaving for Berlin in the morning.

In the week since the horrible encounter with the Gallagher family, he must have called ten times. Each time, she refused to see him. She took a more circuitous route to lectures, fearing he would try to accost her on her way to or from class. Abigail spotted him one day, and she narrowly managed to avoid him.

Her friend insisted she needed to face him. 'Liesl, just meet him once and say what you need to say. Skulking about, avoiding him like you're the one who has done something wrong is ridiculous.'

It was cowardly, she knew, but the thought of listening to some feeble excuse for his behaviour was more than she could bear. Actions spoke louder than words, and Jamie had broken her heart that day. He denied her, not because he didn't want to drag her into it, not because he wanted to spare her, but because he was ashamed she was a Jew. She would never forgive him. There was no going back.

She warned the girls in the house not to entertain him at all. She knew some of them had an eye for him, but she was finished.

But Abigail was right – he wouldn't stop. She'd have to finish it properly. She wouldn't meet him – she was afraid she'd crack as she was so lonely and sad – so a letter would have to do.

She started to write.

*Dear Jamie...*

Then she scribbled out the 'dear' and just wrote 'Jamie'.

She wondered if the letter should be an outpouring of all the hurt and anger, or cold and aloof, simple and to the point? Eventually she decided on the latter. She wouldn't give him the satisfaction of seeing how deeply he'd hurt her.

*Jamie,*

*Whatever we had is over. I will not discuss the matter further. You showed me very comprehensively what kind of person you are last Saturday morning, and so I have no interest in further association.*

*Do not come to my residence or try to contact me again,*

*Liesl Bannon*

Before she had time to reread it or regret her harsh words, she sealed it, put it in an envelope, stamped and addressed it and ran downstairs to the postbox. He'd have it in the morning when she'd be on the boat to England. It was for the best. But it felt like her heart was breaking.

She slept fitfully, everything going round and round in her mind. Part of her longed for him, to feel his arms around her again and to hear him explain why he didn't defend her, give her some perfectly reasonable explanation for his behaviour. But she knew that there was none. Her life experience and the experiences of her family told her that there were few times in life when one was called upon to do the right thing, to stand up and be brave, and those were the defining moments of a person's character. Her father had done it and had paid the ultimate price. Her mother had shown such incredible moral courage so often, it was indescribable. Elizabeth took Liesl and Erich in without a moment's hesitation because it was the kind and decent thing to do; she also defied everyone by defending Daniel when he was accused of spying for the Germans and by getting evidence against the real spy. The children she'd grown up with, who'd been sent away from their families and all they knew, faced the future with fortitude and an inner strength that she knew was so hard to muster. The people of Ballycreggan pulled together during the war, sharing what they had with the Jewish refugees, and put aside whatever prejudice they might have had because it was the right thing to do. All her life, the people around her had shown by example how to put aside what was comfortable and do what was right. And Jamie had failed miserably.

She was relieved to have the debate to focus on. It took her away from Dublin and away from Jamie Gallagher.

* * *

THE FOLLOWING MORNING, exhausted and nervous, she set out on her adventure.

The organisers had thought of everything. A car collected her and brought her to the port, where she caught the morning sailing to Holyhead. The last time she was on the Irish Sea, she was a little girl of eleven years old, fleeing bombed-out Liverpool with Elizabeth and Erich. And as she stood on the deck that February morning, watching the ship pull away from the quay, the biting wind stinging her cheeks, she thought it felt like a hundred years ago in one sense, and in another, only yesterday. She gazed back at Dublin. Where was he now? What was he doing? Did he feel as bad as she did? She doubted it. Tears leaked from her eyes and her heart broke.

The crossing was calm enough for February; sometimes the Irish Sea could be so rough. She'd taken an herbal mixture Willi's mother sent down – Frau Braun swore by it apparently – that was good for motion sickness. She thought about everyone at home in Ballycreggan and how they were so proud of her, and she felt a pang of love and loneliness as she set off on her big adventure.

She'd told them what had happened with Jamie, but she let on that she was better about it than she was. They were worried enough about her travelling without thinking she was in a dark depression into the bargain. Erich had written; Jamie had been in touch with Erich, begging him to intercede on his behalf, but Erich was first and foremost loyal to his sister.

In her bag was a cardigan Elizabeth had knitted, some socks and gloves from her mother, and a book from Erich. It was a romance and not really what she enjoyed reading, especially at the moment, but the image of her young brother going into Mullan's Bookshop on Donegall Place and choosing such a 'girl's book' melted her heart. Daniel had slipped her some money when she went back to Dublin after Christmas to prepare for the trip. She had enough anyway, as her allowance was more than generous. She'd promised him she'd find his favourite chocolates if it was at all possible and bring him home a box. Willi told her about a bar owned by a friend of his, a former member of the White Star, a Berlin-based resistance group, and made her promise that if she needed help, she was to go there. Willi had written to his friend to tell him she was in the city. The name and address were on a piece of paper in her purse. It was unlikely she would need them, but she thought she might just call in and say hello; she'd like to report back to Willi that his friend was well.

Even Rabbi Frank had written to her, congratulating her on being selected. And while he never gushed, she knew he was proud of her achievements. The children left at the farm all made her a good luck card, which was safely tucked inside her suitcase.

The transfer to Folkstone was a long one by train, all the way across Wales and then England, and she gazed out the window, watching the world go by. There was construction everywhere. It was not going to be easy to rebuild a whole country, and after years of relentless bombing, there was much to do.

She bought a cup of coffee at a station when they stopped for a few minutes, watery tasteless stuff, and an egg and cress sandwich. She tried to sleep but couldn't. Her speech, Jamie, the return to Berlin, her memories – they would not allow her to rest. She tried to read the book Erich bought her, a ridiculous tale of a British woman who fell in love with an American horse breeder, but she couldn't focus. She took out her notes and reread them. The facts about the challenges of integration and unity on a continent ravaged by war and division swam before her eyes.

She woke with a start as the train guard gently nudged her shoulder.

'This is Folkstone, Miss. It's time to get off,' he said, his cockney accent unfamiliar.

'Oh…er…right…' Liesl was disoriented and hoped she wasn't drooling. Her hair had come loose from the bun she'd tied in Dublin, and she felt very dishevelled. She began to gather her things; her notes had fallen to the floor beside her.

The young train guard helped her gather everything, and she shoved the items into her bag any old way, embarrassed.

'There's a ladies' powder room on the platform, if you need it,' the lad said, and instantly flushed with embarrassment. 'Not that you do, or even if you do, I don't mind if –' He stopped talking abruptly as an older, more heavyset man in uniform appeared.

'Johnny, please attend to your duties,' the man snapped. He nodded at Liesl but didn't smile.

'I better go…' the young man said apologetically, handing her the last of her notes.

'Thank you.' Liesl smiled and he beamed in return.

'You 'ave a nice trip, Miss.'

Liesl dragged her suitcase and her handbag, now bulging with her notes, off the train and onto the platform. Everywhere she looked, people were bustling about, some still in military uniform. The vast majority of people who served during the war had been returned to 'civvy street' as it was called, dressed in the 'demob suit', a free set of clothes provided by the authorities, and had returned to life as butchers and teachers. The return to some version of normality was hardest on the women, something she would reference in her speech if she could. They'd served in the munitions factories, on the farms and in the services, and now they were expected to toddle back to the kitchen and take care of the family as if they'd never done anything at all. It wasn't fair to give women a taste of independence, of autonomy, and then snatch it away. The social unrest too was palpable, and the rate of divorce was exceptionally high. Men and women were forced back into living together after years apart. They were different people after the war, and it was no surprise to Liesl that things were often not working out. Men were constantly grumbling about how assertive their wives had become. That made her smile.

She went to the powder room and washed her face and hands and took the bun out of her hair. She brushed it and pinned it up again, applied a little lipstick and perched her jaunty little black hat with its birdcage netting back on her head. The powder-blue suit was one Elizabeth had altered for her – new clothes were still hard to come by so they were forever recycling things – but she felt very smart in her tight-fitting skirt and jacket, under which she wore a new silk blouse she'd splashed out on in Dublin.

The ferry to France was due to set sail shortly, so she gave the officer in charge her ticket and walked up the gangway. She was tired and was pleasantly surprised to discover a cabin had been booked for her. She let herself into the little room that contained two bunks and a sink, and after removing her hat, shoes and jacket, gratefully laid down.

## CHAPTER 11

*S*he must have dozed off because she was woken by the
sound of someone opening the cabin door.

'Oh, blimey. Sorry, did I wake you?' A large young woman with an
unruly mop of brown curls dragged a huge case into the tiny cabin.

'Er, no, I just...'

'Are you going to the Intervar?' the young woman asked, noting
the European Intervarsity Debates logo on Liesl's luggage tags, EID in
gold letters on a black background. She spoke with the broad flat
vowels of the north of England.

'I am, yes.' Liesl sat up.

'Me too. I'm the Cambridge rep. Where are you from?' she asked as
she tried unsuccessfully to shove the enormous case under the bed.

'Trinity College, Dublin.' Liesl grabbed the other side of the suitcase, and between them they managed to squeeze it under the bunk.

'Right, thanks for that.' The young woman grinned. 'I heard the
food is dodgy, so I brought supplies. I daresay we'll be together for the
duration now. Emily-Jane Blennet, nice to meet you. But everyone
calls me Millie.' She stuck out her hand and Liesl shook it.

'Liesl Bannon. Nice to meet you too.'

Millie wore a beige dress that was pleated – most unfortunately –

around the waist, making her appear even wider than she was. Her brown hair was pulled into a messy ponytail, and the purple cardigan she wore over the dress clashed with everything.

'Have you been before?' Millie asked, plonking onto the bunk opposite Liesl's.

'No, never.'

'I'm dead excited about seeing Berlin though, aren't you? I mean, we flattened it of course, but they say it's not looking too bad considering. My sister's boyfriend's brother is coming out too, you know, for the World Festival of Youth and Students. He's from Hull. I said to him, our thing is for the brains and theirs is for the brawn. So it should be a right laugh.'

Liesl's face must have revealed she had no idea what the other woman was talking about.

'You know, the thing in East Berlin to show the world that the Reds are really wonderful and life in the GDR is simply smashing.' She gave a theatrical grin. 'It's 'cause of Korea and the spread of communism in China of course – the Russkis are doing a PR job. Still, there'll be lots of fit lads there, so that'll be good, eh? There's over a hundred countries going, so plenty to choose from!'

'Er...yes, I suppose so,' Liesl agreed, though she wasn't sure what Millie was talking about. She hadn't heard of a festival going on at the same time as the symposium.

'I wonder what it's like though, Berlin? We heard so much about it as kids, Hitler and the Nazis and everything to do with the war. And Berlin was the centre of it all. It must have been an odd place before, wouldn't you think, to have turned the way they did.' Millie flopped back and lay her head on the pillow.

Liesl stared at the ceiling and thought for a moment. This was either going to be a secret she never mentioned, or something she said in the early stages of relationships. It was a ramification of the trip that she hadn't anticipated. Everyone at home knew who she was, and in Dublin, her friends knew but it didn't come up much once she told them. But now that she was faced with it, she made a decision.

'It was lovely,' she said.

'What?' Millie leaned up on one elbow. 'I thought you said you were never there?'

'I was never at the competition before, but I was born in Berlin and lived there until I was ten years old. I'm a Jew, and my brother and I were saved by getting a place on the Kindertransport. My father was killed by the Nazis, and my mother survived in hiding for the whole war.' There was more to it, of course, but that was it in a nutshell. It felt strange but liberating to tell her story.

Millie sat up. 'Oh my God, really?' She was fascinated. 'I'm from Yorkshire, and we had some evacuees but they were from Liverpool and Manchester mainly. I knew some Jewish kids were brought in to Britain, but I never met any. There's a Jewish guy in one of my classes – philosophy – and I think he was from Austria but I'm not sure. He's very quiet.'

Liesl wasn't sure how to respond.

'What was it like?' Millie asked quietly. 'You know, having to leave, or before, when your parents were deciding?'

It struck Liesl as strange to launch into such an in-depth conversation with someone she hardly knew, but there was something about Millie she liked. She was open, and Liesl was sure she was a genuine person.

'It was awful,' Liesl said as she recalled those days. 'It was hard to see the whole thing happening, you know? I was just a child, and so I saw the little deprivations first but barely noticed. But then they closed our school, and we weren't allowed to go to the synagogue, or see our friends. My piano lessons stopped, and my brother couldn't play football anymore.'

Millie was hanging on every word. Because Liesl had grown up with Jews, she assumed most people knew her story. But when Jamie had the same reaction, she realised it was a story that people found macabre and horrifying but strangely compelling at the same time.

'Then my papa started saying to my mother to keep us in the apartment when he was at work. My papa was Christian but my *mutti* is a Jew, so we are Jews – that's how it goes. So we had to stay inside that summer of 1939. It was so hot. Before the war, we would go out to the Grunewald for picnics, and we used to go to the Tiergarten on our bicycles, or swimming in the Spree on hot days. But that all stopped.'

'Were you scared?' Millie asked.

Liesl shrugged and smiled as the boat shuddered and set sail. 'Yes and no. Looking back I was, towards the end especially, after they took my father, but before, not really. I thought my papa could fix everything, that he was big and strong and could protect us. It was a slow realisation, I suppose, that my parents didn't have all the answers and they couldn't fight the Nazis. They were too strong, and there were too many of them. We were the lucky ones though – we got out.' She heard the catch in her voice.

'I'm sorry about your dad.' Millie reached over and squeezed Liesl's hand. It was an oddly intimate gesture from someone she had only just met, but it didn't feel awkward.

'Mine was killed in Normandy, on D-Day, Sword Beach,' Millie said quietly.

'I'm sorry.' Liesl turned and faced her new friend. 'I've read about the landings. They were so brave, just crashing onto the beaches with the Germans bunkered in on the shore.'

Millie nodded. 'He was nothing special, just an ordinary bloke, but he loved me and I loved him. Him and my mum got divorced, so she wasn't devastated when he was killed, but me and my sister, Harriet, were heartbroken.'

'Is she older or younger than you?'

'Our Harriet is younger, and she and my mother clash something awful. She's three years younger than I am.'

'My brother, Erich, is three years younger than me too. We're very close though we're like chalk and cheese. He thinks I'm a right old swot, and he's more interested in cars and girls.' Liesl laughed.

'Oh my God, Harriet is exactly the same. All she goes on about is lipsticks and the cinema and this actress and that hairdo. She thinks I'm a disgrace of course, but I don't give a hoot about that stuff, and when I got into Cambridge, she was horrified. She actually said to me,

"Men don't like it if women think they're smarter than them."' Millie chuckled.

'Well, any man who is threatened by a woman's intelligence isn't one I'd want to have anything to do with.'

'Dead right too,' Millie agreed. 'I suppose you've a boyfriend?'

'No, I don't actually.' Liesl felt that pang of pain again. 'I used to go out with someone, but he let me down, so I'm single and happy to be so.'

'Not for long, I'd say. I'm not being funny like, but lads love girls like you, all delicate and slim and sultry looking. They think that's such a sexy look.'

Liesl pealed with laugher. 'If my father heard me described as sultry or sexy, he'd have to lie in a darkened room with the shock and I'd be locked up in the house.'

'I thought your father died?' Millie asked, confused.

'Well, yes, he did. I mean my adopted father, Daniel.'

'Oh, right, you're complicated. Lads like that too.' Millie shot her a wicked grin. 'All mysterious.'

'No, I'm not!' Liesl laughed.

'Well, you are, you know what I mean. And being a survivor of the nasty Nazis makes you even more attractive.'

This made Liesl laugh even harder.

Suddenly though, her new friend looked stricken. 'Oh God, I can't believe I said that! That is so insensitive. I'm mortified.'

'No offence taken.' Liesl dismissed her worries with a wave of her hand.

'So how come you've got two mothers then?' Millie asked.

'Well, my actual mother, Ariella, sent us to my papa's cousin Elizabeth, so she looked after us. We were sure my mother was dead, as we hadn't heard a word in years and years, and we knew for a fact our father was, so Elizabeth and her husband Daniel, an Austrian Jew, adopted my brother and me. But then my *mutti* turned up, and then she remarried a German called Willi Braun who helped to hide her, and now they all live in a village in Northern Ireland.' Liesl spoke as if this was a perfectly reasonable family construction, but of course as she heard the words aloud, she knew it wasn't.

'You should write a book,' Millie said. 'I'm a right boring old sack compared to that.'

'I doubt that very much.' Liesl smiled. 'What are you studying at Cambridge anyway?'

'International relations and public policy.'

'Sounds fascinating.'

'It is. I'm really interested in diplomacy, you know? How stuff happens in the world, who decides what goes on, that sort of thing. I suppose it started when I was a kid. My grandad was in the trenches in the Great War. He came home but wasn't right in the head. Then my dad gets sent to Normandy and is killed. I understand the whole "Hitler had to be stopped" thing, but I'm interested in the way he was managed before he got so powerful that men like my father had to die.' She shrugged. Her broad accent and dropped h's belied a sharp, keen mind.

'So what is your dream?' Liesl asked. It struck her that she'd never asked Abigail or Viola those sorts of questions. It was more immediate with them, less conceptual, but with Millie, for some reason, it was easy to have these kinds of conversations.

'I'd like to be in government. Either run for election or else I'd like to advise the government on handling international problems and try to pre-empt problems by understanding the patterns that lead to conflict.' Then she guffawed. 'Though the men would probably never take advice from me anyway. I'm prepared for being told to go off and have some babies, but things are changing, Liesl, my girl. This war changed things, and we won't go back to being the meek little women we once were.'

'I somehow doubt very much that you were ever a meek little woman.'

'Hmm, you're right. My mum is like Harriet, mortified, wishing I'd pipe down, lose weight and find some bloke to tie me to the kitchen sink. When I was a kid, I knew staying in Middleham wasn't going to be enough for me, so I decided I'd make a plan. I caught the bus to

Cambridge one week and Oxford the next, never told my mum what I was doing, had a wander round and decided on Cambridge. I went up in 1947, the first year women were allowed full membership.'

'And what about the fees? Did she agree to pay them?' Liesl asked.

'God no. That was never in the cards. She'd never do that. No, I got a scholarship.'

'Really? That's amazing.' Liesl was intrigued by her new friend.

'It actually is, 'cause I'm not the right sort at all – too rough and northern. They are such snobs there. But I did the entrance exam and aced it. I had to do one in French and another in German, and I don't know why, but languages come easily to me, so I knew I did really well. They called me for the interview, and I knew by their faces they weren't best pleased – I'm not what they had in mind at all – but I suppose my exam was too good to justify refusing me or summat, I don't know, but I got in anyway.' She said it as if it were nothing.

Liesl knew how hard she'd had to work to get good enough grades to get into Trinity, and thankfully her family could afford the fees, so it made Millie's achievement even more impressive.

'And what did your mum say when you told her?'

'She didn't even look up from her magazine.' Seeing Liesl's face, she chuckled. 'Don't worry, I never expected her to be happy. I walked to the bus myself that first day, and off I went to Cambridge. She never visits. I see Harriet sometimes, but I'm paddling my own canoe as they say.'

'And during the holidays, don't you go home?' Liesl couldn't imagine a life without her family.

'No, I go travelling in the summers. Last year I went to Greece, worked over there. A bunch of us went – it was great.'

'Gosh, that must have been exciting.' Liesl was in awe. Her decision to go to Trinity had been made with her family's input, and this was her very first trip anywhere unaccompanied. She felt like a baby beside the worldly Millie.

'It was. The summer before, we went to Italy – gorgeous. I met an Italian bloke, Paulo.' She sighed. 'He was a right plonker, but oh my, he'd turn heads. Handsome he was. Thick as a brick, mind you!' She laughed. 'Right, I'm starving. What say we go up to the restaurant here and get something?'

'Great, I'd love to.'

As Liesl followed Millie out into the narrow gangway and up the stairs, the smell of diesel oil and fumes filling her nostrils, she felt like a grown-up, maybe for the first time ever.

# CHAPTER 12

*I*t was strange to be speaking German in her day-to-day life again. The first time she heard the accent, someone saying a colloquialism that would not be heard in academic circles, she was immediately returned to the Berlin of her childhood. She started one time as a man yelled something; he was only calling to a friend across the campus, but it made Liesl jump. Men shouting were part of life when she left. But as the week had gone on, she got used to it and began speaking her mother tongue again as a native. She'd studied German and French at university, but living it every day, speaking to German students, staff in shops and cafes, it all felt so familiar. More so than she could ever have imagined.

She was honest and open when people remarked on how good her German was for an Irish person. She told them she was born and raised in Berlin but had to leave when she was ten. To Millie's astonishment, nobody asked anything more. They looked embarrassed and awkward, and she quickly changed the subject. Most of the people she met were her age, too young to have served in the military. But when she spoke to older men, she wondered, *Did you attack Jews in the street? Did you make them dig their own graves and then shoot them beside those graves so you would be spared the job of moving the bodies? Did you herd them on trains? Did you kill my father?* She never gave voice to those questions, but they were there.

There was also the excitement generated by the escalating press interest in the debates. She'd had a mention in the paper that morning. Millie had come screaming in to her with it before seven.

'Listen to this!' she squealed, shoving Liesl awake. She translated the German quickly. 'Liesl Bannon,' she read, 'was born and raised in Berlin and luckily escaped Nazi persecution by securing a place on the Kindertransport with her younger brother, where they spent the rest of the war in Northern Ireland. She is the daughter of the late Peter Bannon, former director of DND Investment Bank Berlin, famously associated with investment in several properties in New York. Miss Bannon's mother is sole heir to the Bannon fortune and survived the war. She currently lives in Northern Ireland. It is wonderful to hear her orate with such poise and elegance, which does nothing to mask what is clearly a deep and inquiring intellect.'

'How did they know all that about me?' Liesl sat up, rubbing her eyes and taking the paper from Millie. 'And what has it got to do with my father's business?'

'Who knows? Felix said a man from a newspaper was around asking about you, and one of the others must have said something. Remember when that girl Heidi asked you how come your German was so good and you told her? Well he must have done some digging I suppose. Your father was well known in financial circles I'd imagine, so it probably wasn't that hard. But it's good, isn't it? You should cut it out.' Millie stood up and the bed sprang back up.

'How was it last night?' Liesl asked, dragging herself out of bed.

Millie had been on a date the night before. Felix wasn't a debater; he was a huge weightlifting Bavarian who was also studying at the university and was representing the college at the other festival, the one her sister's boyfriend's brother was involved with. That was how they met. He really liked Millie too, and Liesl was thrilled for her friend. Felix was over six foot four and enormous in every way, hands like shovels as they might say in Ballycreggan. He made Liesl feel like a midget, but he was a cuddly bear of a man.

'Excellent.' Millie had a victorious glint in her eye, and it was only then that Liesl realised her bed hadn't been slept in.

'Aha.' Liesl smiled. 'Was Felix as fabulous as we've all been led to believe?'

'He was.' Millie flung herself back on her bed with a happy sigh and a twang of protest from the springs.

'Good.' Liesl grabbed her towel. She was happy for Millie, but she had no desire to hear the blow-by-blow account her friend was clearly dying to share. 'I'm going to shower.'

'Hurry up. I need to tell you about last night before the day starts,' Millie called as Liesl left to go to the communal bathroom down the hall.

Later, as they walked across the beautiful old campus, Millie regaled her with the details of her night with Felix, and Liesl tried not to think about Jamie. She knew what it was like to be in love, to want to spend every waking and sleeping moment with someone, and though it felt churlish and she was really happy for Millie, it hurt her to recall all she had lost. Luckily, as Millie was about to get to what she called 'the nitty gritty', some others joined them.

There was great excitement around campus. Hundreds of delegates had been accommodated in Campus Mitte right in the heart of Berlin, and Liesl was enjoying every moment. She and Millie were rooming together and going to all of the debates as well as preparing feverishly for their own. Both girls were through to the quarter finals, and the crowds were growing for each debate. Unlike many of the other delegates, Liesl had only been to one or two parties, though she was constantly being invited. Millie went more often, but it didn't interfere with her preparations. Liesl marvelled at Millie's ability to remember facts. She had a photographic memory, and Liesl was sure she was an actual real live genius.

Liesl had to work a little harder than her friend, but they were a good match. They knew that ultimately if they both continued to progress, they would face each other at some point, but it didn't hamper their support of each other. They worked hard, helping each other with research and delivery, and as a result, they were getting quite a reputation as the ones to beat.

Of the fifty universities represented from all over the world, there were only five women. It felt good to be down to the last eight. They studied the remaining six debaters with intensity, noting their weaknesses, and afterwards, they would try to come up with ways to exploit them. Two finalists were from the United States, one from Stanford in California and the other from Harvard in Massachusetts. Both were erudite and smart, but the Harvard man was a little weak on detail, particularly in relation to the Soviet countries, so that was useful. The Stanford representative was very strong in argument but lacked that ability to think on his feet in rebuttal. He was excellent but could be beaten, they believed. A good-looking and deceptively jovial Canadian was another one left. He came across as a joker and a bit of a flirt, but they both knew he wasn't above snooping or pressing for inside information. There was a French chap who was very quiet, mousy actually, but on the podium he came alive and was very quick in rebuttal. And the last two were both Germans. They of course had home advantage.

Liesl prepared for the quarter finals carefully. She wore her black jacket, white silk blouse and black skirt as usual. Her hair was tied back in a long French plait, and she wore a light-coloured lipstick. They were on day six of fourteen, and she was exhilarated and exhausted at the same time. Once the results of the quarter finals were released, she would know, and if she were knocked out, at least she would have time to explore her former home. Unter den Linden, the beautiful street coming from the Brandenburg Gate, was only a street away, but so far she'd not had time to go there. Millie had asked her if she was scared to venture out into her former home, as she and some of the others had found a coffee shop in the Tiergarten that they enjoyed going to but Liesl refused to join, citing study. The truth was she didn't want to go back, retrace the steps of her childish self, with anyone else. She would have loved to have had Erich, or *Mutti*, but if not them, then she would do it alone. She remembered her mother's stories of that time when she was one of the so-called submerged, a Jew living in plain sight. The incident in which a German soldier asked her on a date; Ariella had to agree to avoid arousing suspicion but then didn't show up. Her mother told her she saw him later, dead in the street, a pool of blood around his head. Her mother used to cross through the Tiergarten regularly, with fake papers in her bag, terrified of being caught or betrayed. No, when Liesl went there, it would be on her own.

After this afternoon, the debating was finished for the weekend, resuming Tuesday, and the organisers had arranged lots of diversion. There was skating on Orankesee lake, frozen now of course, and she remembered going there as a child. The image of her papa and herself laughing at the men who jumped through a hole in the ice-covered lake and then emerged shivering to run to the sauna flashed before her eyes.

She'd explained to Millie that she needed the weekend to explore on her own, to go to her family's places, to look for their old apartment, their school and their synagogue. She'd promised Frau Braun she would check on her house, see who was there now. Not that it mattered, as neither Frau Braun nor Willi was ever coming back to Berlin, but Frau Braun wanted to know if she could sell it to raise some money for the repatriation of the Jewish children.

The motion that afternoon was on the subject of collective memory. The proposal was that efforts should be made to gather first-hand accounts of the events of the war years, and that all citizens in occupied areas should be required to make a deposition before their memories were lost to history. She was arguing against the motion, her point being that it was traumatic enough to have endured it without being press-ganged into reliving it again. She planned to argue that while there was a benefit to the gathering of testimony, what was done was done. Was dragging it all up again so soon going to change anything?

What did she really believe? Should people be asked, 'What did you do? Did you help or hinder the regime?'

She found herself once more on the wrong side of a debate. She personally wanted to know what so-called ordinary Germans did. It was important that people were asked and straight answers given. It was too easy to skulk away and forget the terrible things that were done. Those who were decent and brave and fought against the regime deserved the recognition, and those who didn't, well, the world should know that too. She believed people's children and grandchildren should know if they moved into a Jew's house and started using their things. She wondered who lived in their old apartment, for example – should they never be called to account? Nuremberg addressed the high-ranking officials, but what about the ordinary people? The ones who shoved Jews on trains, the ones who took over their businesses, the ones who bought their goods for a fraction of their value knowing a Jew could do nothing about it? Or was it best to let it go? What good would it do now?

She sighed. She had to focus on the side of the debate she'd been given; to do otherwise would jeopardise her chances. A flash of her father, refusing to argue what he didn't believe, came to her mind, but she dismissed it. She would do what she came to do.

The elaborately decorated hall was packed. Dark wood buttresses winged across the expanse of ceiling, and the walls were adorned with portraits of great German thinkers, from before the time the nation stopped thinking and started following blindly. She'd read that the building had been flattened but had been rebuilt exactly, and she could hear her brother's voice saying, 'With American money.'

The podium spanned the entire width of the hall, ornate staircases on either side, and the lectern was a brass and oak creation, the handiwork of a skilled craftsman.

Millie was speaking on the Spanish Civil War and the impact it had on the rise of fascism. Liesl would have preferred that topic, as she could have argued it more dispassionately, but you got what you were given.

She was sixth to speak, which was good. Millie was second, and Liesl listened keenly to her friend succinctly and with the correct balance of passion and reason explain the rise of Franco and draw similarities between him, Mussolini and Hitler. She held everyone in rapt attention as she indicated what the warning signs were, the indicators that were the road markers to the creation of a totalitarian state. She sat down to thunderous applause.

The French delegate was next. He was representing the Sorbonne and spoke eloquently and with a staggering array of facts and figures on the true cost of post-war reconstruction. While what he was arguing was interesting, Liesl knew he'd overdone it on the data and people were bored. He was losing the audience and had no idea how to bring them back. He would surely be eliminated this time. There were only going to be four people left by the end of today.

His finish was stronger than the rest of the argument, but it wasn't enough. She caught his eye as he returned to his seat beside Millie. He knew it too.

She stood and took a deep breath, inwardly settling herself. The chairman introduced her and she wasn't imagining it – people seemed to perk up. She heard the whirr of shutters coming from the collection of journalists seated in the back corner.

She did what she always did – focused on the panel of adjudicators and ignored everyone else.

'Ladies and gentlemen, academic staff, what I am defending here today is people's right to let the past stay in the past. We must ask ourselves what is to be gained by requiring citizens to relive their worst nightmares for the sake of what? Posterity? Public record? Blame?' She paused and changed her tone slightly on the last word, casting a glance around the room.

'The people of the entire world, not just this continent, are traumatised. Brutalised by six long years of war. The pain that we have inflicted and endured runs very deep. We do not need a full written record of who did what to whom – the various departments of governments have the details of actions taken and what happened. But for ordinary citizens, no good can come of it. We know. We know the how, the when…though the why still remains a matter of discussion –' Liesl stopped mid-sentence. Standing in the middle of the crowd at the back was a young man, about her age, and there was something about him. His long blonde hair was parted in the middle, and his blue eyes bored into hers. He was average height and should have blended into the crowd of spectators, as he was dressed like any other student in a navy round-necked pullover and casual trousers.

She knew him, but she couldn't place him... And then she did. It was Kurt Richter, Nathaniel and Gretel's son. She and he were playmates. His family and hers had been such close friends.

Nathaniel, Kurt's father, had been the one to get Liesl and Erich on the Kindertransport. She wanted to meet him to thank him in person. He and his wife, Gretel, were always so much fun to be around. Seeing Kurt's face now was like a bolt from the blue.

As she dragged her attention back to her speech, it struck her. She shouldn't argue for the suppression of memory; that was wrong. She should stand up and be counted, just as Nathaniel had done, as her father had done, regardless of the consequences. She put down her notes and gazed at the judges.

'That's wrong,' she said, and one could hear a pin drop in the hall. 'All I just said, about letting the past in the past, that there is no good to be had by raking it all up again, I don't believe that and I don't believe for one moment anyone who is grieving for those murdered does either. Plenty of people in this country and beyond are, I'm sure, living in terror of that day, the day when they are asked, "What did you do?" And if they took part, then they *should* be afraid. Not just of the question, but of the fact that for the rest of their lives, their children and grandchildren will know them for what they truly are.

'Edmund Burke said, "The only thing necessary for the triumph of evil is for good men to do nothing." And our generation, better than any before, know that to be true. People who did nothing are guilty. They have blood on their hands. People who exploited those deemed subhuman by the regime, they have blood on their hands. Those who broke Jewish shop windows, those who moved into Jewish homes, those who denounced their neighbours, those who drove the cattle trains – the list goes on and on and on – they all have blood on their hands. So we must know. We simply must. Otherwise justice cannot be served, and that is what distinguishes us from lesser creatures, does it not?

'And what of those who did act on behalf of the vulnerable? Brave men and women who risked not just their own skins but those of their loved ones to do the right thing?' She locked her gaze on Kurt. 'Nobody will build a memorial to the man who got my brother and me on the Kindertransport and saved our lives, but I want the world to know he was Nathaniel Richter. He was a brave man. My father, Peter Bannon, defended a Jewish woman in the street and was sent to a camp, where he died, but nobody knows his name. A Catholic priest, Father Dominic Hoffer, hid my Jewish mother in his church. Before that, a postmistress called Katerin Braun hid her in the attic of her tiny house, feeding her from her own meagre rations. People made false papers, they hid Jews and others, they helped Allied personnel escape so they could continue the fight against the most evil regime the world has ever seen. Just like the list of crimes, the list of kind-nesses too goes on and on.

'So yes, we must ask the question, "What did you do?" And people must answer. We cannot simply forget. We *must never* forget.'

Liesl sat down and the silence was electric. Nobody dared move, and though she knew she'd lost the competition, she didn't care. She'd done, in her small way, the right thing.

The two final delegates spoke. The Canadian was excellent on the subject of connections between the war in the East and that in Western Europe, and the German, from the University of Hamburg, gave a boring but worthy delivery in favour of architectural heritage and its role in reconstruction of cultural identity.

The adjudicators were kind about everyone, but as she anticipated, she was eliminated. She walked off the podium with her head held high.

As she made her way out of the packed hall, wanting to get away from the sympathetic glances, she heard Millie call her name.

'Wait up for God's sake, Liesl,' Millie called, forcing her way through the crowds until she caught up to her. Together, they shuffled out into the cold air.

'Great speech!' Her friend smiled. 'Pity about it being on the wrong side.'

'Thanks.' Liesl grinned.

'So what brought that on? It was incredible, by the way, but what came over you?' Millie led her to a bench.

'I saw someone standing in the crowd. A friend of mine from before. His family and mine were close, but I just never expected to see him, and then when I did, it all came flooding back. I just knew I had to do the right thing, say the right thing, even if it would cost me the competition.' She shrugged. 'I'm fine.'

# CHAPTER 13

*L*iesl was feeling surprisingly serene as all around her, delegates, supporters and spectators milled about.

'Well, we never thought we'd even get this far,' Millie said cheerfully. 'And that was the speech of the competition, despite the result.'

A shadow blocked the late winter sunshine; someone had joined them. She looked up, and there he was – Kurt Richter.

'Liesl…' he began. 'I'm so sorry. I shouldn't have just turned up like that. I…I saw the article in the paper, and I thought surely it isn't Liesl Bannon that I knew. So I came along, and once you walked in, I knew it was you right away. I don't understand why you lost – you were spectacular.'

'Hello, Kurt.' She stood up. 'Please, don't be sorry. Seeing you made me realise something. Yes, I lost. They don't like you to swap sides halfway through.' She smiled. 'But it doesn't matter. I made my point and that's more important.'

Millie watched in amazement as Kurt held his arms out to Liesl. She walked into his embrace, and his arms closed around her.

'Thank God you're safe,' he whispered into her hair.

Eventually he released her and Liesl made the introductions. Felix had joined them by now too.

'Millie, Felix, this is Kurt Richter. His father is the man I mentioned, Nathaniel. He's the reason I'm standing here. I've known Kurt since I was a baby – in fact, I think there was a photo somewhere of us sharing the same pram.' She smiled.

Kurt nodded. 'My mother had it. And remember the one of me and Erich in cowboy suits and you and my sisters in summer dresses when we went to Potsdam for a picnic?' His eyes lit up with the memory. 'We had that in a frame too.'

'I do remember it. And, Kurt, this is my friend Millie and Felix, her...' Liesl paused, unsure of the right word to describe their relationship.

'Millie is my girlfriend,' Felix said proudly, and Millie beamed, moving closer to him.

Kurt shook hands with them all and Felix invited everyone to the café. But Liesl wanted to talk to Kurt; there were so many questions, so much to catch up on. Suddenly the competition was irrelevant.

'No thanks, Felix.' She smiled. 'I'll see you two lovebirds later. Kurt and I have some catching up to do.'

Millie winked and gave her a hug. 'I'm proud of you, Liesl. Well done,' she whispered, before walking off hand in hand with Felix.

'Perhaps I could walk you back to your accommodation?' Kurt asked quietly.

He was as she remembered, a gentle, sweet boy. He looked very similar too. His blonde hair was longer now and he'd filled out and grown taller of course, but he was just a bigger version of the boy she remembered. He'd always been so kind to Erich, and her little brother had hero-worshipped him.

'Thanks, Kurt, that would be nice. I was going to suggest that we go for coffee. I'd like to hear all about your family and to tell you all about us.'

'Of course. I'd love that. I'm sorry to say, my parents are both dead. But I'm glad to hear your mother survived. Did she ever see my parents again, do you know?'

Liesl saw the pain behind the words and felt his loss. Nathaniel and Gretel were lovely people, but just two more in the endless list of war casualties.

'Oh, Kurt, I'm so sorry to hear that. No, I don't believe she did. She went into hiding very soon after we got on the train thanks to Nathaniel, and afterwards, I don't think she ever saw them. What happened, do you mind me asking?'

Kurt shoved his hands into his trouser pockets as they walked. 'They took my father away, the Nazis. He had a radio and was listening to the BBC. I don't know for sure when he died, but we never heard from him again. I think...' – he sighed, then managed to get the words out – 'they sent him to the camps.'

Liesl's heart went out to him. Clearly talking about it was so difficult.

'And *Mutti* died in the bombing, my sisters too. I think it was quick – I hope so anyway.'

'Oh no, that's horrible. Poor Auntie Gretel, and Elke and Kitti... Oh, Kurt, I...I'm so very sorry. So are you all alone in the world now?' she asked, trying to take all this awful news in.

He shrugged. 'Often I wish I was at home when the bomb hit. At least then...'

'So where do you live? Around the same neighbourhood?' Liesl's heart was breaking for her childhood friend.

'No. It was flattened, everything. So I found a job south of the city. I do some casual building work, handyman sort of thing. My boss has a small flat in the yard, so I live there. It's fine for now, but I don't know, perhaps I'll emigrate. I'll have to see.'

'Oh, Kurt, I'm so sorry. I loved your family. We had such lovely times together, our papas joking and playing with us, our *muttis* cooking and laughing together. We never thought it would end. Even though we've lived through it and survived, it seems surreal, doesn't it?'

'It does. My father was so happy when he got you two on that train. I don't think he let your mother know, but it was cancelled several times and he had to pull all sorts of strings. He really wanted to help, especially after your papa was taken.' Kurt kept his eyes on the path ahead, never looking at her.

Liesl had noticed that when people talked about difficult things, it was often easier not to make eye contact.

'I'm really so happy to hear you and Erich and your mother made it. So many didn't. And that you all have a good life now.'

'I know how lucky we are. The reality of it all is so much more stark here, even the little I've seen. We were raised in a kind of bubble in Ireland. Our adopted parents kept things from us inasmuch as they could, and then our *mutti* appeared. The war had taken its toll on her, like everyone, but my father had some investments, so she was able to recoup those. So yes, we're fine. I haven't been out around the city yet, as I was so focused on the competition, but now I've been eliminated, thanks to you.' She laughed.

'Oh, Liesl, I'm so sorry. I shouldn't have just turned up like that. I feel awful...this is all my fault.'

'No, it's fine,' she replied firmly. 'I'm glad actually. Even to get here at all was a wonderful honour, and I felt like I did the right thing. I think my papa would be proud of me. He could never argue what he didn't believe, and it felt good to just be honest. And meeting you again, it's incredible. Sometimes I think I might have imagined my life as a little girl in Berlin, but here you are, evidence that those happy days were real.'

'Thank you. It's wonderful to see you too,' he said quietly.

'And at least now I get to see my old city without worrying about the competition. Maybe it was meant to be.' She managed to smile and he returned it.

'Would you like some company?' he asked. 'If you'd rather not, that's fine. Only if it suits you.'

'Don't you have to work?'

He shook his head. 'It's casual, and he won't mind if I'm not around for a few days. We could start this afternoon, have lunch and then go for a wander around?'

Liesl made a quick decision. 'Let's do it. I was kind of putting it off, I don't know why exactly, but if we go together, I think I can.'

He stopped and turned to face her, taking her hand in his. 'Terrible things happened – it's like a nightmare. I can't believe the way some people behaved. Sure, most of us just did the bare minimum to stay out of the Gestapo's way, and people like my father actively went against them and paid the price. I'm so proud of him, as you should be of yours. I need to tell you, though, that I had to join the Hitler Youth. My mother insisted after my father was taken, as it wasn't safe not to. I hated it, but some people loved it. They won't admit it now, but they enjoyed the power so much, it was sickening. But you probably won't want anything to do with me now, and I couldn't blame you.'

Liesl was quick to reassure him. 'Kurt, you were a child, the same as me. Of course I don't blame you. Auntie Gretel was alone, and she needed to do what she could to protect you and the girls. Of course I don't see you as one of them – you could never be that.'

'It was so horrible, Liesl, the things they made us say, the songs, the way they got inside our heads, filling us with hatred. I resisted, but it was hard.'

'I can only imagine. That's what frightens me, that those people are still here, going about their lives as if nothing had happened. They would still look at me as a filthy Jew that deserves to die. They're not sorry for what they did to my papa, to Nathaniel. I don't want to breathe the same air as them.' The venom in her voice surprised her. She'd been schooled by Elizabeth, Daniel, the rabbi and all of the people who cared for her to not allow the bitterness in, that it was like an acid that would corrode her inside but did nothing to the perpetrators. But here, in this city, it felt good to vent. To her horror, she felt tears well up in her eyes.

Kurt stepped forward, taking her in his arms, and she sank into his comforting embrace. He understood what it was like in ways others couldn't. He had known her papa and understood what a huge loss it was. He knew that her papa wasn't just one other victim – he was Peter Bannon, the strong handsome joker who could sing like a lark and was exactly the kind of man who wouldn't hesitate to intervene if he saw someone in trouble. He rubbed her back as she cried for her father and all they had lost.

# CHAPTER 14

*All* weekend, she and Kurl were inseparable. He was gentle and caring, a perfect gentleman. He was really interested in her mother and Erich, how they lived now, their life in Ireland, and he often expressed a wish to get out of Germany. Unlike her, his family were left destitute by the war. He didn't plead poverty, but his clothes and shoes indicated he was poor. His father's assets were seized when he was arrested and their house had been flattened by a bomb, leaving him with nothing. He'd managed to get that casual job, whatever it was, and a place to sleep, but it didn't sound very appealing.

Liesl didn't say it but felt sure her mother would give him something. She couldn't offer before speaking to *Mutti* but knew there was no way her mother would see Nathaniel and Gretel's boy destitute.

They walked for miles, visiting the remains of her old school, flattened and now being rebuilt as a block of flats. The synagogue too was gone, and as they stood outside the fenced-off site filled with rubble, a man approached them from inside the fence. He'd appeared to just be standing there, lost in thought. He was probably in his sixties, but these days it was hard to put an age on anyone. Everybody seemed to bear the years of war on their faces.

The man was small and wiry, with short grey hair and a beard. His eyes were dark and kind. 'They're going to turn it into some government offices,' he said grimly.

'But why not rebuild it as a synagogue?' Liesl asked, stricken to see the sacred place reduced to this.

'Not enough Jews left.' He shrugged. Then he looked at her again, his brow furrowed. 'You remind me of someone. What's your name?'

'Liesl Bannon,' she replied, not recognising him.

'Ariella's child?' he asked, and Liesl nodded.

'Yes, Peter and Ariella are my parents. Did you know them?'

'Your mother only. She and my wife were friendly. Did she make it?'

Liesl nodded. 'She did. A kind neighbour hid her. She lives in Ireland now. I do too – I'm just here visiting.' She remembered Kurt. 'This is an old family friend, Kurt Richter.'

The man opened the wire that closed the gate and came out onto the pavement. They shook hands.

'I'm Yitzach Moven.'

As he stretched his hand to take hers, Liesl saw the numbers tattooed on the inside of his arm. She'd heard about the Nazi way of marking the prisoners, but she'd never seen it in person. It chilled her.

'Birkenau,' he said. No further explanation was necessary.

'And your wife?' Liesl heard the words before realising she had asked.

'Up in smoke.' He gazed at the blue cold winter sky. 'My Anna went straight up.'

'I'm so sorry for your loss,' Liesl said. 'I'll remember you both to my mother.'

Yitzach nodded slowly and shuffled off.

'Shall we go for a hot chocolate?' Kurt asked kindly. 'That was hard.'

She nodded, and as they crossed the street, he took her hand, not releasing it until they reached the café.

She sat down, peeling off her gloves, hat and scarf, and felt her cheeks redden in the sudden warmth. Much to the disgust of people in Britain, rationing had ended in January of 1950 for Germans, yet there was no end in sight for the victors. She explained to Kurt over delicious hot chocolate and *apfeltorte* how she had to buy some coffee and chocolate for Daniel and some sewing things for Elizabeth. And Erich wanted her to bring him some American cigarettes – not for himself, he assured her, but as bargaining for car parts, which were still in short supply.

Kurt took on the task with enthusiasm, explaining where to get the best and cheapest of everything. They talked about Yitzach Moven and his wife, and her shock at seeing the numbers on his arm. Kurt said that he'd seen the numbers a few times on others but that each time it shook him.

Whenever she talked to him about the war, she noticed he changed the subject as quickly as he could. He didn't want to talk about it, and she couldn't blame him. It was too difficult. His father defied the regime, and he'd hinted that he'd been involved with some underground movement to disrupt the Nazi war machine but didn't go into details. Nathaniel was arrested for listening to the BBC, so it stood to reason that his son would follow in his beloved papa's footsteps.

Kurt extracted a cigarette and lit it with a brass Zippo lighter.

'Oh, where did you get that?' she asked. 'My brother and I have a friend, he's American, and he had a Zippo and Erich loved it. It was a black crackle one because of metal shortages during the war, but Bud used to tell us how "no American would light his cigarette with anything less".' She did a funny imitation of Bud's Mississippi drawl. 'This must be an earlier one to say it's made of brass.'

'Well spotted. An American soldier gave it to me. I helped him out.' He shrugged, lit his cigarette and handed it to her. She read the home-made engraving.

*US 2nd Armored Division*
*Hell on Wheels*
*J. Atlee*

'Who was he, J. Atlee?' she asked, rubbing her thumb over the surface.

'Just a Yank who needed my help.' Kurt stood. 'Shall we go?'

The knowledge that he'd helped the Americans gave her a warm feeling.

She quickly finished her drink. They left and continued walking until they reached a bench opposite Liesl's old apartment. As they sat, she wondered if she should just go and knock on the door, but Kurt cautioned her against it. All Jewish property had been seized and given to loyal Nazis, and knocking was likely to bring her face-to-face with exactly the type of person she was trying to avoid.

'But you should go to a lawyer though – that place must be worth a fortune. Your *mutti* would have to come back and make a claim, but it would be worth it,' Kurt said.

'I doubt she would see it that way. She doesn't need the money, and to be honest, a return visit to Berlin is not something she would ever do.' Liesl sighed, looking up at what once was her home.

'She must be very wealthy to say she can turn her back on a place like that.' Kurt chuckled.

Liesl nodded. 'She is. My father was a good businessman, and some things are just too hard.'

She wondered what it looked like now. She had loved their bright airy apartment on the third floor, with the windows overlooking the park, sunny rooms and high ceilings. It made her blood boil to think someone had just appropriated it, but she could do nothing anyway.

The Braun house, two streets away, appeared to be deserted. Frau Braun's husband was killed in the war. She, Ariella and Willi never went into the details of how or where, and they never mentioned Hubert except to say he was dead.

They peered in through grimy windows and tried to get into the small yard behind to look in the back. There was no sign of life at all.

'We could try the housing office?' Kurt suggested. 'They might have a listing for it?'

Liesl was about to agree with him when a postwoman cycled into the little street. She remembered that Frau Braun delivered mail before the war; perhaps the woman could help. She looked to be in her fifties, maybe older.

She stopped her bike and leaned it against a wall, sorting through a bundle of letters. She made her deliveries and was about to leave.

'Good afternoon.' Liesl approached her. 'I'm a friend of Frau Braun, who used to live at number 11. She worked for the post office.'

The woman eyed her warily. 'Frau Braun didn't have many friends,' she said with a wry smile. 'Who are you?'

'My name is Liesl Bannon. Her son, Willi, is married to my mother.'

'What? Willi Braun is alive? I heard he was killed in Russia.' She seemed surprised but not shocked, as if she were discussing the cost of cabbage, and Liesl wondered at people so accustomed to death and destruction that it was merely a social talking point.

'No. He was injured and lost a leg, but he and my mother live in Northern Ireland now. Frau Braun is there as well.'

The woman laughed. 'So old Katerin made it out, did she?'

Liesl and Kurt shared a glance.

'Well, she always was a wily old bat, I'll give her that. But she just didn't turn up for work one day, and then her Hubert was found, and, well, we put two and two together.' She shrugged as if this made perfect sense. 'So she slipped through the net, eh? Good for her, I suppose.'

'I'm sorry, I don't understand. I thought her husband was killed in the war?'

The woman laughed again. 'That's what she told you, was it? He was killed *during* the war, true enough, but he was battered in his own house. His Nazi buddies found him lying in a pool of his own blood, reckoned he'd been there a week at least. Nobody'd blame her. He's no loss.'

'Oh, I'm sure Frau Braun didn't have anything to do...' Liesl began, horrified at what she'd learned. Frau Braun was a bit of a tartar, no doubt, and she didn't suffer fools at all, but she wouldn't have bludgeoned her husband to death and left his body there to rot.

'You might be sure Katerin didn't have enough of him one day and he got a skillet in the back of the head, darling, but I wouldn't bet my house on it. Maybe she didn't do the actual deed though. Willi hated him too, so...' The woman winked and returned to her bike.

'Wait,' Liesl called, and the woman turned, her eyebrow raised in question. 'Does anyone live there now?'

'I don't think so.' The woman shrugged and got back on her bicycle. 'Oh, and tell Katerin that Heidi says hello.'

'I will,' Liesl said absentmindedly as the woman cycled on.

Over *Wiener schnitzel* and French fries in a *bierhaus* later that night, she talked it all out with Kurt.

'If he did do it, that means your stepfather is a murderer,' Kurt said, his eyes wide in shock.

Liesl dismissed it. 'No, I don't think so. But well... Look, even if Willi did do it, his father was a horrible man. Willi was part of a group called the White Star, which helped with escape lines and disrupted the Nazis as much as possible. Did you know any of them?'

He shook his head. 'Not them, though I knew of them of course. There were lots of different groups, but it was so dangerous, we had to be quiet, give nothing away. And I was only a kid, so not privy to details. I heard of one British agent who got picked up for looking right instead of left as he crossed the street – someone noticed and he was immediately arrested. But I'd rather not talk about it.'

'I understand. *Mutti* is the same. She told us a little about her life in Berlin, those years in Frau Braun's attic and then the even more terrifying months when she was living on false papers, but she can't really go into details – it's too hard. When she came back, at first Erich and I would bombard her with questions, but Daniel and Elizabeth sat us down one night and explained that it was so hard for her, that she'd endured such terrible things, seen such atrocities, and we shouldn't force her to relive them. So we don't ask, and in general she doesn't talk about it. Like you, she wants to face the future without being dragged down by the pain of the past.'

'Did you ever ask her about Frau Braun's husband?'

'No. Any time the subject of Willi's father comes up, they both just say he's dead and it's no loss and move on. I just don't think Willi would do that though, no matter how horrible his father was.

And as for Frau Braun, well, that's just ridiculous. For one thing, she's tiny.'

She'd suggested going to Willi's friend's place instead of the bar they were now in – Willi had said they served good food – but Kurt explained it was closed.

'The owner took off a few weeks ago with an English woman.'

He'd smiled, and she bowed to his local knowledge. It made sense, as the last time Willi met his friend was in London.

The conversation went back to what Heidi had said. Kurt had never met Frau Braun – the families lived on different sides of the city – but he agreed with Liesl that it seemed unlikely an old woman would batter her husband. But then in war, one never knew.

'If he was a Brownshirt, which you think he was, they had a lot of enemies. Even within the whole Nazi structure, they were seen as thugs, a law unto themselves. And when things went bad between Hitler and Ernst Röhm, well, it wasn't good. If he was high up, then you can bet he was not a nice man. None of them were.'

'Anyone with a grudge could have killed him,' Liesl said.

'Exactly.'

Unlike Kurt, Liesl was more and more intrigued by the war years. Kurt liked to talk about the times before the war, when they were children. He recalled so many things she'd forgotten, and as they walked the streets of her city, Liesl found herself feeling like she belonged. She wasn't a tourist like Millie and the others; she was a Berliner. At almost every landmark in the city, Kurt could conjure up a memory, and it felt so good. Her father was brought back to life for her in a more vivid way than ever before, and she could almost see him, hear his voice, as she relived all those precious memories with Kurt.

Of course, reminders of the war were unavoidable. There was evidence of the thousand-year Reich all around them still, and she realised just how insulated she was in Ballycreggan. As impressionable children, they had not been allowed to listen to the news, and Elizabeth and Daniel never got newspapers. When she asked to be allowed to listen to the nightly broadcast on the BBC when she was around twelve, Elizabeth explained that it was all bad, it was all worrying, and there was literally nothing they could do about it except wait and hope. She'd explained in that wonderful way she had, never patronising or condescending, that she didn't think it would be good for her or Erich to listen to such things day in and day out, that it would become their whole lives if they let it, and their parents wouldn't want that. Elizabeth reminded her that Ariella got her and Erich out so they could be free and happy, and listening to the doom and gloom every day would not be honouring her intentions.

As she'd stood outside the Braun's tiny terraced house, she'd looked up at the roof. It was exactly the same as every other one on the street, except that for five years her mother had lived there, in a tiny, cramped, airless, dark attic, protected by a woman who may or may not have battered her Nazi husband to death. It was all so real, so vivid.

# CHAPTER 15

As they walked back to her accommodation, they ran into Millie and Felix on the way out to a party. They'd hardly seen each other for days.

'Aha, the Scarlet Pimpernel!' Millie exclaimed. 'There's a party at Andrews Barracks. The Yanks are stationed there and we've been invited. Full spread laid on and everything. Come on, get your glad rags on, we're going dancing.'

Felix had his arm around her shoulders, and they looked blissfully happy. Liesl was glad. She was enjoying seeing Berlin with Kurt – it felt new but also familiar – and she would have felt bad to have left Millie home alone. But Millie had Felix and was happy.

'Oh, Millie, I'd love to but I actually can't. We've been walking all day and my feet are killing me – I just need to sit down and have a cup of tea.'

'Liesl, are you twenty-one or ninety-one? For goodness' sake, girl, live a little.' Millie was insistent. But then she gave Liesl the look, the one that said 'oh, I see', and changed her attitude.

'OK, you win. You old pair stay home. I'll stay at Felix's tonight, just so you know.' She winked suggestively, and Liesl rolled her eyes with a grin.

Millie leaned in to kiss her cheek, whispering quickly, 'He's cute. Go for it.'

As they left, Kurt smiled. 'She thinks we're…'

'She does.' Liesl chuckled. 'But she's got sex on the brain these days, so obsessed is she with that man mountain. Do you want to come in for a hot drink before you go home?'

'I'd love to. The buses run until midnight, so I have time.'

He followed her up the stairs to the room she and Millie shared. There was a little kitchenette with a kettle and a toaster, and she made tea and toast. She lit the two-bar fire and drew the curtains, and within moments the room was warm and cosy, the aroma of buttery toast filling the air.

'I never drink tea. It's only something *Mutti* used to give us when we were sick,' Kurt said, then sipped the brew suspiciously.

'I prefer coffee, but I always had a cup of tea every night with Elizabeth. Even when things were very bad, when we were in Liverpool for the bombing and we lost our house and everything in it, we always had a cup of tea before bed. It's a kind of habit really, I suppose.'

'It's not bad actually.' He took another sip.

They chatted amicably about the things they missed most from before the war. They reminisced about the family holidays they took together, the parties, the celebrations. So many memories she'd almost forgotten. It was as if Kurt was painting the past she'd locked away in black and white back into colour. For her, Berlin was synonymous with nothing but fear and loss, but Kurt reminded her of the joy, the love, the beauty, and she was intoxicated by it all.

'I remember your *mutti* used to make that cake with the lemon icing and the lemon jam in the middle. Remember? She would bring it to picnics?' Liesl asked. 'And remember one time, she and my *mutti* laid out the picnic and you brought Bruno that black Labrador you used to have and he ate the whole cake? I thought Gretel would kill him that day, and you had to hide him behind you to stop her murdering him.' She laughed at the memory.

'Yes, and Erich and my sisters went paddling but got soaked, and I gave Erich my shirt and just wore my pullover, and you gave Elke your cardigan and she and Kitti fought about it all the way home. They both wanted it, so you wore your papa's undershirt as a dress and gave Kitti your dress.'

'I remember. What a sight I must have been.' She smiled.

'You were beautiful then,' Kurt said, his eyes on the glowing bars of the fire. 'And you're even more beautiful now.'

Liesl didn't know what to say. She told herself over and over that Kurt was like a brother or a cousin, but she knew her growing feelings for him were more than just nostalgia and fondness. He was handsome, kind, funny and gentle. Very different to Jamie. He was slight where Jamie was bulky, and his hair was blonde and silky. Any girl would envy it. They'd been together every day since he turned up in the hall for the debate, and the truth was she was attracted to him.

He turned his head and looked at her, his blue eyes pools of sadness. He'd lost so much, and he was just a boy. She wanted to protect him, to care for him now that he had nobody, but it was more than that.

'Thank you,' she whispered.

'I know I shouldn't say this… I don't want to risk losing you again. And I'm not asking for anything. If you don't feel that way for me, Liesl, I understand…' He paused, trying to find the words. 'But you're due to go home in two days' time, and I…I can't…let you go without saying…'

She said nothing, but her eyes urged him on. She found herself longing to hear the words.

'I think I'm falling in love with you, Liesl.'

She leaned in closer to him, her face inches from his. Words were not necessary.

As she kissed him, she felt his arms encircle her, drawing her close. She could feel his heart beating, and as he kissed her chastely, she knew – she felt the same.

She would have gone on, but he stopped her as she went to put her hands inside his shirt.

'I love you, Liesl, but I respect you too much to do anything that would not be proper. I think you are so beautiful, and I…I can't believe you feel something for me too. But I will wait until it's more appropriate.'

Seeing her shocked face, he rushed to explain. 'You are like a rare flower, to be adored and protected, and I want to be the one to do that. I want to be yours and you mine, and I wouldn't cheapen what we have by…' He flushed and she felt a wave of love for him. 'I hope I can meet your mother and Erich, and I wouldn't like to face them, knowing I'd behaved dishonourably, when all I feel for you is so deep and special. I'm very serious about you, Liesl, and I have never felt this for another girl, ever.'

'I love you too, Kurt,' she said shyly.

Guiltily, she pushed images of her and Jamie's passion from her mind. *This* was how real men behaved, treating girls with respect. Kurt held her in such high regard that he wanted it to be meaningful, not rough and silly and meaning nothing afterwards like it was with Jamie. This was the real thing, this was what true love was, not the joking and fooling around she did with Jamie Gallagher. Real love had to be treated with reverence. Kurt was right, in every sense. Right about not rushing into anything, but also right about how serious true love was.

The remainder of her time flew by, with Kurt loving her and by her side. He kissed her each night but nothing more, and though she burned with desire for him, he always stopped.

She wanted only to be alone with him, but she finally agreed to go to the leaving party with Millie and Felix on their last night, which was on campus. Kurt was reluctant at first, saying that he felt uncomfortable in large groups, but she convinced him. They'd spent every moment of every day together since they'd been reunited. He left her each night and returned the following morning, then they traced the steps of their childhood all over the city. The thought of leaving him now was like a knife in her chest.

They went to the party because to refuse would have been rude. The organisers had put so much into it, and she was anxious her non-attendance at the various social events wasn't seen as sour grapes. She would have liked to join the others at their big table, but Kurt said he'd rather stay separate, so they sat at a secluded table in the corner for most of the evening.

Eventually, she convinced him to dance, and after a waltz in which he held her close, he murmured, 'How can I let you go, my beautiful Liesl?' His hands cupped her face, and his eyes locked with hers. 'I can't be without you, my love. Not now that I've found you. And the idea that your *mutti* and Erich too are alive, I long to see them. I may have lost my family, but yours feel like... I don't know... It's presumptuous of me, but they feel like all I have left.'

Millie and Felix were dancing and smooching. Millie was going home tomorrow too, but Felix was apparently going to visit Cambridge in the summer.

Liesl had a thought.

They quickly gathered their coats and her handbag and slipped outside into the cold night air.

'Don't you want to stay at the party? Your friends...' Kurt began.

'No.' She led him to a low wall under some trees and sat down. 'Come to Ireland,' she said.

'What? I don't understand... Visit you in Dublin do you mean?'

'No. I mean come for good, after my exams of course. I have my finals in May, but after that we could just go from there. Bring everything. You don't have anyone left here. I know *Mutti* and Erich see you as family. We wouldn't have survived if it weren't for your father, so I know my mother would want to help.' She smiled shyly. 'Besides, I love you.'

He stood up, running his hands through his hair. He had his back to her and she was worried. Had she read this wrong?

When he turned, his cheeks were wet and he couldn't speak.

'Is that a yes?' she whispered.

He nodded. His lips kissed the top of her head, and she felt his arms tighten around her, holding her so close. She relaxed. Everything was going to be all right. Together, they strolled back to her room.

Once she was settled with the heater on, he left her to finish her packing and went to get them some food and a bottle of wine. It would be their last night together for a while. Over dinner, they talked about how he would join her in Dublin in the summer.

'You could stay the night if you wanted to,' Liesl said shyly. She didn't want him to think her forward, but she hated him travelling across the city alone at night.

'I will, on that chair.' He smiled.

They ate and drank, and she found a blanket and a pillow for him.

She and Millie talked it over the next morning when Millie returned from Felix's place to pack her bags. The bus to take them to the station was due at noon.

Millie had got all the way to the semi-final in the competition, losing out in the end to the Stanford candidate, although Liesl was convinced Millie had done a better job. Her recall was remarkable, and her ability to think on her feet, to carefully dismantle the opposition point by point was mesmerising to watch.

Liesl had convinced Kurt to come with her to watch Millie in each round, and he'd gone reluctantly. She knew crowded places were not really his thing.

He'd gone to the baker for some fresh bread for breakfast. Her friend was a bit miserable about leaving Felix, but something told Liesl that Millie would not have to wait until July to see her big Bavarian. He was keen, and she told Millie as much.

They talked about Kurt and her invitation, and to her surprise, Millie wasn't as effusive in her excitement as Liesl had thought she would be.

'It's a bit sudden, isn't it?' Millie asked, and Liesl was taken aback and a little offended. Liesl had been so supportive of her and Felix.

'Well, yes and no. I've known him for years,' Liesl answered, bristling.

'Ah, Liesl, I'm not being a moan, but I just don't want to see you make a mistake and then try to get out of it later.' Millie's big brown eyes were kind.

'Why would it be a mistake?' Liesl asked. 'Don't you like him?'

'It's not that.' Millie looked flustered now. 'Look, only a real friend would tell you this and I really hope it doesn't damage our friendship forever, but I can't let you go out with him without saying something. Felix was talking to some guys last night at the party, locals. Well, one of them recognised Kurt and said he was a nasty piece of work. He didn't go into details, but he did say he wouldn't like to see anyone he knew going out with him.'

Liesl was so hurt on Kurt's behalf. She was glad he wasn't there to hear it. 'Millie, you don't know him and I do. He's a lovely person with a kind heart who has been through so much – you've no idea. Whatever those people think they know, it's not true.'

'Why would they lie, Liesl?' Millie pressed. 'You never see anyone – he's keeping you away from everyone because he doesn't want you to know what he really is.'

'Kurt hasn't been keeping me away, Millie.' Liesl was outraged now. How dare her friend say such wicked things? 'I chose to be with him. Is that the problem? Are you jealous that I'm choosing Kurt over you? We've been visiting places from our childhood, Millie.' Liesl was stung. 'You can't possibly understand what it's like for us. Kurt and I were both brutalised by the Nazis. I know England was bombed and there were shortages and all that, but it's different for us. We lost people, we lost our childhoods, and together we're finding some of that joy again. Just because he's not all for going to pubs and staying out all night at parties doesn't make him a bad person, Millie. I understand him, and he understands me.' She could feel her face flushing. She hated arguing with anyone, but how could Millie think her relationship with Kurt was a mistake?

'Those same Nazis killed my dad, Liesl,' Millie said quietly. 'Or had you forgotten that?'

Liesl's stomach lurched sickeningly. She *had* forgotten that. Self-loathing washed over her. 'Of course I hadn't,' she lied, trying to find a way out. 'It's just...' She had no words.

'He wasn't as important as your father?' Millie asked, pain and frustration dripping from every word. 'Nobody has the monopoly on grief here, Liesl, not even the Jews. To lose someone you love is heart-breaking, and it doesn't matter who or what you are.'

Millie rose from her bed and dragged her already packed suitcase out from under it. 'I'm going to spend the rest of my time here with Felix. At least he cares about me.' She threw her remaining toiletries and things lying around the room in her smaller holdall and left without a backwards glance.

Liesl knew she should go after her friend, and was about to when Kurt reappeared, a baker's box in his hands. He looked stricken at her tear-stained face. She told him everything while he soothed and held her.

'I'm sorry that happened to you, my love. That's normal behaviour now, everyone denouncing everyone else for their own petty ends. It was probably some guy who saw you and thought you were beautiful and wanted to put you off me. You were right – other people don't understand us, the bond we have. They think they do, but they don't, they can't...' His voice washed over her troubled mind.

'I should go after her... She'll be at Felix's.' She rose to leave but Kurt took her hand.

'Go if you want to of course, Liesl, but will it do any good? She feels hard done by because you forgot that her father had been killed. It's not a terrible crime. So many have died, how can we remember everyone? We can't. Millie has her own problems, and one of them is seeing you happy.' He drew her back onto the bed and sat close beside her. He gently turned her head to face him, planting a kiss on the end of her nose. 'You're such a wonderful girl, and you never see the bad in anyone. And I'm not saying Millie is bad, but she is jealous. And why wouldn't she be? You are so beautiful and smart, and you have a wonderfully loving family. What does she have?'

Liesl didn't like to hear him running down her friend, but as the thought crossed her mind, he spoke again.

'I know you don't like to imagine that your friend feels that way, but she does and it's not her fault. Well, the fact that she eats too much is her fault, but not the rest of it. Let her cool down, and she'll see the error of her ways. You'll see her on the bus, so let's not waste any more precious time on anyone else, eh?'

'I can't wait to be with you in Ireland,' he said as they had breakfast. 'I wish you didn't have to go.'

'I know, my love. I'm so sad too, but I promise the moment my exams are over, I'm all yours.'

'Will the Irish let me in, do you think?'

'I think so,' Liesl replied, having no idea whether it was true or not. 'And if there's a problem, then I can always come back here. I always envisaged a career in Europe anyway – that's why I studied French and German.'

He shook his head. 'No, Liesl, there's nothing here for either of us now. If not Ireland, we'll go to America. Would you like that? I could show you off on Broadway.' He winked.

Liesl hid her shock. She didn't want him to think she wasn't enthusiastic about them being together. And she could see why Germany held too many bad memories for him.

'I never even thought about going to America. Some of the others, from the farm I mean, are going to Israel, so if I were to go anywhere, I guess that would be the place I thought of. How would you feel about Israel?'

'No, not there.' He was adamant but softened when he saw her hurt face – all Jews wanted to go to Israel at some stage. 'I mean, we can go for a visit sometime in the future if you want, but to live, no. I wouldn't like it. But America now, that's the land of opportunity. But we don't need to decide now. We'll start out in Ireland and see where the wind takes us, eh?'

He poured her more coffee and put some delicious home-made jam on a pastry for her.

'All right.' She smiled, accepting the plate. 'So long as I'm with you, I don't mind where it is.'

After they'd finished breakfast, she rose reluctantly; it was time to gather the last of her things. He helped, and soon her suitcase and small carry-on luggage were packed. He made her a sandwich for the journey and wrapped it in the baker's paper.

'That's so thoughtful, Kurt,' she whispered as he held her.

'I'll take good care of you, Liesl. I promise.'

She fought the stinging tears at leaving him, the uncertainly of how long it would be before she saw him again making the parting much worse.

'I've got to go,' she said as he hugged her again.

In the end it was he who dragged her suitcase, full of chocolate and coffee, downstairs. Felix and a red-eyed Millie and several other students she'd got to know in the first week were gathered. But as the bus came round the corner, Liesl refused to meet her friend's gaze.

Kurt winked and led her away from the gathered group, behind a large pillar.

'What's going on?' she giggled but he held his finger to his lips.

Then suddenly, he was on one knee, his hand in his pocket. From it, he extracted a ring. It was a cheap one, but she didn't care.

'Liesl Bannon, you're the only girl in the world for me. I feel like our fathers brought us together, here in their city. Will you marry me?' he asked, his blue eyes beseeching hers.

Nothing else mattered. This was right for her. Her papa and *mutti*, Nathaniel and Gretel, Kurt's little sisters, all the faces of her life before the war seemed to be around him, encouraging her. Kurt was her past, and now he was her future too. She had no doubts.

'I will,' she spluttered through her tears. 'I definitely will.'

She stood and wrapped her arms around his neck, kissing him in front of everyone. He gently disconnected from her, smiling. He was shy about public displays of affection, she knew, but she giggled. The ring was a little tight, but she didn't care.

'I'll see you very soon, my darling,' Kurt whispered in her ear. 'Don't worry, I'll be travelling light.' He chuckled as several delegates wrestled with large bags and suitcases. 'I don't have much stuff.' A shadow of grief passed over his handsome features once more. 'Almost all of my clothes and books and things were at home and so went up in flames, so my entire worldly possessions won't take up much space.'

He gave her a small smile, and she'd never loved him more. He was so brave, putting a cheerful face on what was such personal tragedy and loss.

'Don't worry about that.' She gave him one last kiss. 'We'll build our new life together.'

# CHAPTER 16

*L*iesl knew as she began the long journey from Berlin to Calais, and then to Dover on the ferry, that she'd not really thought this through. The return journey seemed so much longer without Millie to talk to. She replayed their argument over and over. Kurt was a little aloof – well, he wasn't in reality when you knew him, but she conceded it could seem that he was, as he was just shy and so broken by all that had happened to him.

She was in no doubt that those people Felix said recognised Kurt were mistaken. He had been in the Hitler Youth – he had no secrets from her – but so was everyone, and he was only seventeen when the war ended so hardly a high-ranking Nazi. It was preposterous.

Perhaps Kurt was right that there was no future in Germany. Her mother and Willi felt the same, Daniel had no wish to return to Austria, and now Kurt wanted to leave too. There were other places she could go for work; linguists would always be needed. She had just always imagined Germany because it was the place she knew. She smiled at the memories she and Kurt had evoked this week, the places they visited, the experiences. Those were real. Berlin was where she felt at home, but Kurt was going to be her home now, so wherever he was, that was where she'd belong.

The logistics of the move would have to be ironed out after her exams. She knew it would be hard to focus now with such an exciting future looming, but she was determined to get her first and nothing could distract her, not even Kurt. He loved her so much, and he understood how vital her studies were to her. Unlike the feckless Jamie, who was so fickle, hopping from one thing to another, Kurt was more grown up, more serious and a much better match for her.

She'd never mentioned Jamie and Kurt had never asked. She was Kurt's first proper girlfriend, and he'd just assumed she was new to romance as well. He was so romantic and treated her with such reverence and respect, she could never imagine telling him that she'd slept with someone else. Hopefully she would never have to. It wasn't a lie as such; he just would be appalled and she couldn't bear to see the hurt on his face. He kissed her sweetly, not passionately as Jamie had done, and held her hand. He attended to her every need but never gave in to his passion. He explained how he wanted their lovemaking to be special, and within the bonds of marriage, a sacred, precious thing. It made her feel so loved.

She wondered as the train trundled along if she should tell them in Ballycreggan she was engaged, then immediately dismissed the idea. Mutti and Erich would be delighted to see Kurt, she was sure, but Daniel and Elizabeth would worry about the effect a new romance would have on her exams. They would want to visit and talk about it, and maybe urge her to wait, because to them it would be a week-long romance and they might see it as rash. No, she would say nothing until after her exams. By then Kurt would be in Ireland, and she could bring him home and introduce him properly.

She tried to picture them both arriving in Ballycreggan. Her mother would put him up of course; being Nathaniel and Gretel's son, he was practically family. She imagined the rabbi marrying them in the synagogue; so many of the important events of her life had taken place there. Kurt was a Gentile of course, but maybe he would consider converting to Judaism. He wasn't a devout Christian as far as she knew, and she was certain if she asked him to, he would. Maybe they could work in Ballycreggan. He could help out with Daniel and Erich while at the same time receive instruction from the rabbi, and she could set about arranging the wedding. He didn't speak English very well, which might be a problem at first, but he was smart, he could pick it up, and learning English quickly would certainly make life easier. The less focus on him being a German, the better really, and the Jews were not seen in the same way as other Germans for obvious reasons. She was anxious people liked him, made him feel welcome, so being accepted and loved by her family would be a big step in that direction.

She thought of how well Frau Braun and Willi picked up the language, as had all of the Jewish children, but she supposed they had no choice. Everyone in her family except Elizabeth spoke German as their first language, but they always communicated in English and Kurt would too. She was sure of it.

Few Ballycreggan families were not touched by tragedy. Tens of thousands of Irish people joined up; many thousands more went to work in the munitions factories and on the farms of Britain. They were her people, and she did not want them to see Kurt as the enemy. They'd accepted Willi and Frau Braun, so why not Kurt?

As the green fields and canals of Germany and then France passed by the window, she wondered when she would be back, if ever. She'd envisaged a career in Europe, putting her translation skills to work there in the post-war reconstruction, but Kurt was adamant he wanted to go to America. It wasn't somewhere that had occurred to her to go, and it was so far from her family that she didn't relish the idea, but she would follow him to the ends of the earth if needs be.

Finally, the long train journey was over and they were moved from the platform to the quayside at Calais. She didn't see Millie in the throng. She wished they could patch up their fight. Millie was a good friend and meant well. She was wrong about Kurt, but her heart was in the right place. Liesl didn't agree with Kurt that Millie was jealous of her; Millie wasn't like that. She was open-hearted and generous. But like Millie didn't know Kurt, he didn't know her either.

As the boat bumped across the channel, she practised writing her signature. *Mrs Liesl Richter. Ms L Richter, Mrs Liesl Bannon-Richter.* Each time she wrote it, she scribbled it out, terrified someone would sit down beside her and read it. She missed him like a physical pain. She knew the romance was only a week old, so this depth of feeling felt silly, but she kept justifying the strength of her feelings by saying she knew him for ten years and a week. It felt so good to relive all of those happy memories of the time when Papa and *Mutti* could fix everything, that time before Adolf Hitler.

She reminisced about Berlin, her first and possibly only real home. Nothing about the city was as she'd imagined it would be. It looked fine; there was evidence of the destruction of course, but it wasn't a bomb site by any means. It was a busy working city. The military personnel carried out checks and there was a strong army presence there, but it made her feel safe. If it were not for the building sites and railed-off sites, one could be forgiven for thinking the Nazis had never happened.

She and Kurt had walked to the Brandenburg Gate and stood facing the broad street of Unter den Linden. The university had several buildings there, including the square at the Bebelplatz where the German Student Association, riled up by that monster Goebbels, held one of the infamous book burnings in 1933.

They'd walked and he'd told her about the Berlin Blockade that took place from June of 1948 to May of 1949. He was lucky he lived and worked in the southwest of the city, in the American sector, but he had horrific stories of how Stalin tried to block the road, rail and air access to the areas of the city under Western control.

She was fascinated as he described how the Allies airlifted in supplies of food, medicine, coal, blankets and even goats to resist Stalin's bullying tactics. Kurt was lighthearted about it, but she felt so sad, as if the people of her city hadn't endured enough. He explained how the sector occupied by the Soviets wasn't out of bounds as such, but he warned her not to go there. It was as if the Americans, the British and the French sectors were bright and safe, while the Soviet part of the city was dark, dangerous and best avoided. The Russians were their allies, but she knew from her mother about the terrible things the advancing Red Army did in Berlin in 1945, so there was bound to be mistrust and resentment.

No wonder he didn't want to stay in Berlin; she couldn't blame him. Poor Kurt didn't even have a grave to visit. The bodies of his mother and sisters were never recovered from the rubble of their house, and his father never came back from the camps. He told her how he searched the Red Cross lists every day for months. He had no idea which camp his father had been taken to, and without that information, finding out his fate was close to impossible. He just knew what his mother said, that the authorities burst in one day, found the radio and dragged Nathaniel out. They shoved him in a truck, and his family never heard from him again. He'd been out trying to find food for the family when it happened.

She was lost in her reverie when a shadow blocked the sunlight from the porthole opposite her. Millie stood there, looking nervous and not her usual happy-go-lucky self.

'I'll be going to London, and then on to Cambridge when we dock, so I just wanted to say goodbye,' Millie said.

Liesl looked up at her friend. She could see she was miserable, though whether it was to do with their argument or leaving Felix, she didn't know.

There was a seat opposite her and Liesl offered it to Millie. 'I hate that we fell out,' she said honestly. 'But those men, what they said about Kurt is just not true.'

'Fair enough. You know him and we don't, so...' Millie shrugged. 'I don't want to leave with us not speaking. And I'm sorry. What you do is none of my business, Liesl. I hope you and Kurt will be very happy.' She managed a weak smile.

'We will be.' Liesl was adamant. 'Millie, I'm so sorry for what I said about you not understanding. And you're right, I was so caught up in my own business I did forget that your dad had been killed, and that was unforgivable. I'm so sorry. Of course you know exactly what it's like, and you're right, nobody has exclusive rights to grief. I shouldn't have said what I did. I don't want us to lose touch either.'

'We won't.' Millie reached over and covered Liesl's hands with hers.

'Will you come to Ireland for a visit sometime?' Liesl asked.

'I'd like that.' Millie smiled, her eyes suspiciously bright. 'My dad was a lorry driver before the war, and a mate of his keeps in touch. He's often going to Ireland in his truck, so perhaps I'll hitch a lift sometime?'

'I would love that. You're always welcome.' Liesl squeezed her friend's hand. Everything was fine again, and she was relieved. She changed the subject. 'So was the farewell from Fabulous Felix a joyous one or a valley of tears?' Liesl grinned.

'A bit of both to be honest. I hope it wasn't just a holiday fling, but who knows? He says he's coming in the summer, but he's so gorgeous and he could have anyone...' Millie's voice trailed off, betraying her uncertainty.

'And so could you, but you chose him. He's every bit as lucky as you are, do you hear me, Emily-Jane Blennet?' Liesl pretended to be stern.

Millie relaxed. 'Even if he does come, how's the British public going to react to a huge German wandering about? Over there it was all right, but there's such hatred at home, and you can't blame people, but still.'

'Felix will charm them. You couldn't help liking him, Millie, so don't worry.' She paused. 'Kurt wants to go to America. I always imagined I'd graduate and go to work in Europe, but he doesn't want that.'

'Wow, America?' Millie was surprised. 'Would you like to go there?'

Liesl shrugged. 'I never thought about it, but I suppose we could give it a try. I'd like to see it, but I know it would be hard to leave my family. But then, Kurt will soon be my family.'

Millie's face gave her away. 'What?'

Her friend swallowed, and Liesl had to fight the urge not to get impatient again.

'We're engaged.' Liesl held out her hand to show the small brass ring. It had no diamond or stone and it was dull, but it symbolised the most wonderful fact – she was Kurt's and he was hers.

'When?' Millie asked. 'I mean, congratulations of course, but I just wasn't expecting it…'

'Before we left, he just got down on one knee and proposed and I said yes.' Despite her friend's reluctance, she couldn't help but beam with excitement. 'I'll soon be a married woman.'

Millie's eyes darkened with concern but she said nothing.

'Oh, Millie, please be happy for me,' Liesl begged. 'I know you're worried because we're going so fast, but trust me. I've known him for years and his family and mine were best friends, so it's not a whirl-wind romance. Well, the romance bit is, I suppose, but the love isn't. Honestly, wait until you visit and see him with my family. My brother looks up to him so much, and my *mutti* will love him like a son. Kurt is shy, and that's why he didn't seem that enthusiastic about socialising with you all, and he's so hurt by everything that happened. He's all alone. If you'd seen how close he and his family were… They did everything together, and he misses them horribly.'

'You're right, and I'd like to get to spend time and get to know him properly.' Millie sighed. 'I'd invite you to my home if I had one, but, well, you know that situation.'

'I do.' Liesl smiled. 'But you are welcome any time, Millie, I mean it.'

'Thanks, Liesl. With a bit of luck, I might bring a big beefy Bavarian with me.' Millie chuckled.

'He's more than welcome too,' Liesl said, happy that she and Millie were friends again.

# CHAPTER 17

*P*rofessor Kingston was effusive in his congratulations at her getting so far in the competition, and she explained why she did what she did. He smiled, clearly proud of her achievement and of her taking a moral stand.

'Liesl, my dear, this is a remarkable accomplishment. I'm incredibly proud of you. I have no doubt that you are destined for great things.' He sat back in his leather chair.

She loved his office, lined floor to ceiling with books, the entire room dominated by the beautiful antique walnut desk.

'But now, tell me this, and if I am prying, please feel free to tell me so.' He took off his glasses and cleaned them with his tie, a habit that often made his less dedicated students run a book on how many times he would do it in an hour-long lecture. 'How was the trip for you personally? You expressed some concern, understandably so, prior to it, so I trust it wasn't too traumatic?'

Liesl felt a rush of affection for her teacher. He was a fusty old academic for sure, but he had a kind heart.

'It wasn't at all actually. It felt odd at first, but then I reconnected with an old friend. I had no idea that would happen, but it made the visit easier for me. We explored all of our old neighbourhoods, and even spoke to some people who remembered us, and it actually was nice.'

She thought of Yitzach Moven and his beloved Anna, and Heidi and her extraordinary story of Frau Braun's husband. Then she realised with a shock she was behaving just like Jamie, referring to her fiancé as just an old friend. Why was she denying Kurt? She didn't know. Perhaps because, like her parents, the professor might express concern at the speed of her engagement and she just didn't want to defend her actions again.

'Oh, I am glad, my dear.' He smiled, his bushy eyebrows furrowed slightly. 'I was worried I might not have done the right thing.'

'No, Professor, sending me to Berlin was the best thing you could ever have done.' She saw him relax.

'And has it inspired you to return to Europe once you graduate? I believe you mentioned that was your plan? I'm confident you will graduate with first-class honours, and any of the reconstruction agencies would be lucky to have you.'

'Possibly.' Liesl was deliberately vague. 'We'll have to see. I'm actually thinking maybe of America. I need to study hard for my exams first. The trip was so all-consuming, it's only hitting me now that my finals are around the corner'

'America?' Professor Kingston looked surprised and disappointed. 'But with European languages, and dare I say one as proficient as you, surely Europe is where your talents would be put to best use?'

'Well, I'm not sure yet. I have to finish my exams first.' Liesl felt pathetic. She should have said she was going there with her fiancé, but she chickened out – again.

'Oh, I'm sure you'll do fine.' He stood up, glancing at the clock. 'Freshers philosophy at eleven.' He sighed. 'Perhaps I'm getting too old for this.'

She grinned. 'Never. I loved first-year philosophy with you. It was during your first lecture that it finally hit me I was a student at Trinity College, and the wonder of that has never left me. Thanks, Professor, for the opportunity and nominating me and everything. I can honestly say it changed my life.'

'Well, at least they won't have started betting on how often I clean my glasses with my tie yet.' He winked and opened the door for her. He was more clued in than he let on. 'Goodbye, my dear.'

Liesl made her way across campus to the library. She'd hardly left there since returning from Berlin, refusing all entreaties from Bally-creggan to come for a visit. She told them she needed to study, and the reality was she did, but also she was working hard to keep her mind off worrying about Kurt. He'd written several times outlining the problems he was having obtaining the necessary visa. He had no paperwork, passport or identity card. His birth certificate was also missing, and trying to get a new one was close to impossible, it would seem. Without identification, it was proving very difficult, and she was worried he wouldn't be able to get to her. She wanted to surprise her mother by bringing Kurt home with her for a visit once her exams were over. She often imagined Ariella's face, and Erich's, when she walked in the door with Kurt.

She felt so helpless. He assured her in each letter he would get to her whatever it took. The worst-case scenario was that she would have to wait until after her exams and then go to Berlin again. They could marry there, and then he would be able to travel with her as her husband. Elizabeth had made sure they were naturalised and made British citizens at the time she and Daniel adopted them.

She'd written and suggested that, and he telegrammed back.

*Come now. Marry me. Love you.*

She'd smiled at his impulsiveness. He couldn't wait and neither could she, but she had to stay and do her finals. Going galivanting off once in her final year was bad enough, but twice would be risking her degree, which she couldn't do.

She'd written back; telegrams were expensive and public, and what she had to say to Kurt was for his eyes only. He didn't have an address, just a post office box, but that was common in Germany. She'd explained how she needed to focus on her exams now, but that she adored him and would see him soon.

She remembered she needed some stationery, so she decided to go to Eason's on O'Connell Street. She needed the walk after being cooped up in the library since returning from Germany anyway. It was a beautiful day, the cherry trees in full bloom, and she strolled out the gates and onto College Green. Trinity was right in the heart of the city, which was one of the many things she loved about it. All around her, Dublin was bustling with students, housewives, delivery men. She would miss it when her time there was done.

'Liesl!'

She heard someone call her name as she crossed the road onto Westmoreland Street, and she spun around. The colour drained from her face. Jamie. He was in a large group of lads and girls, but he left them and ran towards her. It had only been a short time since she'd broken up with him, but it might as well have been twenty years so much had happened. She felt that old heart pang as he ran towards her, his broad smile so heartbreakingly familiar.

'Liesl! It's so good to see you.' He panted. 'I got your note and I... Liesl, you were right to be so angry. I was pathetic, absolutely pathetic. I'm so sorry.'

She moved to leave. 'Look, Jamie, I'm not interested, all right? You had your say and –'

'Please, Liesl, just give me ten minutes. I just need to tell you something. Please, ten minutes, five even...' His copper curls caught the springtime sun, and she had to admit he looked like one of those Viking gods. He was wearing a football jersey, and his smile had lost none of its radiance.

'Jamie, I –' she protested.

'Five minutes. I'll get you whatever you want, tea, coffee, wine, a kidney, my granny's right arm, whatever you want.'

She couldn't help but giggle. He could always make her laugh. Five minutes couldn't do any harm. She was engaged to Kurt; whatever she had with Jamie was over and done with.

'Five. And right here. Say what you want to say.' She dropped her bag and sat on a bench, her face warmed by the mid-morning sunshine.

'All right.' He sat beside her, leaving six inches of space between them. He leaned forward, resting his elbows on his enormous

thighs, his huge physique the very opposite of the slender and delicate Kurt.

'Liesl, I am so sorry. I should have stood up to my parents and Fath
– to Brendan when they met you. I should never have allowed my
mother to speak to you the way she did. It was unforgivable.'

She sat there and listened. He sounded sincere.

'I came to my senses after you left. I know that's not much use to
you, but I told them that they were a disgrace and I was mortified by
them. And that you were a wonderful girl and if they were the reason
you finished with me, I'd never forgive them.'

'And how did they take that?' she asked.

'Oh, as you'd imagine.' He sat up and looked at her. 'Called me all
the names going, threatened all sorts, said they'd cut me off, all the
rest of it.'

'And has it happened?'

'They aren't speaking to me, which is fine. I've dropped out of
college. I got a job working in the Cobbler's, you know the bar on
South Anne Street? Anyway, you're right, it's pointless studying something I hate.'

'I'm glad for you.'

He smiled, and she remembered in a moment how she felt about
him. Instantly, she dismissed the thought. She was engaged to Kurt; he
was her future.

'Thanks, but it's all down to you really. So I've got a job, got rid of
my horrible family, and all that's left is to hopefully win back the most
wonderful girl in the world.'

She hated to do it, but she had to tell him the truth. She believed he
was sorry. He might have been spineless in the face of his vicious
mother and his creepy brother, but he was never a liar. If she were still
single, she might consider giving him another chance, but she wasn't
and he needed to know that.

'Jamie, I'm sorry. I believe you, that you regret what happened and
all of that, but the truth is...' She paused, reluctant to hurt him even
though he'd hurt her so badly.

'Please, Liesl, don't say there's no hope for us.' All joking was gone now. 'I know I've been a total jackass – I'm so ashamed of myself – but I swear if you even consider giving me another chance, I'll prove to you I'm a better man than that. I've been so lonely, honestly, Liesl.' His voice was husky with emotion. 'I love you.'

'I'm engaged to someone, Jamie.'

He seemed to register the words but then his face showed incomprehension. 'What? How could you be? I only saw you before you went to Germany, so how can you...' He was distraught.

'I reconnected with a friend from my childhood. We just, I don't know, we fell in love, Jamie. I'm sorry.' Liesl wished the words didn't sound so silly. She and Kurt were the real thing, she knew it, but to everyone else, it sounded like an infatuation.

'Who is he?' Jamie asked, his voice choked.

'It doesn't matter, I –'

'Of course it matters, Liesl, of course it does. If some lad is going to take you away from me because I was so stupid, I should at least know who he is.'

The muscles in his broad back tensed as he returned to his earlier position, forearms on his knees, his eyes on the ground between his feet.

'His name is Kurt Richter. He is the son of my parents' best friends. His parents both died in the war, and so did his little sisters. His family resisted Hitler and so did he.' She hoped Jamie wouldn't press her for details as she had no idea; Kurt had just dropped a few hints but didn't want to relive it all again.

'And he's asked you to marry him, this Kurt?' Jamie asked, each word dropping like a stone.

'He has, and I've accepted.' She could try to explain how they were connected from before, how it wasn't a one-week romance, but there wasn't any point.

'Oh, Liesl.' To her horror, Jamie's huge body shuddered and she realised he was crying.

She put her hand on his back, and he turned, his eyes wet with tears.

'I've lost you, haven't I?'

Slowly and sadly, she nodded. 'I'd like us to stay friends though. Can we do that?'

He stood, wiped his eyes with the sleeve of his jersey and inhaled, steadying himself.

'Goodbye, Liesl. I'm sorry.'

# CHAPTER 18

The weeks went by in a blur. Liesl was at her desk one wet night working on a precis in French for a particularly complex legal document in *Deutsch heute*, which was driving her up the walls. Abigail was gone to her grandmother's house in Ballsbridge for the night; it was her granddad's birthday. There was a knock on her door, and one of her fellow students, a quiet girl from West Cork called Audrey, put her head round the door. 'There's a man downstairs looking for you,' she said, then disappeared.

Liesl wondered who it could be. She had not seen Jamie since the day on Westmoreland Street when she told him about Kurt. Panic struck her – was it Daniel? Had something bad happened at home?

She ran downstairs, and as she rounded the corner of the bannister, she saw him. He was soaked to the skin, his long blonde hair almost reaching his shoulders, a small army kitbag slung over one shoulder. He wore an army jacket over an open-necked shirt and the same khaki-coloured trousers he'd worn every day in Berlin.

'Kurt!' She barrelled downstairs and threw herself into his arms. He spun her round, kissing her on the cheek.

'What? I don't understand! What are you doing here? I thought you weren't coming until June?'

'I told you I'd find a way, didn't I?' He grinned and kissed her again. 'Or would you rather I went away again?' He smiled.

She instantly dismissed that idea. 'No, of course not. It's wonderful to see you. Come up. Oh my God, you're soaked to the skin!'

She took his hand and led him up to her room. Though it was springtime, the evenings were chilly, so she plugged in the two-bar fire.

'Quickly, get out of those wet things before you catch pneumonia.' She fussed over him, hanging his jacket on the chair and putting the kettle on the little one-ring gas stove Daniel had given her when she left Ballycreggan. It had been in the shed since forever but it didn't work, so he took it apart fixed it, and now she enjoyed a cup of coffee or warm soup without having to go to the student dining hall.

As he stood there in the middle of her little room, bare chested, his hair wet, she inhaled sharply. He was so beautiful. Not handsome and rugged like other men, not like Jamie with his bulging muscles and broken nose. But with his delicate features, his perfectly symmetrical face, his slightly slanted blue eyes the colour of the sea on a summer's day, he was perfectly proportioned. He reminded her of Michelangelo's *David*.

She longed to touch him, to kiss him deeply, but as in Berlin, he seemed shy.

'How did you do it?' she asked. 'I thought you were having trouble getting a visa?'

'Where there's a will, there's a way. I got a job on a boat, the SS *Nostrum* as it was, but it was seized by the British in 1945 and sold to the Steel and Coal Company, operating out of Hamburg. They renamed her the *Rosamunde*, and I figured out they would be stopping in Dublin. I got a job, worked my way to here and jumped ship early this morning. I had to lay low of course, but now I'm here.'

Liesl turned from the kettle, shocked. 'But, Kurt, now you are in this country illegally. We can't live like that, with you hiding and me worried all the time...' She couldn't believe he'd done something so stupid.

'Shh, Liesl *Liebchen*, it's all right. You're a British citizen. We'll get married and it will all be solved, simple.' He smiled.

'Oh, Kurt, it's not that simple,' she protested. 'We need papers for you to marry me – we can't just turn up with nothing. They'll ask questions, and once they realise you got in here illegally, they'll report you and you'll get deported, and possibly never be allowed back.'

His expression changed. 'Are you saying you'd rather I didn't come, Liesl?'

She rushed to reassure him. 'Of course not. I would just have preferred if you waited until you had the right visa or whatever you need. This complicates things.'

He pulled a dry shirt from his bag, shrugging it on. 'Surely your family know people? A word in the right ear, an envelope, won't that fix this?'

Liesl shook her head, shocked at his suggestion. 'Elizabeth and Daniel aren't like that. They are very law-abiding, and my mother is the same. Besides, they wouldn't know anyone who could do something like that.' She didn't want him to feel unwelcome, but this situation was far from ideal.

'What about the rabbi? Jews are always well connected wherever they live. Wealthy Jews are all going to America and Israel and wherever they like.'

Liesl did a double take. What did he mean, Jews were always well connected? She dismissed it. Kurt wasn't anti-Semitic; he probably just thought the rabbi was more powerful than he was.

'Rabbi Frank is himself a refugee. How on earth would you imagine he would have connections politically? And even if he did, I couldn't ask him to do something immoral like this.'

Kurt smiled. 'I'm sorry, darling. I didn't mean anything bad by that, just that in Germany before the war, the Jews were well-to-do, you know? They knew the right people, politicians, businessmen… That's all I meant.'

'It's a different time now, Kurt,' she said quietly.

'Oh, Liesl, please don't be like this, ruining our reunion. We'll figure this out. I'll figure it out, I always do. It will be fine. Don't worry, *Liebchen*. We'll live happily ever after, I promise.'

He accepted the warm drink and sat on the chair she'd recently vacated, moving her study notes. Liesl was troubled. How would she cope now? Her exams were in a few short weeks and she needed to focus. But being with Kurt was all that mattered to her. He would find a way.

She gave him a slice of the cake her mother had posted down to her, and he ate it hungrily. Just as she was about to discuss the future, the door burst open.

'Oh, Liesl, my head is pounding. My grandad makes this stuff, slow gin. There is nothing slow about the way he pours it I can tell you, so I've no idea why he calls it that, but we ended up –' Abigail stopped abruptly when she realised Liesl wasn't alone.

'Oh… Oh, I'm sorry… I didn't know…' Poor Abigail was mortified at seeing her friend and a man in their room.

'Oh, Abigail, I'm sorry.' Liesl smiled. 'This is Kurt, my fiancé I told you about.'

Kurt stood up and bowed from the waist, kissing Abigail's hand. Liesl smiled as her friend reddened. Kurt was so old-fashioned and chivalrous.

He grinned. 'Hello, Abigail, it is nice to meet you.' His English was halting and heavily accented, but she loved him for trying.

'Hello, Kurt.' Abigail smiled, recovering from the shock. 'Welcome to Dublin.'

'Ah, yes. *Danke*, thank you.'

'Right, well, I'll let you two at it. I'll go for some coffee in the rec.' Abigail gave Liesl a meaningful look.

'Thanks, Abigail,' Liesl said, her cheeks burning. This was not how she would have liked to introduce Kurt to her friend. Despite the reconciliation on the boat and the letters they'd exchanged since, Liesl knew Millie didn't like Kurt, and she was adamant that Abigail and he would get along better.

Abigail left, and Kurt smiled at her as his eyes locked with hers. He was so attractive, he took her breath away, and she couldn't wait to be his wife.

'Can she speak German?' he asked.

'Who?'

'Your chubby little friend,' he said with a chuckle.

'Do you mean Abigail?'

'Yes, can she speak German?'

'No, why would she?'

'I thought she might be studying German since you are and she's a friend of yours, that's all.' He shrugged.

'No, she's studying Italian and Spanish, but in first year we all took core classes together, then divided into specific languages in second year. By then we were friends,' Liesl explained. 'Abigail is lovely. You'll like her. And I'll explain to her to speak slowly at first.'

'So your stupid German boyfriend can understand, eh?' He smiled but she heard a sharpness in the words.

'Kurt, please don't be prickly. Abigail is one of my best friends, and I really want you two to get along. Can you try, for me?'

'Of course. I'd do anything for you, Liesl.' He put his hands on her shoulders, his eyes boring into hers. 'Anything. I love you.'

'And I love you too.' She smiled and kissed him on the nose.

He murmured, 'Do you pick friends much less pretty than you on purpose?'

'What?' She wasn't flattered, and she didn't like him bad-mouthing her friends.

Reading her expression, he backtracked. 'I just mean you're so beautiful, and your friends are fine, nice-looking girls, I suppose, but not like you. They must envy you.'

'Of course they don't.' She took his empty cup and went to rinse it in the sink.

'I've upset you.' He took her hand. 'Liesl, I'm sorry. I will be charm itself to Abigail, I promise.' He tickled her and she giggled. 'I will do my best Irish accent, and I'll speak that infernal English language, though it makes no sense, and she will love me, and I will like her because she is my soon-to-be-wife's friend, all right?'

'Well, there's no need to get carried away. Just be nice, that's all I ask.'

'Of course.' He clicked his heels and bowed from the waist again, and she hugged him, laughing.

'Now, what are we going to do with you?' she wondered aloud. 'I suppose I could ask Abigail to bunk in with one of the others, and if nobody saw you...'

'Liesl!' Kurt looked shocked. 'We cannot sleep together until we're married, of course not. Besides, I would never risk your position here as a student. If they caught us, they might throw you out, and I would never forgive myself. I'll have to get a place of my own until we get married.'

'But can you afford that? Rent in Dublin is expensive.'

'Well, you know my situation. I've nothing, and coming here cleaned out whatever I had. But could you ask your mother? I'm sure she'd help me. After all, she'll regard me as a son after all our families have shared.'

Liesl flushed. She'd never lied to Kurt, but she'd never said she'd revealed his existence to her family either. Her face must have given her away.

'You haven't told them about me, have you?' The sadness in his voice broke her heart. 'Are you not sure of me? Ashamed of me maybe?'

She knew that feeling, that sense that the person you loved wasn't proud enough of you to tell their family.

'Kurt, I swear to you, that's not it. Of course I'm not ashamed, but I didn't want to tell them before my exams. They'd worry and want to come to Dublin to discuss it, and I just needed to focus on my studies. I had every intention of bringing you home once it was all over.'

He shrugged, resigned to what he saw as her rejection.

'Listen, I have an emergency fund. There'll be enough money there to rent a flat, just about, for a few weeks until my exams are over, then our life together can begin properly, all right? Stay here tonight. You can have my bed, and I'll sleep in one of the other rooms with Abigail. There's bound to be spare beds – there always are this time of year, as lots of people go home to study without distraction once lectures are over.' She knelt before him, stroking his hair.

He nodded. 'All right, let's do that, darling Liesl.'

143

# CHAPTER 19

She arranged to meet Abigail and a few of the others for breakfast the next day, and Kurt was fun and charming. His English had really improved since she'd left Berlin, and he told her and Abigail that he'd gone to the library and got some books out. He worked his way through them with a dictionary in his flat at night after work.

Liesl felt relieved to see Abigail hanging on Kurt's every word.

After breakfast, Kurt left her and Abigail to study for their finals and went out to explore the city. Liesl felt bad telling him that she needed the time, but her finals were so important and she wouldn't throw them away for anyone.

She thought that perhaps she should mention Kurt to the family now that he was here. She knew her mother would be delighted. Elizabeth and Daniel might be taken aback that it was so serious so soon, but she would convince them it was the right thing. Kurt and she were soulmates. He understood her in ways that she couldn't explain to anyone. They were so connected. They could talk for hours, not just about the war but about everything, and when he touched her, it was like an electric shock.

She gave him all her remaining money, as well as the rolled-up notes Daniel had given her and that she'd stuffed in her bag as an emergency fund before leaving Dublin. She knew Kurt didn't have any, though he was embarrassed to take her charity.

'I'll get a job and find a flat,' he whispered as he left.

It was unlikely he would be able to do either of those things, but they would keep him occupied while she studied. Thank God for her emergency fund. Elizabeth and Daniel had insisted on it. Her mother had opened a bank account in her name and put in a monthly amount that she hardly used, so she had enough for a deposit and a month up front. If Kurt could get a job somewhere, they would manage until her exams were done.

To her astonishment, he came back that evening, beaming from ear to ear, brandishing a bottle of wine.

'44 Merrion Square,' he said with a flourish, and dropped on the table a key attached to a buff cardboard key ring.

'What's this?' she asked, raising her face for his kiss.

'I told you I'd find a flat.' He opened the wine with a pop. 'Well, I did. I can move in now. And also I got a job. It's nothing major, just removals and things, but it will do for now and the money is OK.'

'Are you serious?' Liesl asked incredulously. 'You did all that in a day?'

He wrapped his arms around her. 'I told you not to worry, that I would take care of you, Liesl, and so I will.'

'I can't believe it.' She marvelled at the key. 'How did you do all of that without any paperwork? Normally it takes ages, forms to fill out and all of that. I can't believe you got the key and everything.'

He shrugged. 'The guy I'm working for owns it. His tenants were not ideal, not paying rent on time, loud noise or something, who cares, so he gave them notice last week and said I could have it.'

'How much is it?' she asked.

'One pound a week. It's on the top floor, but it's got a bedroom, a bathroom of its own and a kitchenette, so I thought maybe Erich or your mother could visit?'

He looked so enthusiastic and hopeful, her heart ached with love for him. She loved how serious he was about her, how committed, and how much her family meant to him.

'You are amazing. Have I told you that before?' She wound her arms around his neck.

'You have.' He grinned and kissed her briefly. Then his face changed, and his tone became serious. 'I don't know what I would have done if you hadn't come back into my life, Liesl, honestly. I thought so often of…well, of just ending it all. I had nobody, nothing, no memories even, everything was tainted, dirty. It was such a dark, bleak world, the Germany we became, what we did. And then you came back and it was like the clouds parted and the sun came in. I can't ever thank you enough. You gave me my life back.'

'I'm so glad you came that night. And I'm so sorry about Gretel and Nathaniel. And little Elke and Kitti. It all seems so wrong. They were such good people, but then so many were. I'm sure they would be so proud of you, of all you did to resist the evil all around you, of the man you have become.' She paused. 'I know you don't like to talk about it, but I know you did all you could to stop that horrific ideology.'

'It wasn't enough though,' he said sadly. 'This is one of the many reasons I love you, Liesl. You see the good in everyone. You are my angel.' He kissed the top of her head. 'I need to start work tomorrow, so I better get going over there. Not that I have much stuff, but still.'

'All right. And I can pop over to see the place tomorrow afternoon, once you finish maybe? I've a study group arranged for tomorrow morning. Our oral exams are in two weeks' time, and they are going to be tough, so we need to do a lot of practice.'

'But your German is perfect. You're a native speaker.'

'I know, but what I'm being trained for is quite technical, political jargon and so on. One of the lads in my class, Theo Kennedy, he's part of my group of friends – remember the tall chap I said hello to in the café? Well, he did a summer internship at the European Advisory Commission, so he and a few others are getting together to discuss the reduction of German territory to pre-1937 levels. Fascinating stuff like that.' She smiled.

Kurt released her. 'I don't remember him. What's he like, this Theo?'

Liesl was slightly taken aback. 'He's fine, nice, I suppose. As I said, we go around with the same group. His cousin Kevin is in my French tutorial, so that's how I got to know him. He's just part of the gang.'

Kurt looked sad so she hurried to reassure him. 'My friends are lovely. You'll get to know them, and they'll love you too, don't worry.'

'I just can't imagine any men knowing you and not wanting you for themselves. I know you think it's all just friendship, but I know men.'

Liesl pealed with laughter. 'You're so funny, Kurt, and I'm very flattered of course, but honestly I think you're overestimating my appeal.' She decided to be truthful, and now was as good a time as any. 'I had two boyfriends before you, and that was it. Besides, I'm sure the Fräuleins were very much enamoured with you. I remember Gretchen, who lived next door to you, kept stealing your football so you'd go into her garden to get it back?' She began to make some coffee and took some biscuits from the tin.

'We were just kids, and people had more on their minds in recent years than romance. She left for America actually in 1938. Her father had some family there, so they got out. Anyway, who were these boyfriends?' he asked.

Liesl shrugged. 'My first boyfriend was called David. He was a Jewish boy from Dublin who came up to help on the farm at Ballycreggan. He's going to Israel now actually, with my former best friend, though neither of them saw fit to tell me about it.'

'Did you love him?' Kurt asked.

Liesl sighed. 'I suppose so, in the way of first love, you know? But we were very different people. I was boring and studious, and he was religious and a hard worker but no interest in books. It came to a natural end when I came here.'

'And your second boyfriend?' He pressed her for the details.

Liesl was reluctant to talk about Jamie; it was still too raw. 'He was a student at UCD. I met him at a debating competition.' She tried to change the subject. 'So tell me more about this flat. I think I can picture where it is…'

'And how long were you together with him?' Kurt persisted.

'I don't know, a while. Look, it's over and it was before I ever went to Berlin, so like you, I want to look to the future, all right?' She smiled to take the sting out of the words.

'You loved him. Please, Liesl, I'd rather know.'

'Why?' she asked. 'It's over. In the past. I've moved on, and I'm with you now.'

Kurt looked troubled. 'I just don't want any secrets between us. I've told you all about my life since we last saw each other, and so I'd just like the same openness from you.'

Liesl resisted the urge to point out that not five minutes ago he was saying how the past was best left in the past, but she supposed this was different.

'All right. His name was Jamie. He's a very nice chap, and I did love him very much, but he let me down and so I ended it.' Even now, the words hurt.

'Did he have another girl, was that it?' Kurt wasn't going to let it go.

'No, nothing like that. But his family didn't want him seeing a Jewish girl, and he should have stood up for me and didn't, so…' She shrugged. 'Can we leave it now?'

'Did he… How far did you go with him?'

Liesl blushed to the roots of her hair. She couldn't bring herself to tell Kurt she wasn't a virgin. 'Kurt, you don't want to talk about the past, and neither do I. It wasn't a proper grown-up relationship like you and I have. This is the real thing, I know that now, so please, let's just face forward?'

'Sure.' He smiled. 'Have you mentioned me to your family yet?' he asked. 'I thought you might telephone today.'

'No, remember I said last night, I want to wait. It's just a few weeks. Please understand, Kurt.'

'I will wait for eternity if it means I can be with you, Liesl. I'm just impatient, I suppose. These years after the war have dragged on, with nothing to look forward to, no future, my past gone. I'm just excited to finally be doing something. Forgive me.'

'I love you, Kurt Richter.' She sighed, and he hugged her.

# CHAPTER 20

*a* few weeks later, Elizabeth, Daniel, Willi and Ariella were
having breakfast at Ariella's house. She baked every Saturday
morning, and it had become a tradition for the four of them to meet
there. Though they lived in the same village, Daniel was busy with his
business, and Elizabeth had become principal of Ballycreggan
National School when the Morrises retired last year. Ariella spent
most days at the farm, helping the rabbi to wind it all up.

'Is your mother not joining us, Willi?' Daniel asked as he helped lay
the table.

'No.' He shared a grin with Ariella. 'She's up at the farm.'

'What?' Elizabeth asked. 'What's so funny about that. Isn't she up
there all the time?'

Ariella rolled her eyes. 'Willi thinks that the rabbi has a soft spot
for his mother. I think he's mad of course – they drive each other daft
most of the time.'

'Well,' said Daniel with a smile, 'I did wonder. He was talking about
her recently, about what a fine woman she is. I hear she's going to
convert – is that true?'

Ariella nodded as she took the scones from the oven; they filled
her big bright kitchen with their aroma. 'She is. We had no idea, but

she told us a few weeks ago. She feels drawn, she said, and what with Willi and I being Jews and the rabbi and the children... I don't know, she feels like she wants to be part of it, I think. But she spends a lot of time reading now, great big tomes the rabbi gives her, and she's asking questions, so I think she's going to go ahead with it.'

'And it would mean she and the rabbi could...' Willi added, and Ariella swiped him with the tea cloth.

'Will you stop that? If he heard you, he'd have something to say about it, Willi Braun. I think it's nice for them. They spend so much time together, and they are both curmudgeonly of course, but they suit each other. I doubt it would go any further, as they are both too old and set in their ways now, but it's nice that they have that companionship.'

Elizabeth and Daniel shared a glance. Ariella and Willi were another odd match. He was much younger than she was, and in lots of ways, he was very boyish. He joked around a lot and loved to tease her, but they'd endured so much together. They were completely committed to one another.

'So have you heard from Liesl recently?' Ariella asked as she poured tea from the china teapot into Elizabeth's cup.

'I was going to ask you the same question,' Elizabeth replied. 'I got a letter when she came back from Berlin telling about the competition and how she got on there – no mention of Jamie, so we'll assume that's finished for good – but nothing since. I suppose she's studying night and day, so I wasn't going to bother her, but it would be nice to hear from her.'

Worry creased Ariella's brow. 'I got the same, and I asked Erich, but he's heard nothing either. And she normally writes to him every week. He tried phoning her halls a few nights ago, but the girl who answered said she wasn't there. I hope everything is all right?'

'She's fine, I'm sure,' Daniel reassured them. 'You know how much these exams mean to her. She'll be so disappointed if she doesn't get a first, so she'll be stuck in the books.'

'How about we go to Dublin next week, Ariella, just the two of us?' Elizabeth suggested. 'The school is closing for Easter on Friday, so we could go maybe Monday or Tuesday, drag the girl away from her desk for an hour to have lunch with us? If we give her warning, she'll put us off, saying she needs to work, but the child needs to eat too, and if we just turn up, she'll have to come.'

'I'd love a trip to Dublin anyway. Let's do it.' Ariella was thrilled.

'I'll drop you to the train and pick you up afterwards if you like?' Daniel offered. 'I need to go to Belfast for parts anyway on Tuesday, and I've a job I've been putting off down there, so Erich and I could get it done if that would suit you?'

'Perfect, thanks.' Elizabeth kissed his cheek.

'How are Erich's big travel plans coming along?' Willi asked.

Erich had finally told them of his plans to go to Bud's wedding, and they were thrilled for him. It was all he could talk about, and he was forever poring over maps and showing them the route he would take.

The reason he'd not mentioned it to his parents until it was all arranged was he wanted to pay for it himself; he was determined to show them he was a grown-up now. He'd been working as hard as he could for months, with Daniel all day and then in the evenings doing any odd jobs around the village that needed doing. He'd been to the travel agent in Belfast and booked his ticket to Liverpool, and from there to New York. He would then have to take a train to Atlanta, Georgia, change there for Mobile, Alabama and finally a bus to Biloxi.

He'd explained with excitement how he would travel through so many states, New Jersey, Maryland, the Carolinas, Georgia, Alabama and finally Mississippi. Bud's wedding was at the end of June, and he would leave on the first to get there in plenty of time.

'Did you hear Bud asked him to be a groomsman on the big day?' Elizabeth said. 'I thought he'd burst when he got the letter. I think Bud is so thrilled he's making the effort, he wanted Erich to know how much it meant to him.'

'Did we hear?' Ariella answered with a chuckle. 'It's his only topic of conversation.'

They all laughed. Erich was so excited, he couldn't resist telling everyone about his big trip and his American friend.

'I wish I could meet this Bud – he sounds lovely,' Ariella said.

'Oh, he is.' Elizabeth smiled. 'I remember the day he arrived. Erich was only a little lad, and he and some of the others were playing football on the green. This "Yank" as they called him came over and joined in, and you'd swear it was Stanley Matthews himself had joined in the game. He said he wanted to learn German, so Erich offered to teach him, which of course gave him an edge on the other boys. Bud quickly became "Erich's Yank", though in reality it was Liesl who taught him.'

'I can just imagine that.' Ariella loved to hear stories of her children's lives while she was in hiding in Berlin.

'It's a pity Liesl can't go,' Daniel said. 'He'd love to see both of them, though Erich seems happy to do this on his own now that he's a grown-up man.' Daniel smiled. To him, Erich would always be the little boy who followed him around adoringly. Erich had grown up, but he still believed Daniel had the answer to everything.

'He's fine, but he'd rather she was going too, definitely,' Elizabeth said, buttering a delicious scone. 'They are so close, those two. He misses her so much.'

'He'll miss her more once she's qualified and goes off to work in Europe presumably,' Willi said as he topped up the coffee. The leg that he'd lost on the Eastern Front had been replaced with a prosthetic. He'd had it fitted at huge expense in London, and unless you knew, you would just say he walked with a slight limp.

'I know.' Ariella sighed. 'I'm trying not to think about it. She's too bright and clever to clip her wings. She's got such an exciting future ahead of her, but there's a part of me that wishes she'd find a nice local farmer and settle down here.'

They laughed.

'Local farmers might have had an eye for our girl,' Daniel said, 'but she's not got any interest in them, I'm afraid, Ariella, so we'll just have to accept she'll be a visitor from now on.'

'She seemed to like it in Berlin, based on the letter anyway.' Willi sipped his coffee.

'She did,' Ariella agreed. 'And it was odd for me, thinking of her there. I know it's different now, but when I think of what it was like...'

Willi's hand covered hers, giving it a slight squeeze. 'She won't see any of that. It's all gone,' he reassured her.

Ariella nodded. 'I know. And I'm glad she got to go. It sounds like she didn't do much apart from the competition though. She never said in her letter if she visited our old apartment or your mother's house or anything.'

'Well, we'll get more details on Tuesday.' Elizabeth looked at Ariella. 'Where will we go? The Shelbourne or the Gresham?'

'I don't mind. Maybe we could try Restaurant Jammet on St Andrew's Street? I read a wonderful review of it recently.'

'Oh, yes, let's push the boat out.' Elizabeth was enthusiastic. She'd always wanted to visit the famous French restaurant that was mentioned in James Joyce's *Ulysses*. The fine-dining establishment had been a secret gem during the Emergency, as the war was known in the South.

'Oh, no wonder we weren't invited, eh, Willi?' Daniel joked. 'It would be fish and chips in Beshoff's if we were going.'

'Oh, the poor hard-done-by men.' Ariella pretended to be sympathetic. 'Don't think we don't know that all the ladies of Ballycreggan are feeding you cakes and buns everywhere you go, like stray cats.'

Daniel and Willi chuckled. It was true. Willi was going to join Daniel and Erich in the construction business once the farm was wound up completely. They had enough business for three now that their reputation for good work and a reliable timeframe was spreading.

The idea that the farm would cease to be was a good thing, they had to tell themselves that, but there was going to be a significant hole in the fabric of Ballycreggan without the Jewish refugees and those who helped them.

'I was thinking – perhaps we should throw a party before the community breaks up and people leave for Israel and everyone disperses?' Elizabeth said. 'What do you all think?'

'Levi and Ruth would say they'd hate a party,' Daniel said, 'but I think everyone else would enjoy it, and it would give everyone a chance to say goodbye. It will be sad of course, but better to mark it and be sad than ignore it altogether, I think.'

Elizabeth felt a terrible loneliness at the idea that it was all over. 'It feels so strange, after all these years, that it's coming to an end. For so long, we've been thrown together in the most unlikely of circumstances, but we made the best of it and became a community all the same.'

'We couldn't have done it without the people of this village.' Daniel placed his hand on his wife's; he knew how much the school and the farm meant to her personally.

'Nor without you, Elizabeth,' Ariella added. 'I wasn't here, I know, but people always tell me about how you rallied the communities during the bombing, when all the Jews helped to rebuild the village, and then how the people of the village helped with the farm, making it so cosy and homely for the children. They did it because it was in their hearts to do it, but everyone says you were the driving force.'

'And I think this must be one of the few places in the world where you'd find a rabbi, a Catholic priest and a Protestant vicar all enjoying morning tea together in Maisie's tea shop.' Willi smiled. 'Seeing that sense of friendship and respect for others' views has been the making of those kids – they are such a credit to all of you. They are proud of their own traditions but don't see their way as being better or worse than anyone else's.'

They all listened intently, as Willi wasn't one for serious speeches normally.

'That Kindertransport didn't just save their skins,' he went on. 'It saved their spirits too. The children who lived through it in Germany and other occupied places saw such horrible things, such hatred, that it can't but affect them all of their lives. But here they were raised in such tolerance and kindness.' His voice cracked with the unexpected emotion of it all. 'You gave them a home, and me and Ariella too, and Liesl and Erich and even my mother and the rabbi. It should be celebrated... You all should.'

Ariella moved closer to him, and he took her hand under the table.

'Let's plan it for the late summer, best chance of fine weather?' Daniel suggested.

They all agreed, and Elizabeth said she would ask Father O'Toole if they could have the party in the village hall. There would be no problem, as she knew he'd be happy to help. They'd ask him to make an announcement at Mass that all were welcome, as would Reverend Parkes at the Protestant weekly service, nearer the time. Elizabeth sat back as they talked out the details and smiled to herself.

How her life had changed! And while she saw first-hand the ravaged lives in the aftermath of the Nazi ideology, the war had given her children, a husband and dear friends. She thought back to her little life as a widowed schoolteacher in Liverpool, before the letter from Ariella begging her to take her children, the son and daughter of a cousin she'd never met. She didn't hesitate, because it was the compassionate thing to do, but what started out as an act of mercy on her part had proved to be the key to a rich life, full of love, challenge and fulfilment. Everyone in Ballycreggan had been through so much, individually and collectively, but the adversity had united them all, men and women, children and adults, Protestants, Catholics and Jews. Hitler was burning in hell if there was any justice, and his abhorrent vision for the world had wreaked havoc undoubtedly, but in the midst of it all, the world showed the best of itself. The kindness, the bravery, the altruism, the humour – all of it showed the world what it was to be a human being. Nationality, language, skin colour, religion – none of that mattered. People just saw each other as people, with hearts and minds and spirits. She'd lived through bombings, she'd found a warm, friendly community, and most importantly, the war gave her Daniel, Liesl and Erich. She knew that she was a very lucky woman.

'What will become of the rabbi, do you think, after all of this, when the farm is closed?' Elizabeth asked. Though she and Rabbi Frank respected each other deeply, she wasn't a Jew and he tended to confide more in the Jewish men. He was getting on now, in his seventies at least, and he'd made such enormous concessions over the years. He would have been very traditional, a Chassidic Jew, but when he found himself the caretaker of all manner of children, many of them from secular backgrounds, he rose to the challenge beautifully. Though he was serious and devout, he was loved by the children because they knew without doubt that he cared so deeply for each and every one of them.

Ariella worked closely with him, corresponding in several languages with agencies all over Europe trying to repatriate the children. She had passed her talent to her daughter. Liesl astonished everyone by even getting the highest marks in her class in Irish, which she took as an elective subject when she went to university. She'd never studied the language before in her life.

Frau Braun and Ruth ran the house, took care of the cooking and cleaning and managed the hens and vegetable gardens, and Willi did most of the maintenance, but it was Ariella who worked tirelessly with the old rabbi.

'He will probably go to Israel, I would think,' Ariella speculated. 'I haven't asked him and he hasn't said for sure, but his wife died years ago and they had no family, so I think when the farm closes, he'll retire to Tel Aviv. He has lots of contacts there.'

'It's hard to imagine him retiring. He's such a ball of energy, isn't he?' Daniel said.

'He is,' Ariella agreed. 'But he is getting on in years. Though he hates the sun, so how he'll fare under the Middle Eastern skies, I don't know. And the paperwork, oh, it drives him up the walls. Another thing for him to moan about, I suppose.' She grinned. The rabbi was not known for his patience when it came to bureaucracy.

'He could stay here if he wanted to. I mean, we could suggest it to him?' Elizabeth said.

'That's not a bad idea, Elizabeth,' Willi said. 'I know everyone assumes he'll go to Israel, and maybe he will, but his home is here. His life is the farm, but there are going to be a few Jews around here for years to come – all of us, the children who stay, as well as the Jewish community in Belfast.'

'Well, do you think I should mention it?' Daniel asked.

It went without saying that Daniel would be the one to speak to him on any such matter. The two men were close friends, and Rabbi

Frank had been Daniel's spiritual teacher from the moment the two men met. Daniel embraced his Jewish identity, despite coming late to the faith. Because of his upbringing, he didn't accept all the rules, and he and the rabbi frequently clashed on points of doctrine, but Daniel was his own man and refused to bow down to rules he saw as draconian or anti-women. It was a source of amusement to the community that he refused to cover his head as men were expected to do, because Elizabeth preferred him without a hat or kippah, but despite their differences the two men had a deep respect and affection for each other.

Ariella nodded. 'I think you should, he sees you as the representative of the entire community so he'll know if you are suggesting he stays, then it's what we all think.'

Willi agreed, 'He needs to know we want him to stay.'

# CHAPTER 21

*E*lizabeth and Ariella were dressed to the nines. It was so nice to have access to nice things again, having made do and mended for so long. Both women liked fashion and had treated themselves to a shopping trip in Belfast the day before in honour of the visit to the girl they thought of as their daughter. It struck them both frequently how remarkably easy it was to share Liesl and Erich. Elizabeth and Ariella had become so close, and they told each other everything.

'I was terrified and thrilled at the same time when you came back,' Elizabeth had admitted in the weeks after Ariella's miraculous arrival in Ballycreggan. Nobody had heard from her in years, so they had been more or less convinced she was dead. Elizabeth and Daniel had even adopted the Bannon children, so to have their birth mother turn up was a shock for everyone. 'I wanted you back for them of course – it was what I prayed for every single night – but I was so afraid of you taking them away from us.'

They'd agreed there and then that Liesl and Erich had lost a lot, though not nearly as much as some of their friends, and that there would be no more loss. So Ariella and Willi settled in Ballycreggan, and both couples shared the children harmoniously. No jealousy, no differences in parenting styles – they both deferred to the other – so it was a smooth and peaceful transition.

They were catching the last train to Belfast at 5 p.m. and it was eleven thirty now, so they had plenty of time to liberate their girl from the books. They were in high spirits as they walked from Amiens Street Station to Trinity Hall. The communal door of the halls was open, and the bright spring sunshine spilled across the green linoleum.

Everywhere students were feverishly revising, alone or in groups, and the hum of activity was unmissable. They knew which room was Liesl and Abigail's, having helped her move in four years earlier, so they climbed the stairs.

Liesl's door was closed, so they knocked. Inside, they heard a chair scrape across the floor, followed by footsteps. They were just about to call, 'Surprise!' when Abigail opened the door.

'Oh, Abigail, how are you dear?' Elizabeth giggled. 'We were being silly. We're looking for Liesl.'

Years of teaching had taught Elizabeth that it was close to impossible for a young person to lie to an adult's face. Only a rare few could do it, and Abigail wasn't one of them.

'Oh...um... She's not here, Mrs Lieber. She's...' Abigail's face flushed deep crimson and she averted her eyes.

'Oh no, that's a pity. Do you know where she went?' Ariella asked. 'We only came down for the day to surprise her, and we have a table booked for one o'clock.'

'She's with her boyfriend, I think...' Again Abigail paused, biting her lip.

'So is she back with Jamie? Is that where she is?' Ariella asked.

Elizabeth would have been surprised if that was the case. Liesl had told them why she finished with him, the way he stood by and allowed his mother to hurl abuse at Liesl.

'Jamie?' Abigail seemed surprised that they would mention him. 'Oh, no. Look, it's not my business. I'd rather you spoke to Liesl...' The poor girl was in a dilemma, they could see. She was loyal to her friend but hated having to lie.

'That's exactly what we would do.' Elizabeth smiled reasonably. 'But Dublin is a big city, so I'm afraid you'll need to give us a clue where to find her if we are to do as you suggest?'

Abigail deliberated, and then sighed. 'He's got a flat on Merrion Square, number 44, I think, top floor.'

Elizabeth and Ariella shared a look of confusion. Something was definitely going on. It wasn't like Liesl to be secretive, but whatever it was, they would need to speak to her face-to-face and not extract it word by word from this poor girl.

'Thank you, Abigail, we'll go and see her.' Ariella smiled. 'I'm sorry we made you tell us. I know you wanted to be loyal to her, and that's a wonderful quality. Liesl is lucky to have a friend like you.'

Poor Abigail nodded miserably, and the two women took their leave. They hailed a taxi and went immediately to the beautiful Georgian square.

'Well, whoever this lad is, at least he lives in a nice part of town,' Ariella said as the taxi rounded the corner. The beautifully symmetrical red-bricked terraced houses with their ornate fanlights and coloured front doors exuded middle-class opulence. The women paid the taxi driver and stood outside number 44.

The bottle-green door had a highly polished brass knocker, but to the side of the door frame were several doorbells. The numbers were faded, so Elizabeth decided to press the top one and see what happened. She and Ariella stood expectantly, but nobody came. They tried the other bells one by one, but nobody appeared to be at home. It was the middle of the working day, they supposed, and these flats would not be for people who were unemployed.

They stood back, stepping onto the road, and looked up for signs of life, when suddenly the door opened and a middle-aged man, carrying a briefcase and an umbrella, emerged. Without a word, Ariella smiled and brushed past him into the house, Elizabeth on her heels.

The hallway was dark and a little dreary, and there were two flats on the ground floor. The women walked quickly upstairs until they reached the top floor, which thankfully only had one door.

They looked at each other, then Ariella knocked. They listened keenly, and yes, there was movement inside. She knocked again, and then they heard footsteps. The door opened and there she was.

'Elizabeth! *Mutti*... I... How did you find me here?' Liesl was flustered and shocked to see them.

'Liesl? *Wer is da?*' A very striking-looking blonde man, obviously a German, walked up behind her.

Elizabeth didn't notice Ariella pale as she saw who it was.

'Er...c-come in.' Liesl stuttered over the words. 'What a surprise! I didn't know you were –'

'Clearly,' Elizabeth said wryly. 'So then, Liesl, would you like to explain what's going on, and introduce us to your friend?'

Liesl stood back, and Elizabeth watched in complete astonishment as the young blonde man stepped forward and embraced Ariella, his eyes bright with tears. Despite being taken aback, she noticed that the embrace wasn't reciprocated, that Ariella was frozen and wooden in his arms.

'Liesl, I don't understand...' Elizabeth began as the man released Ariella and extended his hand to her, which she took. He was very handsome, with a perfect profile, a straight nose and a square jaw; his long blonde hair was held back in an elastic. He was slight and a bit shorter than Liesl, who was five foot ten. He looked askance at Ariella, who seemed frozen, and turned his smile to Elizabeth.

'My name is Kurt Richter, and you must be Mrs Lieber? Liesl has told me so much about you. We can never thank you enough for what you did for Liesl and Erich. Ariella and Peter were my parents' best friends in Berlin. Liesl and I were friends as children, and now we're engaged.'

'I'm sorry, I don't...' Elizabeth was lost for words.

'I'm sorry. I should have told you, but I wanted it to be a surprise for *Mutti* and Erich,' Liesl began. 'I met Kurt – well, I should say he found me in Berlin, and we...well, we got together, and then I came back and he followed me.'

'And you got *engaged*?' Elizabeth was struggling to remain calm. This behaviour was so out of character for Liesl.

'Yes.' Kurt put his arm protectively around Liesl. 'I just knew when I found her again that she was the one for me, and so there's no point in waiting around. We just need to be together.'

'Well, you seem to have achieved that,' Elizabeth said, glancing around the small flat.

'Please, Elizabeth, *Mutti*, I know this is a shock, and I didn't want you to find out like this, but we love each other and we want to be together. Please be happy for us.' Liesl's eyes seemed to beseech her mother, who had yet to say a single word.

'And besides the fact that I love Kurt, he's alone in the world.' She turned to her mother. '*Mutti*, I'm so sorry to tell you this, but Nathaniel and Gretel and Elke and Kitti are all gone. Kurt is the only one left. Nathaniel was taken away for resisting the Nazis, and Gretel and the girls were killed by a bomb.' Liesl's eyes were bright with tears at the memory of their old friends.

Ariella spoke, her voice sounding husky. 'That's terrible. When did it happen?'

Kurt placed his hand on her shoulder, smiling sadly. 'They wouldn't have known anything, at least that has given me comfort. It happened on the twenty-fifth of April of 1943, when the brave men of the RAF decided to give Hitler a birthday to remember.'

Ariella nodded. 'And your father?' she asked, her face a mask.

'Poor Papa was betrayed.' Kurt's face hardened. 'We used to listen to the BBC, and someone told the authorities. He was, as you know, a brave man and he wasn't going to be dictated to by the likes of Goebbels, but someone came and dragged him out. To this day, I wish I'd been there, done something to defend him, but I wasn't. I was out trying to buy food, and when I came back, *Mutti* and the girls were distraught. I did my best to comfort them. I tried to find out where they'd taken him, but I was just a child and they wouldn't deal with me.' Kurt's voice lowered to an emotional whisper. 'I did all I could do, and continued with his work.'

Ariella nodded but said nothing.

'He would have been so proud of you, Kurt.' Liesl stood by his side. 'Your father is the reason Erich and I survived, isn't that right, *Mutti*?'

'He is,' Ariella said, but her voice sounded distant, not herself. Elizabeth assumed it was the shock of learning the fate of her dear friends.

'And he would have wanted you, Kurt, to carry on what he started,' Liesl went on. 'It was because of people like you and him and Frau Braun and Willi that *Mutti* survived.'

Kurt nodded and put his arm around her. The four of them stood there, a strange tableau in silence for a moment.

'Well, Kurt, it's lovely to meet you, and welcome to Ireland.' Elizabeth decided to take control of the situation. 'Now, we have a table booked for lunch at one at the Restaurant Jammet, so would you mind if we whisked Liesl away for an hour?'

Liesl looked uncertain. 'Perhaps Kurt could join us?'

'Oh, certainly another time. If he's going to be part of the family, there will be lots of reasons to celebrate in the future, I'm sure, but we had hoped for a girls' lunch, if you don't mind, Kurt?' Elizabeth smiled sweetly, and the German had no option but to agree.

'Of course,' he said, though his smile didn't reach his eyes. 'I must report for work anyway. It's my first week, so I'm trying to make a good impression.'

'Very wise,' Elizabeth said dryly. 'Now, ladies, shall we go?'

# CHAPTER 22

*E*lizabeth led the way from the taxi to the table, following behind the liveried waiter. She and Liesl had prattled meaninglessly in the taxi, but Ariella had not said a word. Whatever was going on, it was something very serious. She'd never seen Ariella so rattled. Liesl was aware of her mother's odd reaction, and Elizabeth could see the girl was nervous. Once the three women were seated and the waiter had taken their order for three gin and tonics – given by Elizabeth without consultation – they sat for a moment in silence.

Realising neither Liesl nor Ariella was going to speak, Elizabeth began. Something was wrong here. It could be the news that her friend didn't survive the war, but Elizabeth had a gut instinct that it was something else as well.

'Right, how about we start at the beginning, Liesl?' She smiled kindly. 'We accept you are a grown woman and perfectly entitled to live your life wherever you wish and with whom you choose, but you must understand that we are a little taken aback. We're happy for you if it's what you want, of course, but it's just a bit…well, unlike you, if you don't mind me saying?'

Liesl glanced at her mother, who was sipping her drink and

keeping her eyes on the immaculate white linen tablecloth. The décor of the long room was exquisite, and normally they would have been admiring the surroundings, but they had other things on their minds.

Liesl sat beside Elizabeth and opposite her mother and now gave Ariella a nervous glance before speaking. 'I should have told you, I know I should, but my plan was to finish my exams and then bring Kurt to Ballycreggan. I thought it would be a lovely surprise for you, *Mutti*, to know that one of the Richter family at least had survived. Even if Kurt and I hadn't fallen for each other, I would have thought that you would have been delighted to see him?' Liesl addressed her mother.

The silence hung heavily between them.

'*Mutti*, what's wrong? Please tell me!' Liesl pleaded. 'Are you disappointed I didn't tell you? Is that it? Because I explained –'

'That's not it,' Ariella interrupted, her voice like a whip.

Elizabeth waved the waiter, who was coming with menus, away as Ariella seemed to try to gather herself.

'The last time I saw Kurt Richter was in 1945. He didn't see me.' Her eyes were locked on her daughter's across the table. 'He was swaggering down the street towards Nathaniel and Gretel's house in Berlin, near the Tiergarten, looking very pleased with himself in his Nazi youth uniform.'

'But, *Mutti*, they made all boys join that.' Liesl was frantic now. 'Auntie Gretel made him join after Uncle Nat –'

Ariella held her hand up to stop her. 'They did, but I'm afraid your boyfriend took to it like a duck to water.' She swallowed. Clearly the memory of their last encounter was something more than a mere passing in the street.

'But *Mutti*…' Liesl tried again.

'Let her speak, Liesl.' Elizabeth put her hand on Liesl's arm.

'I was a Jew, alone in the city without a friend, and I thought perhaps Nathaniel and Gretel could help me. Frau Braun had told me I needed to get out of her house because the Nazis were going to use it for billeting bombed-out families and soldiers back on leave. It was too dangerous for me to stay in the attic.

'I had nobody to turn to except Nathaniel and Gretel. Peter was gone, friends from the synagogue had been long rounded up by then, and people I saw as neighbours all seemed to be supporting the regime, so it was too risky to approach anyone else. I went to their house. They were Aryan, not that any of that mattered when we were friends.

'Their house was visible from the Tiergarten, so I just watched and waited. I eventually got up enough courage to knock on the door, and when Gretel answered, she nearly jumped out of her skin. She looked terrible, worn and haggard, and she blurted that Nathaniel was gone and that I should leave. She more or less closed the door in my face, but it wasn't that she didn't want to help, I know that. She was simply terrified.'

Ariella took a sip of her drink, and Elizabeth saw the tremor in her hand. This was in 1945. Kurt said his mother had been killed in 1943. Something was wrong.

'I begged her to talk to me, so she whispered that I should come the next day, and then she was gone. I walked back into the park, and as I stood there, trying to imagine where I could go or what I could do, that's when I saw him. He walked down the middle of the pavement, almost causing an older man to be pushed into the traffic.' Her breath was ragged now, her normally stoic demeanour gone.

'Go on,' Elizabeth encouraged her. Ariella spoke so rarely of those days that nobody but Willi and Frau Braun knew what had really happened.

'Well, then, when I went back there. I had to go around the back, and Gretel let me in. Kurt and his sisters Elke and Kitti were out at the various Nazi youth groups, and she told me then.' Ariella glanced at Elizabeth, their eyes locking for a moment. 'Kurt was the one who denounced his father. He's the reason Nathaniel was picked up and sent to a camp. He boasted to her and Nathaniel about the Jews he'd had rounded up – he was the kind to harass and abuse Jews in the street – and he was commended by his senior officers for the alacrity with which he attacked his task. Nathaniel had fought with him – I can't imagine it, as Nathaniel was gentle and kind and adored his boy when he was little – but Gretel was sure that was what motivated Kurt to tell the authorities that his father had a radio. She said he smirked when Nathaniel was dragged from her arms. He enjoyed watching it and mocked her grief afterwards. She was so terrified of him, her own son. She said he beat her and his sisters and threatened them all the time that he would have them taken away too. She lived with that boy Liesl now thinks she loves, but she was afraid to death of her own child.' Ariella paused. 'He wasn't press-ganged into it, and any stories that he told you about involvement with the resistance, well, I wouldn't accept them as truth. Kurt Richter was a true and loyal Nazi and loved every minute of it.'

Tears flowed unchecked down Liesl's face as she listened to her mother. 'It's not true. I don't know about dates, maybe he got mixed up, but Kurt isn't what you think he is. He told me he was in the Hitler Youth, but listen to what you are accusing him of, *Mutti*. He was twelve when Nathaniel was arrested, *twelve*! A child! He never denounced his father – it's ridiculous to even suggest it. He was so excited to meet you again. He's lost everyone and everything. Please, please, don't do this, it's not true. He had to join, everyone did, and anyway, people do things in war. What about Willi killing his father?'

Elizabeth was shocked but Ariella's face was inscrutable.

'We met someone in Berlin who told us what he did. I didn't believe her, but maybe it's true. Either way, I don't condemn him out of hand, so it's a bit rich from you condemning poor Kurt for doing what any child would have done!'

Liesl was near hysterical now, and people were looking. Elizabeth knew she needed to get them out of this situation before it turned into a scene. She threw some money on the table for the drinks and stood up. 'Come on, let's go somewhere we can discuss this in private.' Elizabeth tried to coax them.

But Liesl wasn't having it. She stood and took her coat and bag. 'There's nothing more to say, Elizabeth. I'm sorry it's come to this, but Kurt is my future. We plan to marry once my exams are over. Kurt wants to go to America.'

Elizabeth sat back down in shock. She then garnered every ounce of her strength. The idea of Liesl going to America at all, let alone with a new German husband who seemed to be someone entirely different to what Liesl thought, was horrific. She needed to keep the lines of communication open with the girl so decided to play along as much as possible. Ariella looked physically deflated, having told her story.

'America, my goodness. Does he have friends there, or a job?' Elizabeth tried to keep her tone light and gesturing that Liesl should sit, she could not let the conversation end like this.

Liesl reluctantly sat back down. 'No, we don't know a soul – except Bud, I suppose. But Kurt's had enough of Europe and wants a fresh start.' Liesl tried again to get her mother's attention. 'You can understand that, *Mutti*, can't you? That's what you wanted too. Maybe you think you know something, but it isn't true. Poor Kurt lost everything and everyone he loved. He's been through so much, and now he just wants to forget all of that and move on. With me,' she finished quietly, and Elizabeth's heart broke for her.

Suddenly she was in Liesl's shoes, younger even, just eighteen, and her mother had cut her off for marrying a Jew. She didn't care, or at least she told herself she didn't. Rudi was all she wanted, and perhaps they would have stayed happily married forever, who knew. The Great War had different plans, and poor Rudi was killed on the morning of the eleventh of November of 1918. Elizabeth had been so angry for so long. His needless death happened after the armistice was signed but before the ceasefire was announced. Someone thought it would look nicer in the history books – 11 a.m. on the eleventh day of the eleventh month. She was a young girl then, in love and carrying her first child, which she later lost to miscarriage. A thought struck her – was Liesl pregnant? Was that the reason for the sudden rush to marriage and all the secrecy?

'Darling, you know you can tell us anything.' Elizabeth tried to sound reassuring. 'Anything at all, and we won't be shocked or horrified. We have both made decisions in our lives that our parents mightn't have agreed with, so please, if there's anything you want to tell us, please do, without fear of any negative reaction from us.'

Liesl smiled sadly. 'I'm not pregnant, Elizabeth.'

'Good,' Ariella said, the first unprompted word since she'd finished speaking. 'At least that.'

'*Mutti*, please trust me?' Liesl begged, the anguish badly disguised on her beautiful face. 'Can't you give him the benefit of the doubt? For me?'

To Elizabeth and Liesl's astonishment, Ariella stood up, forcing her chair to scrape noisily on the polished parquet floor, and simply mumbled, 'I will not let that monster ruin your life, Liesl. No matter what it takes, I will stop him, even if you hate me forever for it.' She grabbed her bag and coat. 'I'll see you on the train, Elizabeth.' And she made her way quickly out of the restaurant.

'Let her go.' Elizabeth placed her hand on Liesl's arm as she was getting up to follow her mother. They were now undoubtedly the floor show.

Elizabeth desperately wanted to go after her friend, but her poor broken-hearted daughter needed her more. Ariella was tough and had been through so much. She would be all right. Elizabeth would find her later and discuss everything, but poor Liesl was so sad and deflated, she couldn't just abandon her.

She led Liesl out onto the street, and together they walked. Elizabeth knew Ariella was telling the truth – she just knew on a deep intuitive level – but she needed more than ever to keep Liesl close now. If this Kurt had her so wrapped up in him, she needed to keep the lines of communication open.

Though there was no doubt in her mind the engagement was a terrible idea, she encouraged Liesl to talk about him. 'Tell me about Kurt,' she said as they walked along arm in arm.

'You don't believe all those awful things *Mutti* said, do you, Elizabeth?' Liesl pleaded. 'You know me better than that. If Kurt was what she said he was, I'd know, and it's just not like that.'

'I think she thinks it's true,' Elizabeth said diplomatically. She could not afford to have Liesl think she was taking sides.

Liesl's eyes lit up as she told her tale of the night of the quarter finals, the instant connection, the tramping all over Berlin. She even explained what the postwoman said about Willi and Frau Braun killing Herr Braun.

'Do you think Willi killed his father?' Liesl whispered, her eyes wide.

'I've no idea,' Elizabeth replied. 'But I do know he was a horrible man, and a committed Nazi to boot, so maybe if he'd found out that Frau Braun was hiding Ariella... Who knows what happened.' Elizabeth sighed. 'I remember about two years ago – you know the McGoverns that live out on Hawthorn Road?'

Liesl nodded. Mr and Mrs McGovern were silent people, but they came into Ballycreggan for service and to get a few groceries once a week. 'I do. Mrs McGovern always reminds me of a little bird, and he had that big booming voice.'

'Well, apparently Willi was doing a job out there – Daniel asked him to go because he was stuck on another job in Bangor – and Erich was with Willi, that's how I know. They were fixing a leak, and they saw Mr McGovern be rough with his wife. Apparently Willi hit him a belt that nearly knocked McGovern into next week. And when McGovern threatened him with the police, Willi said everyone, including the police, knew he beat his wife and that he'd better not do it again.'

'Really?' Liesl was astonished. Willi was not an aggressive man at all; she couldn't picture it.

'Well, according to Erich, on the way back, Willi said his father had beat his mother and he couldn't do anything when he was a boy, but as soon as he was older, he did.'

'So you think it might have been Willi who killed his father?' Liesl was even more incredulous now.

'As I said, I've no idea, but it's probably all best left alone anyway. No good will come of digging up that bit of the past. It sounds like no matter who did it, he was no loss to the world, so we won't shed any tears for him.'

Liesl exhaled. 'If it is true, then it makes it even worse that *Mutti* is being so horrible about Kurt.'

'I wish I had the answers for you, darling, I really do, but I haven't a clue,' Elizabeth said wearily.

# CHAPTER 23

*E*lizabeth left Liesl to return to her halls and made her way to the station. Elizabeth had managed to glean from Liesl how she and Kurt got together, and had even heard about the fallout and reconciliation with Millie. Whatever lies he'd spun, he certainly seemed to make Liesl happy, so she encouraged the girl to talk about her new-found love. Information was power.

The train was at 5 p.m. Elizabeth scoured the platform for her friend, but of Ariella's distinctive red hair there was no sign. She walked the length of the train, finding her in the last carriage.

'Are you all right?' Elizabeth asked, settling herself beside her friend.

'We have to get her away from him somehow.' Ariella was determined. 'He's an awful person, but she isn't the first woman to be charmed by a liar and a manipulator. He exploited her most precious thing, her childhood memories of her father, and used them to his advantage. That's why she's so obsessed with him – she feels he understands. But, Elizabeth, I didn't put her on that train – and you didn't raise her – to lose her to a monster like Kurt Richter. We can't let it happen. If I have to kill him with my own hands, I'll do it.'

Ariella was frighteningly intense. Elizabeth rarely saw that side of her friend's character. Once or twice when relatives rejected their Jewish refugee children, she'd seen flashes of cold fury, but never like this.

Elizabeth nodded. 'Well, we must not be hasty or do anything rash, and all the talk in the world won't get her to leave him – she's convinced we have him wrong. I've seen it before. She's under his spell, and we have to be careful. The last thing we want is to drive her further into his arms. So in theory, I agree that we need to do something, but we must be careful. If they up and go to America, we may never find her.'

The train journey was long, and all the way home, they tried to make sense of the day. Whichever way they went around it, they had to acknowledge that Liesl was an adult and entitled to be with whomever she chose. But there was no way they could allow this.

Eventually the train pulled in, and to Elizabeth's relief, her husband was on the platform.

'Had a nice day wining and dining while I was slaving away?' he joked, kissing her and then taking her bag.

'No,' Elizabeth said wearily. 'We didn't.'

On the way home, they told him everything that happened, and he was as concerned as they were.

As they drove into Ballycreggan, the village was in darkness.

'We need to tell Willi,' Ariella said as Daniel slowed down for their turn-off.

Daniel swung the car up the avenue to their house.

'Can you both come in?' Ariella asked. 'We need to make a plan together.'

Daniel followed Elizabeth into the sitting room. Willi had lit the fire, and there were two tumblers and an open bottle of whiskey on the coffee table.

'Can I get you a drink?' Willi offered, taking two more tumblers from the sideboard.

'It looks like we're going to need it,' Daniel said, accepting the glass. Willi poured a generous measure, first for Elizabeth and then for Daniel.

'What's up?' Willi asked, noting his wife's stricken face.

Ariella told him, then she, Daniel and Elizabeth sat down as Willi refreshed their glasses. He perched on the arm of the chair where his wife sat, his hand on her shoulder. Only the clock ticking on the mantelpiece and the crackling logs in the fire made any sound. The four of them sat still, absorbing this new reality.

'Is there any way Gretel could have got it wrong?' Daniel asked gently. 'I'm not doubting you, but all you saw was him on the street after what his mother said?'

Ariella shook her head. 'She adored him. It killed her that he'd gone the way he did.'

'I think Ariella's right,' Willi said. 'But I could easily check with some people I knew who were involved in resistance, see if they knew of him. Berlin is a surprisingly small place, really, and if he was involved with our side, someone would know.'

'So he's spun Liesl a load of lies to worm his way into her affections?' Daniel spoke with cold fury. Liesl Bannon might not have been a blood relative of his, but she was his daughter in every single way that mattered and he would not sit by and allow her to be treated like that.

'Yes,' Ariella whispered. 'He told her that Nathaniel was picked up – that part was true – but not that he was the reason. But he said that Gretel and the girls died in a bombing raid in '43. I spoke to her in 1945, so that's not true.'

'So what do we do?' Elizabeth asked.

'Well, I'm for going down there and ripping his head from his shoulders,' Daniel said darkly.

'She is so besotted with him,' Elizabeth said, 'I wouldn't risk doing anything like that. She is convinced he's the love of her life. He was the gateway into her happy past, and he shared her memories. If you'd heard her talking about him... I don't think she'd listen to a bad word about him.'

'She will from us,' Daniel disagreed, but Ariella sided with Elizabeth.

'You didn't see how she looks at him. They say they are going to marry and move to America.'

'Over my dead body!' Daniel was furious, and the other three watched in astonishment. Daniel was always the level-headed, reasonable one, and this wasn't like him. But he adored Liesl and Erich and wouldn't stand for anyone hurting either of them.

Willi spoke. 'I can check with some friends of mine, just to be sure. He may have been a double agent…'

'He had his own father killed, Willi, and he beat his mother. I saw the results of his handiwork with my own two eyes.' Ariella's eyes flashed with hatred for that innocent-looking boy. 'Don't let the façade of carefree student fool you. He should hang.'

'But how can we get Liesl to listen?' Elizabeth wasn't at all sure that Liesl would simply accept what they said and finish the relationship. Liesl had Ariella's steely determination, and though she wouldn't easily defy or hurt them, she would not be dictated to either.

'We need to make her listen,' Daniel said. 'Before it's too late.'

# CHAPTER 24

*E*lizabeth and Daniel hardly slept, and both rose early. They were surprised to find Erich at the kitchen table, reading a letter.

'Who's that from?' Daniel asked as he filled the kettle.

Erich looked up. 'Jamie, Liesl's old boyfriend.' He looked troubled.

'What's wrong, Erich?' Elizabeth asked.

'Here. Read it for yourself.' He passed the letter, and Daniel read it over Elizabeth's shoulder.

*Dear Erich,*

*I'm really sorry to write to you like this, but I feel like I have to. As you know, Liesl and I split up, totally my fault, and I wish every day it wasn't so. But I swear to you, this is not sour grapes on my part. She's seeing this German – he knew her from before, when you lived in Berlin, Kurt something – and she and he are engaged. But we are all worried about her. There's something not right there. Since he turned up, she's not seen any of her friends, and any time he is in company, he seems very strange. I know his English isn't great, but it's more than that.*

*Last night he threatened a chap we know, Theo, and his cousin Kevin. He told them that he would injure them badly if they made any contact with Liesl. He made some very strange remarks to the girls too, asking*

177

*about Liesl being with other men and being really graphic about it. I won't go into details, but you can guess, basically suggesting she had lots of partners before him. He also asked Abigail if she'd been to Ballycreggan and if she thought your family were very wealthy. He laughed it off when she was taken aback, but she and I and everyone really just thinks he's very strange.*

*Liesl mentioned to Abigail that a friend of hers, Millie, had said that Kurt wasn't all he seemed, so Abigail found her address and wrote to her. She too was really worried, and her boyfriend, Felix, is sure Kurt is bad news too, so they've come over to Dublin. We are all worried about her, and I thought you'd want to know.*

*It's not my business who she sees, I know that, but I care about her a lot and I could never live with myself if anything happened and I never said anything.*

*You can call me at the pub where I work if you like. It's called the Cobbler's on South Anne Street, Dublin 2376.*

*Jamie*

'The only Kurt I can think of is Kurt Richter. He was –' Erich began.

'It's him all right,' Elizabeth said darkly, then filled Erich in on everything that had happened.

Erich was speechless. 'Kurt Richter was a Nazi?' He was incredulous.

'It seems so, and judging by that letter, he's not changed much,' Daniel said.

'Well, we need to go down there, rescue her if that's the case. We can't just sit here and do nothing.' Erich was upset at the thought that someone would hurt his sister.

'I agree.' Daniel turned to Elizabeth. 'Let me talk to her. Now that some time has passed, she might listen to reason. Let me try at least?'

Elizabeth knew that if Liesl would respond to anyone, it was Daniel. Her mother was like a red rag to a bull, and she'd already told Elizabeth everything. Elizabeth wanted to maintain the semblance of a myth that maybe she was on Liesl's side.

'I think you should,' she agreed.

'I'm going too. I'll find Jamie, see if we can't do something,' Erich said.

'OK, let's go.' Daniel shrugged on his jacket and took the car keys. 'Tell Ariella what I'm doing. I hope she doesn't think I'm going over her head, but I have to sort this out.'

'I will. Be careful.' She kissed him and hugged Erich, and they left.

* * *

DANIEL AND ERICH split up in the city, as Erich went in search of Jamie and Daniel went to Liesl's halls. But she wasn't there. They'd arranged to meet in Jamie's pub in two hours. Daniel knew where to find Liesl, so he went straight to Merrion Square. Luckily, a janitor was sweeping out the hallway, so he waited until the man's back was turned and ducked into the building. As he climbed the stairs to Kurt's flat, he tried to rehearse what he was going to say. He hoped to see Liesl alone, but he could handle Kurt if things got nasty.

He knocked on the door, but there was no sound from inside. He tried again, but still silence.

Glancing over the bannister down to the deserted bottom floor, and realising the janitor was gone and the door closed, Daniel took out the Swiss army knife he always carried in his pocket and managed to pick the simple padlock.

There was nobody inside so he had a quick look around. There was a single bed, made neatly, and an army kit bag on the bed. Apart from that and a few bits of delph, the flat was empty.

He lifted the bag. It felt strange. Something was rattling around in the bottom, though when he looked inside, it only seemed to contain a few items of clothing.

The bag was lined with a heavy card base that wasn't sewn to the canvas, and Daniel reached in and pried it up. He was right; there was another compartment underneath the clothes. He didn't want to alert Kurt by tearing the bag, so he thought if he could extract the contents without damaging the bag, he would.

He pulled the cardboard back enough to get his hand in, taking care not to crease it. He felt what seemed to be a leather pouch of some kind, a book, some papers and something metal, as well as a roll of fabric. Carefully, he extracted the items.

One was a dagger, issued to the Hitler Youth. Daniel took it out and examined it. It was encased in a black leather scabbard with a leather attachment for a belt. The handle was a chequered design with the Hitler Youth insignia set into it. Daniel pulled the knife from its sheath. Engraved on the blade were the words '*Blut und Ehre*'. Daniel felt a wave of profound revulsion. What people like Kurt did had a lot to do with blood and absolutely nothing to do with honour.

He'd seen those kids, barely out of primary school, after the Anschluss, parading around the streets of Vienna. They had daggers just like this one proudly tucked in their scabbards, and everyone knew that if the children who carried these deadly weapons used them on anyone perceived to be an enemy of the Reich, there would be no repercussions. Had Kurt used this on Jews? Probably. He unrolled the fabric to reveal medals; there must have been more than twenty. Various designs – diamond shaped, square, round – but all emblazoned with the swastika. Some had the HJ insignia of the Hitler-Jugend.

The pamphlet was one issued to the Hitler Youth, all full of rubbish about the superiority of the Aryan race and the inferiority of everyone else.

Daniel didn't touch the medals or the pamphlet; the idea of holding something in his hands touched by the devil was repugnant to him. If Kurt denied ever being an enthusiastic Nazi, why keep the trophies?

The book was a small cheap notebook and on the first page was written:

*Shares in USA – Estimated value unknown*

*House in N Ire. – Substantial dwelling house on own grounds (five bedrooms)*

*Apartment in Berlin – Three bedroom, four reception rooms, two bathrooms*

*Adopted parents – house and engineering/building business + teacher's salary and pension*

Daniel swallowed his fury. Kurt obviously thought Liesl's family was wealthy and was trying to capitalise on that.

He replaced everything and relocked the bag, leaving it on the floor. He slipped out and walked to the pub, where Jamie and Erich were in deep conversation. He filled them in on what he'd found.

'I still can't believe it,' Erich said as Jamie put a pint of beer each in front of him and Daniel. 'I mean, I do, but Kurt. It's just so hard to picture.'

Daniel sighed. 'He's bad news, all right. We need to get her away from him, but a young girl in love is a stubborn thing, and a cornered Nazi is a dangerous one. We'll need to be clever. We can't go in there all guns blazing, much as I'd like to strangle him with my bare hands. We don't want to go bringing the police in on top of us. If we could send him on his way, over to England maybe, I could get a word to the right people. I'm sure there are several of Willi's former colleagues who'd love a crack at him.'

'Look, how about this.' Erich seemed to be thinking aloud. 'I'll try to get Liesl to come out, say I've just come down to Dublin, let on I know nothing. She knows you lot never tell me anything anyway, so that's not that much of a leap. We'll get her out with everyone. It's going to be tricky though this close to the exams, but I'll just have to do my best. Jamie, Abigail, Millie and Felix and I will all meet her, and we'll tell her about what you found. We'll make her listen. She knows we wouldn't all lie to her.

'Meanwhile, Kurt won't go – Jamie told me he hates meeting her friends – so I'll just convince her to come out with me. Then you go up to the flat and have a word with Kurt, making sure he never comes within ten yards of her ever again.'

'Sounds like the best plan,' Jamie agreed. 'Unless you want me to come with you, Daniel?'

Daniel took a sip of the beer. 'No, thanks. I can handle him.'

'OK. How about we get Millie and Felix in on this as well. They show up at his flat, saying they looked for her in her halls and

181

someone directed them to Kurt's. They can say they're newly arrived in town. She won't be able to refuse to meet them, after them coming all this way. She needn't know they've been here for a few days.'

'OK, let's do it.' Daniel stood.

Jamie went off to contact the others while Daniel pulled Erich to one side. 'I'm going back to the van. I need to get a knife or something. That little Nazi is armed, so I'm not taking any chances. Do not let our girl out of your sight, right?'

Erich nodded. 'I won't. Don't worry. Be careful.'

# CHAPTER 25

*A*fter the disastrous lunch, Liesl walked alone in Phoenix Park for the rest of the afternoon, all hope of study gone as she was so upset. She had to tell Kurt something, give him some explanation for her mother's reaction to him. She went back to her room without seeing him that evening, feeling cowardly, but she needed to sleep on it all, to figure out what she was going to say.

She tossed and turned all night and early the next morning went around to Kurt's.

'She knows you were in the Hitler Youth and she thinks you were, I don't know, enthusiastic. She had the wrong end of the stick, I know, but she seems convinced.' Liesl was miserable. 'She also says she met your mother in 1945.'

'What? She thinks I'm lying that my *mutti* was killed? Why would I do that?' His innocent blue eyes raked her face for an answer. 'I was in the Hitler Youth, everyone was. We would have been in trouble if the girls and I didn't join those organisations, but the idea that I had my papa arrested? Liesl, I swear on my life that's untrue. You saw him and me – we were so close. I adored him. And as for hurting my *mutti*...'

He swallowed. 'I never told you this as I didn't want you to think badly of her, but *Mutti* and I did argue, that part is true. She... Well, I hate to say this, Liesl, but she had another man. It was before my father was picked up, and I found out about it. I was just a child, but I saw them together.' He shuddered visibly. 'I confronted her, and maybe that's why she told your mother a big pack of lies. I swear I never hurt her – I could never do that – but I threatened to tell Papa and she went mad. The man, he might have had my father arrested, got him out of the way... I don't know. But anyway, it didn't matter because they were killed. *Mutti* and I weren't speaking when she died, and I...I can't...' His shoulders were shaking.

'Oh, Kurt...' Pity, but also a stronger emotion, flooded through her. This was the explanation. Gretel was having an affair. It seemed hard to imagine, but it happened, and if the man she was seeing was jealous, he could have had Nathaniel arrested. And when Kurt confronted her... Well, it explained everything. Gretel was the one telling lies to protect her reputation with her old friend.

'I knew there would be some explanation, I just knew it. I'll explain.' She held him in her arms. 'It's all going to be all right, Kurt. I promise we'll sort this all out and everything will be fine.'

He sat up, his tear-stained face worried and frightened. Then he stood and crossed the room, going into the bedroom and picking up his bag from the floor. She could see him through the door.

'I could have sworn I left that on the bed,' he said, his brow furrowed. He looked around the room, gazing at everything suspiciously.

'What, Kurt? What's the matter?' Liesl asked.

'I think someone was in here while we were out. I just...' He rooted in the bag, throwing a few shirts and some underwear on the bed.

'Kurt, nobody was here, why would they? It's not like there's anything to steal.' She gave a small smile. 'Look, let's just try to have a nice evening. Please don't be upset anymore, and thank you for telling me the truth about your mother.'

He turned and his face was inscrutable. He gazed at her for the longest time. Then the doorbell rang.

'I'd better go and see...' she began.

'Leave it. Just ignore it and they'll go away.'

'I can't ignore it, it could be anyone.'

She stood, and without waiting for a response, she let herself out and went downstairs. She opened the heavy front door, and to her astonishment, found herself enveloped in a huge hug.

'Surprise!'

Millie and Felix stood in the doorway, their combined bulk filling the space.

'Millie! Felix! I can't believe it… What are you doing here?'

'Well, you said to visit, and Felix came over to Cambridge, and we just decided, spur of the moment thing. My dad's mate, the lorry driver I told you about, was coming over on the ferry, and we cadged a free spin. He's going back tomorrow, so we just came on a flying visit. I went to your halls and your roommate said you were here. I should have given you notice, I know, and now I realise you have exams shortly – ours aren't for another month. So we've booked into a hotel and we promise we won't get in your way at all. But maybe you could spare some time to meet us for a few drinks tonight?'

Liesl tried frantically to find a reason not to meet them, but they'd come all this way. She knew she had to go, but the timing could not be worse.

'That would be lovely. When and where?' she asked weakly.

'Well, your roommate, Abigail, said there was a band playing tonight in a pub, Madigan's, I think she said. We had a cuppa with her – she's so nice,' Millie gushed.

'We're looking for a real Irish pub.' Felix grinned, clearly delighted to be in Dublin.

'Well, Madigan's will fit that bill all right.' She smiled with as much enthusiasm as she could muster. All her college friends would be there – it was their favourite haunt – and maybe this was a good thing.

The last few days had been so intense, maybe a night out with her friends was just what she needed. Suddenly returning to her carefree student life, just for one night, was so appealing. Every interaction she'd had of late was either an argument or highly emotionally charged; she longed just to step away from it all.

Kurt didn't like socialising. He said her friends spoke too fast; he even accused them of doing it on purpose so he wouldn't understand. He claimed he could watch films in English and understand them easily but that her friends were unintelligible. She'd tried to explain that the Irish spoke very quickly, that it was just their way. She tried to get him to see the funny side, explaining it came from necessity. When the Irish were under British rule, it was useful to communicate incognito. The British had long since outlawed the Irish language, so the Irish developed a way of speaking quickly, using lots of native words and peculiar syntax, to confuse the enemy. She'd made him laugh in the end.

'Super.' Millie beamed. 'Oh, Liesl, it's so good to see you. And how's Kurt?'

Liesl thought back to Millie's reservations about him and dismissed them yet again. Millie didn't know him; nobody did.

'Oh, he's fine. He's in Dublin too actually, came over a few weeks ago to surprise me. It's great to see you too.' She changed the subject. 'I'll see you in Madigan's later?'

She felt terrible. Millie and Felix were her friends and she should invite them in, but now was a terrible time to host anyone.

'Wonderful, about seven?' Millie didn't seem to mind. 'We're going to explore this beautiful city of yours. See you then.' She hugged Liesl once more, and they were gone, happily walking down the street hand in hand. Liesl was happy for her friend that it had all worked out. She knew Millie was really smitten with Felix, so she was glad he'd come good on his protestations of love back in Berlin.

She was just about to back up when she heard her name being called. Erich ran to her from the other side of the street.

'Erich! What are you doing here?'

'Well, that's a welcome!' He grinned, his dark hair flopping over his eyes as always. He looked so much like their father.

'I'm sorry, things have been a bit...' She looked at him quizzically. 'Have the parents sent you?'

'No, I just decided to come down before my big trip to the USA. Spur of the moment thing to get some bits and pieces. Thought we might have a get-together. I haven't seen them in a while myself, as I've been busy getting organised.'

His innocent chatter reassured her that at least they hadn't poisoned her little brother against Kurt. From the sounds of it, they'd not even told him Kurt was here.

'Well, actually, I have a surprise for you.' She smiled.

'What?' He grinned. 'If it's dollars, I'm happy to take it.'

'No, it's not dollars, but it's someone you haven't seen for a while.' She turned and gestured he should come in. She ran upstairs and Erich followed her.

'What's this fancy place about?' Erich asked as they climbed up. 'I thought you were still in halls? I went there and some girl, not the gorgeous Abigail unfortunately, told me you were here.'

'Yes, well, that's all part of the surprise.' They eventually reached the top floor. The key was in the door and she turned it and pushed it in. Kurt was where she'd left him on the sofa.

Erich did a double take. 'No way.' A dawning delight spread across his face, and Liesl felt herself relax; they hadn't got to him.

'Kurt!' He crossed the room in three paces as Kurt rose to greet him. 'I don't believe it! Oh my, what a surprise!'

'Hi, Erich, great to see you, buddy.' Kurt grinned. They embraced.

'I can't believe you're here.' Erich turned to Liesl. 'Why didn't you tell me? Does *Mutti* know? Tell me everything, how are the family?' he gushed, excited to hear all of Kurt's news.

'They're gone, Erich, *Mutti*, Papa and my sisters. The Nazis got my father, and a British bomb got my mother and sisters,' Kurt said sadly.

'Oh, Kurt, I'm so sorry. They killed my papa too,' Erich said, the pain only slightly diminished with years.

'I heard. I'm sorry.' Kurt put his arm around Erich's shoulders. 'But we survived, and we're here and we're reunited, so we should be happy, right? That's what they'd want, for us to be happy?'

'They would.' Erich nodded. 'Oh, Kurt, it's so good to see you. How did you find Liesl? You two weren't in contact before, were you?'

'No. I found Liesl when she came to Berlin. She was a famous university debater, and her name was in the paper, and…well…here

187

we are.' He slung his arm around Liesl and kissed the top of her head.

'Hold on.' Erich looked even more amazed. 'You two aren't...'

Liesl smiled shyly. It felt good to have at least one member of her family happy for her.

'We're together,' Kurt said proudly.

'I...I can't believe it, but I'm so happy for you, I...' He ran his hand through his hair. 'I can't believe it.'

'We're engaged actually,' Liesl said with a smile.

'Oh, congratulations!' He hugged his sister. 'You're getting married! Have you told them at home yet?'

She and Kurt shared a split-second glance. 'The thing is, Erich, they're not happy for me. They have some kind of cock and bull story about Kurt, from back years ago, and they believe it. There's a logical explanation – we just need to explain it to them.'

'What kind of a story?' Erich asked, accepting a cup of coffee from his sister.

'They say I was in the Hitler Youth, and I don't deny it. I was – you had to be. We would have been persecuted if I didn't join. Elke and Kitti were in the girls' version. But your mother believes I was more enthusiastic than I was. It's a long story and I don't really want to go into it, but that's enough to condemn me in her eyes it seems.'

'But that's not fair, you were only doing what you had to do.' Erich seemed frustrated. 'I can't understand why... Have you explained to her?'

'She never gave us a chance. She just made a decision.' Liesl said, her hurt at her mother's reaction still raw.

'But Kurt and all the Richters are like family. We all spent so much time together, and she should know that Kurt would never do anything to Jews or anything like that. We've been friends forever.' Erich seemed agitated.

Liesl assumed her usual role of soothing his anxiety. 'I don't know, Erich, I really don't, but we can explain and she'll realise it was all a misunderstanding. Kurt and I are meant to be together. We love each other, and he's not the kind of person she thinks he is.'

# CHAPTER 26

*L*iesl, Erich and Kurt spent the afternoon happily reminiscing about life in Berlin before the war. Then Liesl remembered her plan to meet Felix and Millie.

'Oh, Kurt, I forgot to tell you in the whole excitement of Erich turning up that my friends from Berlin – you remember Millie and Felix? They arrived in Dublin last night, a last-minute thing, and they're going to Madigan's tonight. Some of the old college crowd will probably be there too, Abigail and a few others. So I said I'd pop in.' She hoped he'd just accept it. He didn't enjoy socialising and said he was always afraid other men were looking at her. It was nonsense of course; he was just insecure because of everything that had happened to him.

'I feel bad that I can't entertain them, but they understand it's exam time. They just got a last-minute free trip over with a friend of her father's.'

'Liesl, come on, don't be ridiculous. We're not going to Madigan's,' Kurt said quietly. 'I don't feel like it after everything. Besides, Erich has just turned up. Why can't we just spend some time together?'

'Well, I'd like to go, especially if the lovely Abigail is going to be there,' Erich joked.

'I'm sure she will be, though I doubt a schoolboy like yourself is what she's after, little brother,' Liesl teased.

'We'll see. You haven't seen my full-on charm offensive in action.' Erich winked.

'I'm too tired to go out. Besides, I have work tomorrow,' Kurt said, and Liesl heard that hard edge to his voice, one that was becoming more frequent, and she didn't like it. She knew he was damaged and hurt, but she had a life.

'Well, if you don't want to come, I could just take Erich and you could rest here. I'll come back here to say goodnight after I've made an appearance. He's got a crush on Abigail, so he'll be happy to see her again.' She smiled, hoping to lift his spirits.

'I don't want you going out tonight, Liesl.' Kurt spoke as if it were the most reasonable request in the world and she was being a particularly obstinate child.

Liesl felt a surge of annoyance.

Erich looked awkward and kept his eyes on the floor.

'Kurt, I have a life,' she said. 'My friends are visiting from England, my brother is here from Ballycreggan, and I'm going to go to the pub and see them. You're welcome to come – in fact, I hope you will – but either way, I *am* going to go.'

'And that's it, is it? You do what you want, going out to bars with all sorts, and I just sit here and wait for you to come back?' A muscle ticked in his cheek and his eyes were bright. She thought he might cry, but she wasn't going to let her friends down.

'I love you, Kurt, you know I do, but it's been hard on me too, you know? I have to do my exams, and I hate falling out with my family. So how about after my exams are over, we can go to Ballycreggan, explain about your mother and why she lied, and they will see you're the lovely sweet man I know you are?'

The silence hung heavily between them.

'So you're refusing to do as I ask? Is that it?'

Liesl felt the tears well up. The last while had been so stressful, and now this. 'I just want a night out with my friends. It's not a bad thing, and it's not too much to ask. I have invited you and you won't come, so I'm going,' she said quietly.

'And you won't change your mind?'

'No, Kurt, I won't,' she said sadly.

She didn't want to hurt him, but she felt bad enough that she couldn't put Millie and Felix up and show them around Dublin; she was the only one they knew in the city. And Erich loved a night out with her college friends; it made him feel very grown up.

She took her light-pink summer jacket and buttoned it over her red dress. The jacket was Vogue – Elizabeth had made it from a pattern – and everyone admired it on her.

'All right, I'm off. Come on, Erich.' She smiled and went to kiss Kurt. He sat stock-still, staring forward, saying nothing, never meeting her eye.

'That was a bit intense,' Erich said as they let themselves out onto the street. 'He's different to how I remember him.'

Liesl sighed. 'It's complicated, Erich. He's just hurt and confused, and he thought *Mutti* would be happy to see him and she wasn't. Look' – she linked his arm – 'can we just not talk about it? I'm tired of the whole thing. I love him and I love *Mutti*, and I have my exams next week, and it all just feels so overwhelming.'

Erich smiled. 'Sure, let's just go and have some fun. Tonight will be the night Abigail will fall for my charms, I can feel it.'

Liesl chuckled and cuffed her brother gently on the head. 'Righto, Romeo, though she's old enough to be your big sister at least.'

'Ah, the path of true love is...something... What is it again?' he asked, never the scholar.

'Poor Elizabeth was wasting her time trying to drill Shakespeare into your thick head, wasn't she?' Liesl grinned as they walked towards the pub on the quays.

'Absolutely. Could never see the point of it myself. All those old poems and stuff, on and on droning about flowers and coffins and other things nobody cares about. Wasn't there one about a Greek vase? I mean really... Daft, the whole lot of them.'

She smelled beer on his breath. 'I thought you were shopping? Were you in the pub, Erich Bannon?' she asked with mock sternness.

'I was, my dear sister,' he admitted with a chuckle. 'I've become a martyr to the demon drink.' He did a theatrical Irish accent.

'Oh, where'd you go?' she asked as they walked. 'There are some dodgy places in Dublin for an innocent country boy.'

'I went to a pub off Grafton Street, can't remember the name. It was nice.' He was non-committal.

'Jamie works in a pub on South Anne Street, just off Grafton Street. It wasn't that one, was it, the Cobbler's?' She was surprised to see her brother flush.

'It… Well, it was actually. But he wasn't there. I borrowed a football magazine from him when I was down, and I wanted to return it. I didn't say 'cause you two were broken up…'

'Oh, right.'

'So is the lovely Abigail ready to fall into my arms, do you think?' he asked, changing the subject. 'I could read a few sonnets to her?'

Liesl giggled. 'I doubt it. Besides, as I've told you fifty times, you're too young for her.'

'Let's let Abigail be the judge of that,' he said as they crossed the busy road. 'So how are you for the exams? Ready?'

'Well, I was. I mean, I am, I suppose. I've worked hard, but the last few weeks… Well, it's been a bit hectic, I suppose. It's great to have Kurt here and everything, and he's so supportive. I start with German lit on Monday morning, and then French on Wednesday. I have two oral exams on Thursday, both in German…'

'I'll never speak that language again, never,' Erich said, unusually serious.

'It's over now, Erich. The Germans are not all Nazis, you know. Look at Willi and Frau Braun and Kurt,' Liesl protested.

Erich shook his head. He almost never went against her, deferring to her on everything since the day he stepped on board that train in Berlin with his little hand in hers when he was seven years old.

'I know that, but I…I hate even to hear it. It reminds me of that day…' He swallowed, and the confident happy-go-lucky man he had become was suddenly gone; he was that little boy again. 'Do you remember when we left the apartment, and we were so hungry?' He spoke quietly as they walked. 'And *Mutti* had you on one side and me on the other. We passed Herr Bruner's, where Papa used to get pastries for us on the way home from work, and the aroma of fresh bread and cakes was torture. I stopped to tie my shoe, just to smell the baking. You and *Mutti* walked a little ahead, and he came out, brushing outside his shop, and he muttered, "That's right, get out of here, you filthy Jewboy. Your father is gone and we don't want you here."' He sighed. 'That was the last sentence in German I heard before I left, and I'll never forget it.'

Liesl stopped, and though she longed to hug him, she knew he'd shove her off for embarrassing him in the street.

'I don't mind you studying it, but I won't ever go there, or speak that language ever again.'

'I understand, Erich.' She had to ask. 'But you don't hold it against Kurt, do you? I know why *Mutti* is saying those things, and I know they're not true, and...' She felt the tears well up in her eyes.

'They never said anything to me, Liesl. Honestly, I never spoke to them about him, so maybe they just think you're too young, or it's getting in the way of your studies.'

Relief surged through her; at least she had one person on her side.

They continued walking and arrived at the pub. Abigail, Millie, Felix and Jamie were there. She was surprised to see her ex-boyfriend but kind of relieved too to see his smiling, welcoming face.

'Hello, Fräulein,' he said, using the pet name he had for her.

'Hi, Jamie. I thought you'd be working in the bar tonight?'

'Ah, all work and no play makes Jamie a very dull boy.' He winked as he accepted a lemonade from Felix.

Once everyone had a drink, Liesl noticed they were all acting strangely. There was none of the usual banter and teasing. Erich sat on one side of her, Jamie on the other, and Abigail, Felix and Millie sat opposite.

'So how are things? Not regretting your decision to drop out?' Liesl asked Jamie, then sipped her orange juice.

193

'Are you not on the wine tonight?' Jamie asked, nodding at the juice. 'Aren't we a perfect pair? The Liesl I knew could drink for Ireland. 'Twas like throwing water into a barrel of sawdust.' He nudged her playfully, and she laughed.

'You make me sound like an alcoholic,' she replied indignantly.

Jamie grinned. 'Anyway, to answer your question, no, I do not regret it for one second. I'm no doctor – I don't know what I am – and the blood and guts will have to be someone else's department.'

'I'm happy for you.' Liesl meant it. 'And how are things with your family?'

He looked at her, and she felt confused. This was the boy who let her down, who hadn't the guts to stand up for her. So why did he make her stomach lurch still? She was engaged to Kurt; he was the man for her.

She glanced around the table. Abigail and Erich were chatting now and Millie was showing Felix something in a guide book, so nobody was listening in.

'They came up to Dublin. We had it out. Mam is sorry – she asked me to tell you if I ever saw you. Brendan is never going to speak to me again apparently, but that's actually a mercy. He's a pain in the arse with all his sanctimonious pontificating. But Mam and Dad saw how heartbroken I was when I lost you. I went down home for a bit, everywhere in Dublin just reminded me of you, and I… Well, anyway, they could see how much you meant to me and how terrible I felt at letting them speak to you like that, and they realised they did wrong. Mam went to the priest at home, confessed it all, and he gave her a right good talking to about Germany and the Jews and everything, so she's changed her tune. My father thinks what she tells him to think.' He rolled his eyes. 'Too late now, but still.' He shrugged sadly.

'I'm glad you are all speaking again. I've fallen out with my mutti. But at least I have Erich here now. He came down to visit before his big trip to America. He called into your pub today actually, wanting to return some magazine?'

Jamie looked confused. 'Oh right… Did he? Sure I can get it from him another time.'

He seemed to catch Millie's eye and then Abigail's and Erich's. Something was going on.

'What? You're all being weird. What is it?' Liesl asked.

'OK, Liesl, don't freak out or leave please,' Erich began. 'Just hear us out, right. We all love you.'

'Oh God, not this again. It's about Kurt, isn't it?' She stood up.

'Please, Liesl, just listen to what we have to say, and if you want to go, then go.' Jamie grabbed her hand.

'Daniel went to Kurt's flat today,' Erich said sincerely, his eyes never leaving his sister's, 'and he found some things – Nazi medals, his Hitler Youth knife, propaganda about the Jews and a book listing the property and assets of our family.'

Liesl felt her stomach lurch. Kurt had said someone was in the flat – was it Daniel?

Then it was Abigail's turn. 'He asked me about Jamie and about any other boyfriends you had and if you'd slept with them. He suggested he knew you'd been with lots of men. He used really disgusting language, and it was honestly, Liesl, such a creepy conversation. And he threatened Theo and Kevin, said that he thought they were interested in you and said he'd make sure they never got near you.' Abigail glanced at Millie. 'Look, I'm so sorry, but I was worried. You said you'd had a falling out with Millie about something Felix had said in Berlin, so I wrote to her and she and Felix came over.'

'My friends weren't lying, Liesl,' Felix said. 'I swear, I double-checked afterwards. He was only seventeen, but did you know he was decorated by Hitler himself? He denounced so many people. He beat an elderly man to death one night because he refused to get down and lick the streets. He did those things, Liesl. I'm sorry, but it is true. I would not say it if I wasn't completely sure.'

Liesl was blinded by tears. She needed to get away.

'Please, Liesl, don't go back to him.' Erich was upset now, and she couldn't take it anymore.

'I just need the toilet,' she said, and stumbled to the back and to the ladies' room.

The barrel store was downstairs and had a service door, so she let herself out. It couldn't be true. She didn't believe it, but she needed to confront Kurt, tell him what they said and look in his eyes when he told her it was wrong. It was just one story that got legs and arms. She had no idea why the people she loved were doing this, but she needed to sort this out for once and for all. Kurt would never hurt her; she knew that as sure as she knew her own name. There was an explanation – there had to be.

She slipped out into the Dublin night, heading for Merrion Square.

# CHAPTER 27

'Wake up, Richter.' Daniel kicked Kurt awake. He'd found Kurt sleeping on the bed, and had already taken his bag and thrown it over the bannister.

'What? Who are you?' Kurt asked groggily in German. 'Where is Liesl?'

Daniel bent down and grabbed Kurt by the hair, yanking him up so that their faces were level. Then he spun him round and twisted his arm up behind his back, pressing him to the wall.

The German yelped in pain as Daniel exerted pressure.

'Listen carefully.' Daniel spoke in German as well. 'I am Liesl's father, and your worst nightmare. You are going to leave Liesl alone. You will go to America and never come back and never again attempt to contact her for any reason, do you understand?'

A stream of expletives poured out of the German, so Daniel punched him hard in the ribs with his free hand, winding him. Kurt whimpered and looked terrified.

'You will do this,' Daniel went on. 'It's not a request. We know *who* you are, we know *what* you are, and there are a great many people around the world who would be very interested indeed to know the whereabouts of one of Hitler's most loyal little boys. We're giving you a chance to scurry away like the little rat that you are.'

'Liesl doesn't believe this. She won't,' Kurt hissed.

'Oh, she will, because right now her friends, the people who actually care about her, are telling her about your precious possessions, your medals and your little book, the pamphlet showing what you really think about us Jews, your dagger. You'd hardly have brought them all the way to Ireland with you if they were meaningless, would you?'

Kurt's face registered something. Shock? Fury? Daniel didn't care.

'So you will go tonight, and don't ever show your face in Liesl's life again or I swear to you, Kurt Richter, you will find yourself at the mercy of people who will not show such clemency. You hurt our daughter and we will not stand for it. If you think I'm bluffing, by all means try your luck, but know it would be very foolish.'

Kurt was about to say something – his blue eyes flashed – but Daniel shoving his arm up further behind his back stopped him.

'So you'll go?' Daniel asked.

Kurt at first made no reply, then muttered, 'Filthy Jew.'

Daniel pressed a little harder. Kurt screamed, but Daniel grabbed his hair once more and slammed his head against the wall. Blood trickled from Kurt's forehead.

'It's a simple question. Will you do as we demand or won't you?'

The pain registered on Kurt's face, and a tear trickled down the side of his head. Daniel increased the pressure on his arm, and Kurt whimpered.

'Please, stop…' he gasped.

'Oh, does it hurt, Kurt?' Daniel asked. 'Poor you. Now, back to the question…'

'I'll go,' Kurt muttered through gritted teeth.

'Good.' Daniel released his hand. 'Now, not a word to Liesl – just go. You can write a note saying it's over, but nothing else. And you catch the boat out of Dublin to Liverpool, and from there to America, or wherever the hell you want to go. I don't care, but I never want to see your face again for as long as I live. Is that clear?'

'Yes,' Kurt replied, rubbing his arm and wiping his head with his sleeve.

Daniel checked his watch. He needed to get to Madigan's and collect Liesl. He'd bring her home to Ballycreggan directly and drive her back down for her exams. He was afraid the conversation with the others wouldn't go well, and he didn't want her coming back and finding Kurt still there.

'This flat is being watched,' Daniel lied. 'First thing tomorrow morning, you're on that boat, and if you're not, I'll know all about it. It sails at seven.' He threw some money on the floor. 'For your fare.'

Daniel let himself out, carrying Kurt's bag in case Liesl needed more evidence, and headed to Madigan's.

# CHAPTER 28

*L*iesl took her shoes off and opened the door, hoping Kurt was asleep. There was a middle-aged couple living on the first floor, but they both worked at St James's Hospital – night shifts she thought, as she rarely saw them – and there was an elderly lady on the second floor who was very hard of hearing, so it was unlikely she would disturb anyone.

She was so tired and confused. She longed to just feel his arms around her and drift off to sleep, locking the whole world and its negativity and bigotry out.

Kurt would have an explanation, of course he would, and she would tell him she'd go to America. Perhaps she could retake her last year there; Professor Kingston would vouch for her. She needed a new start, somewhere everyone wasn't determined to break her and Kurt up. They didn't understand he wasn't just her future – he was her past as well. He connected with her in a way that nobody did. Liesl was only ten years old when she got on the Kindertransport. That was the day her childhood ended. She was responsible for Erich from that day on.

Kurt had given her back her life. She could talk to him about her papa, and it wasn't hard. *Mutti* remembered him but she was married to Willi now, and Erich was so small then that his memory was patchy. Nobody else had ever met him. And Erich preferred to look to the future. With Kurt, she felt whole, like a full person who was born, had a childhood, parents, a life. Nobody else could give her that.

Something drew her to Germany. She'd chosen German to study at University, and she knew Erich and her mother were baffled as to why. She'd felt at home in Berlin when she visited. She loved Ballycreggan, of course she did, but whereas Erich saw it as his only home, for her it was only part of the story. A big chunk of her personal history was missing, and Kurt filled it with his love.

He wasn't asleep; he was sitting on the sofa in the dark.

'You came back.' His voice was flat.

'Of course I did, darling.' She reached for the light switch.

'Leave it,' he said, his voice like a cracking whip.

She took her hand off the switch and crossed the room to sit beside him. 'I shouldn't have gone, but...'

'And who was there?' he asked, examining his hands. She spotted the empty whiskey bottle on the floor.

'Um...Abigail, Millie and Felix, Erich...'

'What about Jamie, was he there?' He turned. His face was a mask of cold fury and he had a cut on his forehead. His blue eyes bored into hers, but the love that normally was there was absent. 'Don't deny it, Liesl. I know he was, probably pawing you and you loving it like some cheap *whore*.' He spat the last word.

'I... Kurt, I don't know what you're talking about...'

He stood up, and shouted, 'Don't lie to me!'

She stood too. 'Kurt, you're scaring me –'

But before she could go on, he grabbed her hair, twisting her head painfully and frogmarching her to the bedroom.

'Kurt, stop this!'

The sting of his hand across her mouth was followed by a dull throbbing pain, then Kurt shoved her towards the bed. Blood spurted from her lip.

'I thought you might like it a bit rough? All you Jews are the same. You try to look respectable, but you are all just lying, thieving cockroaches.' He smirked, a horrible grimace. 'I should have let him have you back. I would never defile myself by having a dirty Jewess in my bed.'

Liesl felt nauseous. 'I'm not staying here to listen to this...' She knew she needed to get away. She made a run for the door.

'Oh, you're going nowhere, Liesl, nowhere without me,' Kurt said quietly, shutting the bedroom door, then turning the key in the lock and pocketing it.

'Kurt, please,' she begged, frightened now. She needed to reason with him. 'I'll go to America. That's what I decided tonight, that we'd go together, tomorrow if you like. Please, Kurt...' She looked down. Blood was dripping down her chin now, onto her Vogue jacket.

'No. We're not going now. We're staying here in Dublin.' He was suddenly calm, and she realised he was doing something at the dressing table. All at once a pungent, solvent smell filled the room. Kurt turned, and she saw he was holding a large glass bottle. He walked around the bedroom dousing everything with the contents. It was petrol.

He spoke calmly. 'You see, Liesl, I tried to love you. I did. I just shuddered inside when I could sense your feral heat wanting me like a cat in heat. I tried not to think of it. I mean, you are beautiful, but the problem is that you always show your true colours. It's like putting perfume on a stinking corpse. Sooner or later, the perfume fades and the stench is still there. No escaping it. It was useful that your Jews have lots of money. If that article in the Berlin paper had not mentioned that your mother survived and was heiress to your father's fortune, I would never have reappeared, but I knew your father had money. Now he was a decent man, I'll give you that, but he sullied himself by laying with your whore mother, so...' He shrugged. 'But then you lot always do, don't you? No matter what happens, the Jews will always come out on top. And then that Jew who says he's your father had the audacity to come here and threaten me. Did you know he was going to do that? A big ugly brute of a fellow, threatening to hand me over to some other Jews who were spending the rest of their pathetic lives hunting down the Führer's followers.' He laughed.

'Kurt, no!' she screamed. 'You'll kill us!' She rushed to the eight-foot-long window, its sill only inches above the floor. It was a sash, so she pulled up the bottom section, opening it to allow in the night air. 'Help!' she screamed into the deserted dark street before he grabbed her by the hair once more. He'd crossed the room with surprising speed, and now he dragged her back and threw her across the bed. Then he continued sprinkling the petrol, now onto the bed and her dress and jacket. Once the bottle was empty, he cast it aside and hunkered down beside her, his hand pressing on her chest.

'Kurt, please, let me go... I don't know why –'

He grabbed her hair again, jerking her head back painfully. 'Shut up, you dirty little Jewess,' he hissed into her ear. 'You should have gone up in smoke years ago, just like your father did. Your mother and Erich too if we'd have managed to catch them, but you lot are slippery, like vermin. Not that smart but hard to catch.'

'What? Kurt... I...' Liesl couldn't believe she was hearing these words come out of his mouth. This was not the man she knew. He even looked different with his snarling mouth and cold blue eyes full of malice.

He slapped his hand over her mouth, the smell of the petrol making her eyes water.

'I would have given you everything. We could have made a new start. Nobody would ever have known your dirty Jew secret. I could even have made myself lie with you, I suppose, but it wasn't enough for you. That was always the problem with you vermin – nothing was ever enough. Greedy, mean, viscous, poor efforts at humanity, always taking, taking, taking, sucking decent people dry. Don't you see? It's all your fault, all of it.' He removed his hand and wiped her blood on his trousers, his lip curled in disgust.

He was terrifyingly calm. The fumes from the petrol drifted up from her clothes and made her gag. The entire room would go up in a second if he struck a match. He had the key to the door, but the window was still open if she could just get there.

She tried to get off the bed, but he forced her back. Then he climbed on top of her, pinning her beneath him with his weight.

His breath smelled sour, and to her horror, he began kissing her. His three-day stubble was sharp and coarse on her face as she struggled beneath him. He was bigger than her, and heavy despite his slim frame, and as she tried to resist, she could feel him pulling at her clothes.

Using all the strength she could muster, she pulled her knee up, trying to kick him where it would do the most damage... But it didn't work. He positioned himself between her legs and seemed more secure than ever. He was chuckling,

'Yes, fight me, little Jew, fight back. I like that...' His breath was warm and moist in her ear. 'How about we keep going, and then I'll light the match, eh?' He laughed again, a horrible sound. 'What a way we will die together. We were born within months of each other, spent our childhoods together – it's only fitting we should die together.'

Liesl was helpless pinned beneath him, and she racked her addled brain for a plan. Her head was pounding now – maybe it was the fumes. Her eyes were sore and she had to keep blinking to see.

'Please, Kurt, think of your parents, your father and mother. If they could see you now, how ashamed of you they would be. They wouldn't want you to hurt me. I know you are lonely, you feel alone. I do understand it. But I'm your family now, and your parents are in heaven, watching over us...'

Kurt stopped kissing her and pulling at her clothes, his ardour suddenly gone. The mention of Nathaniel and Gretel must have worked, brought him to his senses. Liesl used the opportunity to roll him off her and she stood. She could call out the window, but it was late; nobody would hear, she was sure. Perhaps it would be better not to antagonise him further, but instead make him believe she forgave him, that they still had a future.

He lay on his back on the bed, staring at the ceiling.

'Kurt, darling, please. Let's just get out of here, go for a walk. We can talk about everything, make our plans for the future. This room is too dangerous.'

He never looked in her direction; his eyes were focused on the crack in the ceiling that he had joked was just like the Danube. 'They're not dead,' he said, his tone entirely neutral.

'Who are not dead, Kurt?' she asked gently, wondering if she could get close enough to get the key out of his pocket if she couldn't convince him to leave. She tried moving towards the bed, but he held his hand up to stop her, shooing her back. She sat on the bedroom chair in front of the dressing table.

'Gretel and my sisters.'

He felt in the breast pocket of his shirt for his cigarettes. As he opened the box, she screamed, 'No, Kurt, don't light up a match!'

He glanced her way and smiled. 'Oh, yes, I forgot.' He replaced the box in his pocket.

'Where are they?' she asked, terrified of the answer.

'They went to stay with my father's sister, Lena in Dresden. Her husband Martin came home from the Eastern Front. He's useless now of course, but he did come back. So they went to live with them for a while. But I heard they came back to Berlin when it looked like the East was being taken by the Reds.'

'So there was no bomb?' Liesl asked.

He grinned. 'Oh, there were plenty of bombs – your British friends saw to that. And the house was hit, but they weren't in it. They left before that happened.'

'That's wonderful news, Kurt,' she said genuinely, meaning it. 'I'm so pleased.'

He shrugged. 'They might as well be dead. I won't ever see them again.'

'You don't know that . . . Maybe you could –' she began, glad to at least be having a conversation. He seemed calmer, less manic.

'No. They left to get away from me. They probably pray I was killed in the bomb.'

'Kurt, your mother loved you so much. I don't think she would just stop, no matter what you did.' She kept her voice gentle and soothing.

He sat up a little and rested back on the pillows, and if it weren't for the pungent smell of petrol, an observer might think it was a perfect domestic scene.

He shook his head. 'She's stupid. A fat moron of a *hausfrau*, who hadn't the imagination to see what we could have done, the civilisation we could have achieved. Her tiny brain wasn't good enough to comprehend. Same for my two dull sisters. They got every opportunity, every chance to be part of it. They look all right and they would appeal to the Führer with their blonde hair and blue eyes, but they weren't committed. Like so many others, they let him down at the end.'

'But you didn't?' she asked, hating this conversation but trying to buy time.

'No.' He was adamant on that. 'I met him, you know. In those last days, some of us were trying to hold the city, keep the barbarian Reds back, and he came out of his bunker and met us. Oh, Liesl, it was... Despite everything – the destruction of our city, the lack of food, fuel, weapons, forget about all of that, that was incompetence and laziness – it was' – he sighed – 'a wonderful day.'

He crossed the room and stood beside her. 'If that Jew hadn't stolen my bag, I could have shown you.' The pride in his voice was unmistakable. 'I got a medal for archery, and one for wrestling.'

Liesl had no choice but to listen.

'And one when we were brought into the fire service after the Allied bombing raids.' He shoved his hands in his pockets as he reminisced happily, just as he'd brought her back to the picnics and skating of their childhood.

'Most medals were diamond shaped, with the swastika in the centre. But then I got one like this.' He opened a drawer and took out her fountain pen, the one she'd got from Rabbi Frank when she started at Trinity. He grabbed a piece of paper and drew a symbol. 'Do you know what this is?' He held it up to her.

She knew. 'It's the Iron Cross,' she whispered.

'Yes, it is. For bravery in battle.' He dangled the paper in front of her nose. 'Even if I had it, I couldn't let you touch that one. The Führer gave it to me. He touched it and then he gave it to me, and he patted my shoulder and said I did my country and my Führer proud.'

Liesl heard the catch in his voice, the emotional pride at the memory.

'So I couldn't let you touch that one, being a Jew. You understand, don't you? It wouldn't be right.'

She nodded. He leaned down, his face inches from hers, swaying slightly. He was drunk. The sour smell of his breath from the whiskey mingled with the fumes from the petrol, making her even more nauseous.

She saw her heavy glass perfume bottle on the dresser; it had been in her handbag. In one quick movement, she grabbed the bottle and sprayed it in his eyes with one hand. She reached for the fountain pen with the other and drove the point deep into his neck. She had no idea if she had managed to do any real injury, but his face registered shock. Suddenly he seemed to come back to his senses and pulled the pen from his neck as blood spurted out.

She ran from him, screaming, 'Help! Help!'

Kurt managed to stagger across the room, his neck bleeding profusely, and he grabbed her again.

'Liesl!' She heard a voice call her name, then others. Jamie? Was that Erich, Millie? She couldn't see them. Was she dreaming?

She wrestled free of Kurt as his grip had weakened. But then she saw him reach into his pocket and extract his brass Zippo lighter, the one the American gave him. Everything slowed down. His face was pale, almost ghostly, and she knew she had no option.

Liesl ran, and without pause, she climbed through and jumped from the third-floor window.

# CHAPTER 29

*T*he bus pulled into the main bus station in Berlin as the skies opened for a summer shower. They'd taken the bus from the airport, having flown from London. For Ariella and Liesl, it was their first time on a plane, but Erich explained everything to them with great authority as Bud had taken him flying when he was in America. Bud's wedding went ahead a month after Liesl's fall. She insisted Erich go, as she was being very well cared for by everyone in Ballycreggan and Jamie had moved up as well. Erich had been reluctant to leave, but she promised him she was in good hands and Jamie gave him his word to not let Liesl out of his sight.

Ariella reached over and took her daughter's hand. Erich stood and grabbed their cases from the overhead rack, taking them outside before returning to help his mother and sister off the bus.

'Liesl, are you ready?' he asked, trying to hide his trepidation and distaste at being back in the city that had treated him so badly. If it had been for any reason other than this, he would not have come.

'I'm fine, stop fussing.' Liesl grinned and leaned up to place her arms around her brother's neck.

He swung her up into his arms, used to the manoeuvre by now, as the driver unloaded the wheelchair from the storage compartment of the bus. Ariella helped him unfold it and make it safe, then Erich settled her in, placing the blanket Frau Braun had crocheted over her knees.

'*Danke schoen.*' Liesl smiled her thanks at the driver as her mother pushed the chair and Erich carried the bags.

'*Bitte schön,*' he replied, and she tried not to see the pity in his eyes. She hated that more than anything.

'The hotel is only across the street. Should we wait for the shower to stop or make a run for it?' Ariella asked.

'Let's just walk slowly. We'll get wet, but who cares?' Liesl smiled. 'It's hot summer rain. I remember this from when I was little. The rain is never hot in Ireland, so let's just feel it again?'

'If you say so.' Ariella grinned and pushed Liesl out from under the protective canopy of the station, letting the deluge do its worst.

It had been three months since the night of the fire, and in lots of ways, it felt like years. Jamie, Erich, Millie, Abigail and Felix had apparently stood in horror as first they heard Liesl scream and then watched as she came hurtling out the window of the tall red-bricked house, followed by the explosion of flame as Kurt set the flat alight. Jamie and Felix had rushed to her and together broke her fall, Jamie breaking his own arm in the manoeuvre. Kurt was killed in the blaze, as was poor old Mrs Moriarty on the second floor. She was asleep and never knew a thing. The couple from downstairs were at work, so mercifully, further loss of life was averted.

Had her friends not been there, Liesl's injuries could have been more catastrophic. The doctors were hopeful she would walk again one day, and she was too, but rest and allowing her broken bones to heal were all she could do for now.

Ariella originally wanted to go to Germany alone to find Gretel and the girls, but Liesl insisted on accompanying her despite her injuries, and Erich said there was no way he was allowing them to go alone. Everyone, including Jamie, had begged her not to go. She smiled at the memory of him pleading with her to remain in Ballycreggan where she was safe and he could care for her, but she refused. Willi too wanted to accompany them, but Ariella explained that this was between the Bannon and the Richter families only, and while they appreciated everyone's concern and love and were grateful for it, this was a trip she and her son and daughter would make alone.

Ariella, Rabbi Frank and Frau Braun had worked tirelessly, using all of their contacts to trace Gretel, and finally they did through the Red Cross. They had a last-known address, but Ariella didn't want to write. She needed to do this in person.

They checked in to the hotel and arranged to have dinner in the restaurant. Over their meal, Ariella told her children everything about her time in Berlin, filling in the gaps that they had been too young to hear when she first was reunited with them. Over chicken schnitzel and Riesling, they talked and cried and laughed a little as they recalled their memories, and they raised a toast to Peter, who died doing the right thing.

'*Mutti*,' Liesl asked, 'can I ask you something?'

'Of course, my darling, anything.'

'Did Willi really kill his father?'

To Liesl and Erich's astonishment, Ariella smiled slowly. She took a sip of wine, then gazed at her beloved children. 'He did.'

Before they could express their shock, she went on. 'Hubert Braun was a bully. He was a violent Nazi, and he deserved to die. Don't waste one shred of your sympathy on him, my darlings. He was a truly terrible man.'

Erich raised his beer glass and took a sip. 'If you say so, *Mutti*.' Then he grinned. 'Why can't I just have a normal family?'

\* \* \*

THE FOLLOWING MORNING, they decided to walk the three kilometres to the address in the Kreuzberg area of the city. The summer sun shone down, and the city looked remarkably well considering all it had been through in the past decade.

'Plenty of American money,' Erich said bitterly as they saw construction and progress on every corner.

'Well, what's the alternative, darling?' Ariella challenged her son. 'Allow people to live on in the ruins, barely scraping by? What good would that do? They were left with nothing in Germany after the Great War. Versailles was so harsh. It is dangerous to leave a country like Germany with nothing to lose. It's better they are built up and watched carefully.'

'I just find it sickening that they are being rewarded with a shiny new city, behaving as if nothing had happened after what they did,' Erich said through gritted teeth as a well-dressed young couple walked past, laughing and joking.

'Not all of them. Remember what I told you about Willi and his friends, about Father Dominic, Frau Braun, the forger, Gretel, Nathaniel? There were and still are lots of good people here, and who knows how anyone would react under such tyranny? We can't know, Erich. We just do what we can and hope.'

He shrugged, not convinced but willing to let it go for his mother's sake.

'I want to go to St Johanniskirche before we leave, light a candle for Father Dominic. He was such a good man.' Ariella smiled sadly at his memory.

'We'll do that, *Mutti*, and we'll go to the Tiergarten, and have coffee and cake at Café Kranzler – remember how we used to go there at Christmastime? It was flattened, but it's recently reopened,' Liesl said, happy to be back in the city.

She'd walked these streets as a child with her parents and Erich, and then with Kurt, and she'd wondered how it would feel being back again. But it was good, even if she was in a wheelchair. The doctors didn't want to give her false hope – they constantly said there was a chance of recovery but it was slight – but she was trying to will herself to walk again. Kurt had almost cost her everything she loved – her family, her home, her education, her very life – and so even if she was confined to a chair, she'd had a lucky escape. But she hated it, much more than she ever let on to anyone. People spoke differently to you when you were in a chair, like it was her brain that was affected and not her spine.

Kurt. She went over and over it as she lay all of those long weeks in the hospital. How could she have been so blind? All the signs were there. She thought he was being respectful and romantic by not touching her, but the truth was he found her repulsive. He was only interested in her family's money. There were telltale signs all along the way. She'd tortured herself remembering triggers that should have alarmed her. The suggestion that the rabbi would be able to circumvent the law 'because Jews can do that'. Or the constant questions about her mother's house or the investments in America.

She mentally shook herself. She could not live in the past. There had been no body after the fire, so there was no need for a funeral. Kurt was gone and good riddance.

In the first few weeks after that fateful night, she would wake in the hospital, screaming with nightmares. Jamie sat beside her bed every moment he wasn't working in the bar. He normally charmed the nurses into allowing him in during the small hours of the morning after he'd cleaned up, and he would sleep on a chair beside her. When she woke, drenched in sweat and terrified, he would soothe her back to sleep, until eventually the nightmares stopped.

There was always someone there, and in those weeks, it was a blur of faces she loved. Elizabeth, Daniel, Erich, Millie, Rabbi Frank and even Frau Braun came to see her, bringing gifts and cards from Ballycreggan. Wrapped in their love and support, she got through the nightmare.

She would never forget Daniel's huge bear hug when she finally came home after so long in the hospital. Her family and friends had made a visitation rota, so she had never been lonely there. The physiotherapy was excruciating, and so often she cried as they manipulated her legs and back. But Jamie was there, beside her every step of the way.

She'd begged him to go, to leave her, but he refused. She told him she was not the girl he knew, that she'd been through too much and he deserved to be with someone like the old Liesl. But he said he loved one girl and that was her, and that he was going nowhere. He loved her and she loved him. She'd never stopped really, but something about Kurt and Berlin and all the memories seduced her. They talked it out and Jamie assured her, chair or no chair, degree or no degree, if she would have him, he would never leave her side again for the rest of his life.

After eleven weeks, she finally got to leave the hospital. Daniel had called to see her the week before she was to come home and told her of his proposition. He wanted to clear it with Liesl first, and of course she was delighted.

As they waited for the doctor to come and sign her out, Jamie and Daniel, who'd come alone so she could stretch out on the back seat of his car for the drive to Ballycreggan, sat at either side of the bed. Jamie was unusually quiet. She knew he was happy for her but sad that he wouldn't see her every day anymore.

'Do you like the bar work, Jamie?' Daniel asked.

'I do actually. It's a good way to make a living, I think,' Jamie replied. 'My mother is appalled of course. She thought she was making a doctor of me and here I am a lowly barman.' He smiled, and Liesl felt a rush of love for him. Jamie's parents had sent a big basket of fruit and a card apologising for their behaviour and wishing her a speedy recovery.

'Well,' Daniel said nonchalantly, 'maybe you'd have no interest, but Johnny O'Hara is crippled with arthritis, the poor man, and he's not able for the bar anymore. He's thinking of selling up and going to live with his daughter in Omagh. So there's a bar for sale in Ballycreggan, probably at a good price too if you knew who to ask.'

Liesl looked at the man she loved every bit as much as her real papa. His turn of phrase had become so Irish, even though he still had an Austrian accent – she thought it an endearing combination.

Jamie looked puzzled as he caught her eye. 'If you're suggesting I buy it, Daniel, I would in a heartbeat if I had a brass farthing, but I don't.' He sighed.

Daniel shrugged. 'No, but I do, and maybe you could run it for me, and then in time, see what you two want to do? If Liesl here wants to go off and work in Europe or wherever, you could do that and I'd just get someone else, or if you didn't want to, there would be the option of buying it from me?'

Jamie stared incredulously at him. 'I couldn't ask you to do that for me, Daniel, it's too much...'

'Well, it's not for you really – it's for that troublesome minx.' He nodded at Liesl in the chair. 'I think we'd have a hard job keeping her at home if there was a certain person drawing her back down here, or worse to County Kerry. And besides, it's the only pub in the village so it's a good investment. It's a bit run down. Johnny wasn't able to do much in recent years, so it will need work, but if you're interested, then we can talk about it?'

It had all happened seamlessly, and within weeks of her returning to Ballycreggan, Jamie was installed in O'Hara's as the manager and they were together and happy. She loved him and he loved her, and it was simple and easy.

He was so sorry for how he'd behaved when his mother and father met her, and they were too. She told him she was in no position to take the high moral ground, as she'd been so stupid over Kurt.

Jamie's parents asked if they could come up to Ballycreggan to visit. Jamie was reluctant at first, but Liesl asked him to allow them to come, and after a nervous start, it went well. If anything, Jamie was too quick to jump in if his mother looked like she was going to say anything even remotely hurtful, so much so that Liesl ended up siding with Mrs Gallagher on several points of conversation. Mrs Gallagher had explained how she was wrong and said she hoped Liesl could forgive her.

Liesl would ring Jamie later. He was worried about her taking the journey, but she'd assured him she would be fine.

Ariella consulted the map, and soon they were at the corner of the street where Gretel and the girls were last known to be living. They all hoped their friends were still there.

Ariella pushed her daughter along the newly restored pavement until they got to number 17. It was a much more modest house than the Richters' previous one near the Tiergarten, but it was spotless and cared for. The tiny front yard was filled with flowers, and the windows gleamed in the sunlight.

Erich opened the little gate, and Ariella went forward, her children behind her, and knocked on the door. There was someone there all right. Through the stained glass in the door, they saw a shadow, and Liesl could tell that Ariella's heart sank. Whoever it was, they were too tall to be Gretel or the girls.

# CHAPTER 30

*A* man stood there, staring, and nobody spoke. Ariella's hand went to her mouth involuntarily. He looked much older, more stooped, his hair grey and cut so short it was almost bristles, but there was no denying it.

'Nathaniel,' she finally managed.

He never said a word but opened his arms, tears coursing down his lined cheeks.

Behind him came Gretel. 'Nathaniel, who is it –' She too stopped in her tracks, dropping the tea towel she held in her hands. 'Ariella, is it really you? Oh my God, I thought... Oh, I can't believe it... And...' She gazed at the Bannon children she'd not seen since they were young, now grown adults. 'Not Liesl and Erich? Liesl, *Liebchen*, what happened to you? How are you in that chair? Oh my darlings!' She wiped her eye with the edge of her apron. 'Come in, come in... Oh, I just can't believe it... It's like a miracle...'

She led them into the small tidy house that smelled – as had every house the Richters ever lived in – of fresh baking. Gretel had filled out a little since the last time Ariella had seen her, and though both she and Nathaniel had aged decades, they looked well. Gretel's hair was iron grey now and she seemed stooped in a way Ariella didn't remember, but her kind hazel eyes were as warm and full of love as ever. Her husband, once tall and slightly overweight, was now skeletal and gaunt. His eyes seemed sunken, and his hair, once lustrous, dark and thick, was now silver and less than a quarter of an inch long.

'Sit, sit! Tell us everything.' Gretel fussed and found chairs for everyone in the small kitchen. 'First, Liesl, my darling girl, what happened to you?' Her voice was filled with concern.

'It's a long story, Auntie Gretel. I had a fall, but I'm going to be all right. The doctors hope I'll walk again, but it will take time.'

'Oh, you sweet girl, you look just the same, just a grown-up version.' Gretel placed her calloused hand on Liesl's cheek. 'And Erich, oh my... It could be Peter standing there. It feels like he is here.' Gretel was stumbling over her words. She kissed his cheek. 'Oh, you were just a little boy in short trousers, and now look at you, a strapping young man. Oh, your papa would be so proud of you both.' Tears coursed down her wizened cheeks.

'Nathaniel, we were sure you were...' Ariella was overwhelmed. 'I can't tell you how good it is to see you.'

Her husband's best friend just nodded.

'He can't speak, Ariella,' Gretel said gently. 'We don't know why, but he hasn't spoken since he came home. But we don't care – the girls and I just wanted him back, and he knew it, didn't you, darling?' She laid her hand on her husband's face with such love. 'He survived Theresienstadt and was liberated, and he found us. His sister Lena and her husband were at their house in Dresden, Martin was invalided home from the Eastern Front, and Nathaniel made it there and found us.'

Ariella took her old friend's hand. His grip was strong. 'Well done, Nathaniel, well done on making it through. I'm so proud of you. But you always were brave. If it weren't for you, I wouldn't have those two.' She nodded at Erich and Liesl. 'I hid in Berlin all through the war. I survived because they did, and they did because of you. So we owe you so much.'

He smiled and nodded, taking her hand to his lips and kissing it.

'And the girls, are they all right?' Ariella asked, turning to Gretel.

Gretel nodded. 'Yes, Elke is working for the housing authority, and Kitti works at a hotel in town. They're both fine. We're all fine. Kurt...' A shadow crossed her face, and Ariella felt Nathaniel's grip on her hand tighten slightly at the mention of her son's name. 'We don't know where he is, nor do we want to.' The pain was still there, even now.

Ariella glanced at Liesl. They'd decided she should be the one to tell the story.

'Auntie Gretel, Uncle Nat, I have something to tell you. It's not a good story. Kurt is dead. He died in a fire in Dublin.' Liesl began slowly, hating to bring more pain down on the heads of these kind people who'd already endured so much, but as she told her story – meeting him in Berlin, his following her to Dublin, that terrible night – the reaction she saw on their faces was not what she expected. There was grief certainly, but there was something else.

'He's dead?' Gretel asked, her hand on Nathaniel's shoulder for strength. 'You are sure?'

Liesl nodded. 'Yes, I'm sure.'

'Oh, thank God.' Gretel exhaled, with what sounded like relief.

Nathaniel stood silently and wrapped his wife in his arms, his lips on her hair.

Gretel cried, her tears absorbed by the cotton of her husband's shirt. 'It's over. Our boy is dead. Our darling boy. Oh thank God.'

Erich caught Liesl's glance, unsure how to respond. They sat in the small kitchen, the sunlight streaming in, as Nathaniel and Gretel Richter clung to each other in grief, relief and gratitude at the news that their first-born child was gone.

* * *

THE REST of the day passed with food and conversation, hugs and tears. The girls came home from work and were astounded to find their house full of the Bannons, their childhood playmates. A bottle of home-made schnapps was opened, and reminiscences and laughter found their way through the web of pain that had separated and then reunited them.

Elke and Kitti suggested taking Erich and Liesl down the street to a café where a band were playing, and they looked questioningly at their mother.

'Go. You youngsters have fun.' Ariella smiled. Erich had refused to speak German since landing, but since none of the Richters spoke English, he had no choice. He was rusty, and they gently teased him as he tried to remember basic words of the language he'd not spoken since he was a child. As usual, he deferred to Liesl, who gave him each word he forgot, and within a few hours, he was speaking easily again.

Once they were gone, the three parents sat in the sitting room, sipping their schnapps. Gretel, curled up beside Nathaniel on the small sofa, explained how Elke managed to find them this house to rent and how grateful they were to have it. The rent was high, but all rent in Berlin was because property was in such short supply.

'The girls are wonderful. They pay the rent between them. We'd love to move out of the city, live somewhere quiet and peaceful, but then the girls need to work and there are no jobs out there. But maybe someday. There's a constant military presence here. I know it's the Allies, but it's hard for Nathaniel. He hates to see the uniforms and the trucks, so we stay inside mostly. The girls bring us groceries, but we're just so happy to be together again.'

Nathaniel was still and silent. This man was nothing like the big, loud, confident man Ariella remembered, the Nathaniel who could make anything happen, the man who got her children two tickets on the last train out of Berlin.

'Now I'm going to say something, and it's a statement, not a question.' Ariella spoke firmly, knowing her friends would react to what she was about to say. 'It requires no answer nor any reaction from you, so I'm telling you now, I will brook no argument.'

Nathaniel and Gretel looked at her and then each other, a shadow of fear crossing their faces. They'd had so much bad news, they seemed constantly cowering, waiting for the next blow.

'Don't worry, it's something good.' She smiled. 'Peter made investments in America, and thankfully I was able to liquidate those. I also recently received reparations for our apartment here that was confiscated. This has left me with more money than I need, so I'm sharing what I have with you.' She took an envelope from her handbag. 'My husband Willi and I have a lovely home in Ireland, and Liesl and Erich are well provided for. In that envelope is enough money for you to buy whatever house you wish, wherever you want to live.'

She saw they were about to object, so she raised her hand. 'You saved my children's lives, Nathaniel, and, Gretel, you gave me your friendship when I had nothing, even though it risked your life.'

'But Kurt, what he did to Liesl, she could have –' Gretel began.

'This is nothing to do with Kurt or Liesl. This is to do with us. Nathaniel and you and Peter and me. We were friends since before our children were born, and we were the family we chose for ourselves. Very rarely in our friendships are we called upon to do the hard thing, to make a huge sacrifice, but how we behave in those times – believe me, I know – that is the value of a friendship. You two are true friends, and you have my eternal gratitude – Peter's too from heaven, I know – so this is nothing.' She pushed the envelope towards them. 'We three survived, somehow, against every single one of the odds. We made it through this, and now we all deserve a life of peace. Please take the money, buy your house and get settled, and then come to Ballycreggan to visit us. We have so many people we want you to meet.'

The Richters looked at each other, Gretel's eyes searching her husband's for an answer.

Nathaniel stood, his tall gangly frame almost filling the small room. He picked the envelope up and put it in his pocket. He took Ariella's hand, bringing it to his lips and kissing it gently. 'Thank you, Ariella,' he whispered.

# EPILOGUE

's the place all right, do you think?' Jamie was worried. The back room, as it was called, in O'Hara's had been the repository for all of the junk in the village for years: floats from long-forgotten parades, bits of scenery from the dramatic society's plays, sandbags from the days when they were needed during the war and hundreds of other bits of rubbish. Erich, Jamie, Daniel and Willi had worked tirelessly to clear out the area, paint it and turn it into the warm, bright, welcoming space it now was.

Liesl put her arm around his waist and gave him a reassuring squeeze. She'd walked with her crutches from the house to the pub, and though it was slow-going and she needed to rest several times on the 700-yard journey, every day she could feel herself getting stronger. The wheelchair was almost obsolete, and though she did get very tired in the evenings and her back ached, she was thrilled to be up on her feet again. The doctors were really happy with her progress, and they had ruled out the need for surgery.

'It looks lovely, so clean and bright, and you wait till the ladies of Ballycreggan get at this with their bunting and tablecloths. It's going to be marvellous.' She kissed his cheek. 'I'm so proud of you, Jamie. The departure of so many people from the farm for Israel could be a sad thing, but we'll have such fun here, and there's going to be music and dancing and everything, and I guarantee there will be enough food to feed twenty armies. It's going to be a night for everyone to remember. I know Father O'Toole said we could use the church hall, but this will be so much better. People can have a drink, for one thing!' She chuckled.

'I hope so. But maybe if this works out, we could look at renting it out for functions, dances, weddings even?' Jamie was full of enthusiasm. He had turned O'Hara's from a dingy, dirty little shebeen into a lovely bar with a separate lounge area. It had been Elizabeth's idea to have a place the ladies could meet in the evenings. They wouldn't like to sit in the bar with the men, so there was a carpeted lounge where ladies-only card games happened and even the Women's Institute had their meetings. They all loved Jamie, with his handsome easy charm, and he was as happy to supply cups of tea as pints of beer. The fact that he wasn't a drinker himself seemed to be a bonus. The clergy were happy he was running a moral house, and the police knew there would be no illegal gambling or after-hours drinking. Jamie Gallagher ran a tight ship.

'That's a wonderful idea. You definitely should look into that.' She glanced at her watch. 'What time are your parents getting here?'

'Around three, I think. My father insisted on driving all the way. I told them to get the train, but he's a stubborn old bat so as usual he refused.' Jamie shrugged. 'They're bringing Derry and Sean now as well. Apparently they're dying to see the new pub.' He grinned with pride. There was no mention of Father Brendan. Jamie and he would never see eye to eye, and it was best if they kept their distance.

'Now, you need to go home for a rest,' he said. 'I promised Elizabeth I wouldn't let you do too much, so go on, be off with you.' He glanced around and for once they were alone, so he kissed her.

'I'm grand. I'll be dancing tonight, Jamie Gallagher, just you wait.' She sighed happily.

'Not with me you won't. Daniel would kill me with his bare hands if he thought you were dancing, Fräulein.' Jamie kissed her again.

'Urgh, can you two stop pawing each other for five seconds? I'm only after my lunch.' Erich groaned theatrically as he came in with a stack of chairs.

'Well, Abigail is on the train as we speak – she rang this morning – and Millie and Felix arrived off the boat into Dublin last night. Apparently the party is all anyone can talk about, thanks to you talking up Ballycreggan like it's Las Vegas. So we'll see later on who's being all soppy and romantic, won't we, Jamie?' Liesl teased her brother, who just chuckled.

'Ah, when you've travelled the world like I have, Liesl,' Erich said theatrically, 'you'll come to realise what a great place Ballycreggan is.'

Jamie and Liesl groaned. Erich and his 'travelling the world' stories had been retold so often since his return from Biloxi, it was a running joke in the family now.

'So what are the final numbers, do you know?' Erich asked Jamie.

'I think around two hundred. I just hope we can squeeze everyone in,' Jamie said as he helped Erich put out the chairs.

'Well, the men will probably congregate in the bar anyhow, so it will be the women and kids in here.' Erich tried to reassure him.

'I can't see Rabbi Frank, Father O'Toole and Reverend Parkes propping up the bar somehow, Erich,' Liesl said, leaning on her crutches.

'OK, well, the women, kids and clergy in here.' He winked. 'I'm sure you'll have a lovely time.'

The doors opened again, and this time it was Daniel and Nathaniel carrying the long trestle tables borrowed from the church hall. The Richters had come for a visit, and it was so lovely to have them. Though their English was poor, they were trying, and enough of the Jews spoke German that between them, Daniel, Ariella and Willi, they were managing fine. Gretel had been baking since she arrived in preparation for the feast, and Elke and Kitti were really enjoying the holiday after working so hard for so long.

'Are the girls gone to the beach, Nathaniel?' Liesl called.

He nodded. Though he spoke now occasionally, and it was such a relief to Gretel and everyone that he'd found his voice, he was naturally quiet these days. He looked so much better now though compared to when they'd met in Berlin. His hair was longer and his skin had a healthier glow. He hadn't gained any weight despite Gretel's best efforts, and Liesl noticed he only ate tiny amounts at each meal.

He and Gretel bought a gorgeous house beyond Spandau, to the west of the city, a lovely place with a stream in the garden, and they kept chickens and goats and grew their own vegetables. They'd invited Liesl and Jamie for a visit once she was well enough to travel, and she was looking forward to showing Jamie her Berlin. Elke and Kitti opted to live in the city, and there was enough money left over to buy them a little apartment, so they were all much happier.

Nathaniel crossed the hall; he would never shout. 'They are. They swam in the sea yesterday, and they said it was lovely.' He smiled. 'Everything – the beach, the cliffs – is beautiful here.'

'It is,' Liesl agreed. 'We landed on our feet the day we came here, Uncle Nat, that's for sure.'

He put his arm around her shoulder and gave her a squeeze. 'You all right? Your back? Legs?' he asked, and she knew he and Gretel felt responsible for what their son had done, though they were in no way to blame.

'I'm improving every day. The doctors are delighted with my progress.' She hoped he was reassured.

'Good.' He released her, and as he did, she saw the numbers. He'd rolled his sleeves up to move the table, something he normally never did, so she'd not seen them on him before but knew they were there. He saw she noticed, and as he rolled his shirt sleeve down and closed the button at the wrist, he shrugged. 'I'm one of the lucky ones.'

She nodded. Elizabeth had found a clinic in London that would remove the tattoo at Nathaniel's request. They were going to go back to Berlin via London and have it done. Some people wanted to keep theirs as a symbol, so that people couldn't forget, but he wanted rid of it.

Liesl went home as instructed and rested before preparing for the party. The scars on her body would heal, and the scars on her heart were healing too, the balm of her family's and Jamie's love diminishing the pain every day.

She needed help dressing so she called Elizabeth, who was ready and dressed in a stunning rust-coloured dress. The bodice was fitted to the waist, a sweetheart neckline showed off her youthful décolletage despite her approaching her fifty-first birthday, and the skirt was full and lined with a petticoat. Her dark wavy hair, normally in a tight bun, was pinned up loosely, with several tendrils framing her beautiful face.

'I need to stop eating strudel,' Liesl commented as she sucked in to allow her mother to fasten the buttons all the way up the back of her cream fitted dress. The dress was tight all the way from the neck to the knee, and it was just as well she couldn't dance because the dress left very little wriggle room. She had wondered if it was too figure-hugging, but she'd shown it to Viola yesterday and her friend assured her it was gorgeous. Viola and David and Jamie and Liesl were good friends now, and it felt nice that they would be going to Israel without any bad feelings.

Viola had knocked on the door the day after Liesl left the hospital and appeared nervous as she was shown into the room where Liesl lay.

'Liesl, I'm so sorry you were hurt. I heard from Rabbi Frank and I was so worried...'

They talked it all over, and Liesl told Viola all about Kurt and Berlin, and about the accident and Jamie, and in turn Viola explained how she felt so guilty about David and how they hated not telling her but honestly felt like she was all tied up with college life and was distancing herself from them. They ironed it all out, and David was invited on the next visit. He'd carved her a little bird, one that balanced delicately on a stand, and she placed it on her windowsill. It was an inspiration to walk again someday.

'So how does it feel to be closing the farm?' Liesl asked Elizabeth as Elizabeth finished doing her buttons.

Elizabeth sighed. 'A million emotions.' She took the brush and began pinning Liesl's dark hair into loose curls. 'It feels like yesterday

I was in this room, putting a skinny ten-year-old you into my old clothes and cutting them down to fit. But then in other ways, I don't know, so much has happened.'

'Are you sad about the farm closing?' Liesl probed. Elizabeth was at the centre of Ballycreggan, and the children of the school, Jew and Gentile, were in her heart.

'Yes and no. I'll miss them all of course, but they are going on to live their lives, and that makes me very proud and happy.' Elizabeth's eyes were suspiciously bright.

'It's all right to be sad, Elizabeth. You're the reason they have such happy memories. You gave us all so much.' Liesl felt her eyes well up too.

'And look what this life has given me.' Elizabeth kissed the top of Liesl's head. 'You and your brother, Daniel, Ariella and Willi, friends – I got so much, Liesl. Before you two burst into my life, it was a small lonely existence, but you and Erich changed all that. I never need your gratitude, darling. If anything, I should thank you.'

Daniel stuck his head around the door and gave an appreciative whistle. 'Well, won't I be the proudest man in Ballycreggan tonight with these two beauties on my arm?' He grinned. 'Are we ready?'

Elizabeth gathered her things, and Daniel helped Liesl downstairs.

The party was in full swing when Jamie came to find her. He'd employed Erich's friend Simon and two other local lads to work the bar so he could mingle and make sure everything went smoothly.

Just as Liesl had predicted, the tables were groaning under the weight of cakes and cold meats and salads, and tea was flowing as quickly as the beer was in the bar adjoining.

He found her just as the rabbi made his way slowly to the podium, leaning heavily on the cane he used nowadays. Liesl felt a rush of love for this old man, who'd seemed so scary and strict when they first arrived but now was so loved and adored by everyone in Ballycreggan. He was their guide and champion, and not one of the refugees ever doubted how much he cared for them. The esteem in which he was held was evidenced by the fact that every single one of the Jewish children who came on the Kindertransport in 1939 had gathered in the hall, twelve years later. Even the ones who had moved on, returned to Europe or even gone to America, had come back for tonight.

He wasn't just their rabbi; he had become their father, their grand-father, their teacher, their advocate. He did more than just care for them over those uncertain years – he made them feel part of something. Those who lost their families, which was most of them, now had another family, that of the Jewish community of Ballycreggan, and Liesl knew that she would attend their events, their weddings and funerals, just as certainly as if they were blood relations. The bond between the children of the farm was all because the rabbi fostered it, and it would endure no matter where they lived, for the rest of their lives. He had taken a bunch of lonely, lost children from all over Europe, united only by their faith, and made them a family.

The respect and regard everyone had for him was palpable as the crowd came to a natural hush. The men crushed into the back of the hall from the bar until there was standing room only. The rabbi had a long grey beard and his curled peyot hung from his temples. He was never seen in any colour but black, but he wore a white shirt when he was working on the farm. His hat made him look taller, but in reality he was small and wiry.

In preparation for the speeches, Daniel had erected a small podium so everyone could see.

Liesl looked around at the gathered crowd. Beside the stage were Elizabeth and Daniel, Willi, Frau Braun and her *mutti*. Ariella looked radiant as always. The Richters too were seated near the front, with Levi and Ruth. Viola and David were there as well.

One evening last week, when they'd called to the pub, they made her and Jamie promise to visit them in Israel. Jamie was all for it, though she joked that his pale Irish skin would burn to a crisp under the hot Israeli sun. He asked her later if she wasn't curious to see if that was where she belonged. He had been clearing up in the bar after another busy night, and she was perched on a stool finishing a glass of wine.

'No, I know I don't.' She'd smiled.

'So the quest continues, does it?' he asked. He knew about her sense of constantly searching; she'd explained it to him in the hospital.

'No.' She shook her head. 'I'm not searching anymore,' she replied with certainty.

'Why not?' he asked, casually lifting two heavy barstools onto the counter at once.

'Because I've found where I belong.' She sipped her drink. 'I realised belonging isn't to do with geography. It's to do with people. Home is where my people are.' It was so simple now, this thing that had plagued her since she was ten years old.

'That's good.' He smiled at her, and she felt her stomach flutter. 'And am I one of your people?' he asked shyly, standing before her, his arms circling her waist.

'You *are* my person, Jamie Gallagher,' she'd whispered before he kissed her.

Erich and Abigail were squeezed into the corner with Millie and Felix, who towered over everyone. Millie raised her glass, catching Liesl's eye, and the friends exchanged a smile. Millie had stayed on in Dublin after the night of the fire and had been such a great friend. She prepared for her own finals beside Liesl's bed, and though Liesl would have to defer her exams until the autumn resits, she was ready because Millie made sure she studied just as soon as she was able. Millie spoke to her in French and German every day and insisted on keeping the pressure on while Liesl recovered. Liesl was so glad she had and now was feeling confident about her performance in next month's exams.

Millie, of course, did spectacularly well in her finals at Cambridge, of that there was no doubt. And though the results were yet to be announced, she'd been contacted by her professor, who offered her a post-graduate scholarship at the university – a pathway to a teaching job there. Millie must have turned out to be their sort after all. Felix reckoned he could wrestle in England as well as anywhere so was moving there permanently.

The people of Ballycreggan gathered and waited for the rabbi to speak.

Bridie from the sweetshop, old Johnny O'Hara, who was delighted and amazed with what Jamie had done with the place, Miss McGovern from the village tea room, Major Kilroy and his grouchy housekeeper, Mrs Dawkins, Mr and Mrs Morris from the school, her school friends – these were her people. An odd group for sure, a community divided along sectarian lines before the war, Protestants wary of Catholics and vice versa – they had been united by the arrival of a bunch of bedraggled, frightened children. They took them to their hearts, and the differences that had seemed so important before, overnight became meaningless.

The rabbi clapped his hands. 'Ladies and gentlemen, Father O'Toole, Reverend Parkes.' He addressed the crowd, his accent still as strong as the day he left Germany. 'Friends, neighbours, children, thank you all for coming to our little gathering. Shalom. I have been asked to say a few words, and I am happy to do it but sad too, because this is, for some of us anyway, goodbye.'

Liesl blinked back the tears and noticed she was not the only one.

'But we must, before we take our leave, have the saying of some things.'

Liesl smiled. Though the rabbi had mastered English, he always spoke in a kind of pedantic way, his delivery slow and deliberate, that made the children chuckle. Elizabeth was convinced he did it on purpose and often caught him winking at the gigglers when he made a mistake.

'As you all know, the reason we came here was because we were refugees. Some adults, more children were lucky enough to escape the grip of National Socialism and found an oasis of calm and peace here in this little corner of Northern Ireland.' He smiled. 'Now, through the bravery of many thousands of military people as well as civilians all around the world, that beast has been slain and we are free once more. For some of us here tonight, we are going home. Home to a land we've never seen, Israel, the Promised Land. But I know I speak for all of us when I say that though Israel is our spiritual home, Ballycreggan is in our hearts and it always will be.

'There are too many people to thank to name each one. Each and every one of you over the years has done or said something kind, something that made us feel loved and wanted in a world where we were not. You did this without making us feel bad, or that we were a burden. You opened your hearts and your homes freely and with such love. We thank you all. But I must pay special tribute to the Lieber family, especially Mrs Lieber, without whom we might have stayed a disparate and divided community. She pulled us together. We have comforted each other in times of hardship, we have cheered our combined victories, and we have given each other courage in the darker days.'

The crowd clapped and several people wiped their eyes.

'Now, I would like to invite all of the Kindertransport children to the stage. Many of you are no longer children, but nonetheless, in the eyes of this village and my old eyes, you will always be children.'

In the crowded hall there was movement as grown men and women and some teenagers made their way to the stage and surrounded the rabbi. Finally, they were all gathered.

He addressed the crowd once more, his arm out to the gathered Jewish refugees. 'These people live because of you. God worked through you to save us all. You are all righteous amongst the nations.' He smiled. 'Not just alive, but they are happy, educated.' He nodded at Elizabeth. 'They are people who don't just hear about the goodness of people – they have experienced it first-hand. At a time in their young lives when they were frightened, lonely and lost, you gave them hope and love and held out the hand of friendship. Their children's children will know of this place, and they will visit. I have decided to stay, if you'll have me. These old bones would not do well in the sun, I fear.'

There was more applause.

'But on behalf of the Jews of Europe, these children's families who did not survive, and on behalf of every one of us, we extend our most heartfelt thanks. We will take your love with us in our hearts wherever we go.'

The rabbi smiled then. 'And I think we can call the football match that began in 1939 and that at last count was' – he pulled out a piece of paper and read – '17,219 goals to 16,963 in favour of Ballycreggan, a local victory.'

Loud cheers and clapping filled the air. The football match that never ended was a running joke.

He gave Ruth a nod and she went to the piano.

'We will sing for you now. It is a prayer of thanks to God for giving us another glorious day of life. Life is precious, and we must not take it for granted. If any generation understands that, it is all of us. This song starts each day at the school here in Ballycreggan, and we've all sung it together every day for all these years, Jews and non-Jews alike, so please join with us.'

*Modeh ani l'fanecha*
*Melech chai v'kayam*
*Shehechezarta bi nishmati b'chemla*
*Raba emunatecha*

The voices of young people, from Ballycreggan to Berlin, were raised in song, and the sound floated out into the summer night air, rising high over the village and out over the sea.

The End.

# THANK YOU

I sincerely hope you enjoyed this book. I loved writing it. The characters of Liesl and Erich are so dear to my heart, and represent for me the many children who survived the darkest of times due to the kindness of strangers. They also represent the many millions more who did not. May they rest in peace.

The research for this series made me face the whole gamut of emotions. Horror, despair, grief, but also compassion, and relief. The evils of the Nazi ideology are well known, but those that resisted, that helped their neighbours, friends, and even strangers, at such enormous personal risk still gives me such hope. These were ordinary people, from all walks of life, all religions and none, who were compelled to act, to defend the vulnerable from the strong. Their blood runs in the veins of our generation, and so many of them remain unsung.

If you enjoyed the book I would be so grateful of you would write a review here:

mybook.to/HardWayHome

If you want to hear more from me, go to my website www.jeangrainger.com and join my reader's club. It's 100% free and always will be and you get a full length novel to download when you join with my compliments.

# ABOUT THE AUTHOR

Jean Grainger is a USA Today bestselling Irish author. She writes historical and contemporary Irish fiction and her work has very flatteringly been compared to the late great Maeve Binchy.

She lives in a stone cottage in Cork with her husband Diarmuid and the youngest two of her four children. The older two show up occasionally with laundry and to raid the fridge. There are a variety of animals there too, all led by two cute but clueless micro-dogs called Scrappy and Scoobi.

*The Hard Way Home* is her twentieth novel.

**f**

# ALSO BY JEAN GRAINGER

**The Tour Series**

The Tour

Safe at the Edge of the World

The Story of Grenville King

The Homecoming of Bubbles O'Leary

Finding Billie Romano

Kayla's Trick

**The Carmel Sheehan Story**

Letters of Freedom

The Future's Not Ours To See

What Will Be

**The Robinswood Story**

What Once Was True

Return To Robinswood

Trials and Tribulations

**The Star and the Shamrock Series**

The Star and the Shamrock

The Emerald Horizon

The Hard Way Home

**Standalone Books**

So Much Owed

Shadow of a Century

Under Heaven's Shining Stars

Catriona's War

Sisters of the Southern Cross

Made in the USA
Coppell, TX
01 July 2021

58390563R10141